CRANFORD

MACMILLAN AND CO., Limited
LONDON · BOMBAY · CALCUTTA
MELBOURNE

THE MACMILLAN COMPANY
NEW YORK · BOSTON · CHICAGO
ATLANTA · SAN FRANCISCO

THE MACMILLAN CO. OF CANADA, Ltd.
TORONTO

Miss Matty

CRANFORD

BY

MRS. GASKELL

WITH A PREFACE BY

ANNE THACKERAY RITCHIE

AND ILLUSTRATIONS

BY

HUGH THOMSON

MACMILLAN AND CO., LIMITED
ST. MARTIN'S STREET, LONDON
1907

First Edition printed November 1891.   *Reprinted December* 1891
January, February, and September 1892, 1894, 1895, 1898, 1900, 1901, 1903, 1907
Reprinted with Coloured Illustrations October 1898.   *New Edition* 1907

Printed by R. & R. CLARK, LIMITED. *Edinburgh*

I

My father has written of the memories connected with the writing of books, and of the scenes and feelings which are printed on the pages, quite other from those which they recount. And there are also the associations of the readers as well as of the writers. One scene in Cranford *always comes back to me, not only for its own most pathetic value, but because I saw my father reading it. I can still remember him coming through the doorway just as I had finished the chapter, when not without some agitation and excitement I put the close printed number of* Household Words *into his hand. It was in the little dining-room of his house in Young Street, by gas light, just before dinner-time. The story was that of Captain Brown and he sat down and read it then and there, and afterwards told me the writer's name. But indeed I did not think of it as a story at all, it seemed to me rather*

*that I had witnessed some most touching and heroic deed,
some sad disaster, and though I was a grown girl at the
time I had a foolish childish wish for my father's sympathy, and a feeling that even yet he might avert the
catastrophe. Dear Captain Brown! in his shabby wig and
faded coat, loved and remembered far beyond the narrow
boundaries of Cranford—the city of the Amazons, the
home of Miss Pole, and Miss Matty, and Miss Jenkyns,
the place where economy was always 'elegant,' where
'though some might be poor we were all aristocratic.'
Ever since the winter's evening when I made my first
acquaintance with that delightful place it has seemed to
me something of a visionary country home, which I have
visited at intervals all my life long (in spirit) for refreshment and change of scene. I have been there in good
company. 'Thank you for your letter,' Charlotte Brontë
writes to Mrs. Gaskell in* 1853. '*It was as pleasant as
a quiet chat, as welcome as spring showers, as reviving as
a friend's visit; in short, it was very like a page of*
Cranford.' . . . *The quotation breaks off with little dots,
but I am sure that each one of them represents a happy
moment for Currer Bell, who had not many such in her
sad life.*

*There is a most interesting notice of Mrs. Gaskell in
the* Biographical Dictionary, *in which Lord Houghton is
quoted as writing of* Cranford, *as 'the finest piece of
humoristic description that has been added to British
literature since Charles Lamb.' I had been thinking of*
Elia *after re-reading the book, and I was pleased to find*

myself on the steps of such a critic as Lord Houghton. One could imagine Mrs. Sarah Battle and the poor relation dwelling in Cranford, and if Charles Lamb could have liked anything that was not London, he too might have fancied the place. Perhaps Miss Austen's ladies may also have visited there, but I feel less certainty about them, *they belong to a different condition of things, to a more lively love-making set of people, both younger in age and older in generation than the Cranford ladies. Cranford is farther removed from the world, and yet more attuned to its larger interests than Meryton or Kellynch or Hartfield. Drumble, the great noisy manufacturing town, is its metropolis, not Bath with its succession of card parties and Assembly Rooms. At Cranford love is a memory rather than a present emotion ; the sentimental locks of hair have turned to gray, the* billet doux *to yellow, like autumn leaves falling from the Tree of Life, but there is more of real feeling in these few signs of what was once, than in all the Misses Bennett's youthful romances put together. Only Miss Austen's very sweetest heroines (including her own irresistible dark-eyed self, in her big cap and folded kerchief) are worthy of the old place. I should give the Freedom of Cranford, were it mine to bestow, in the usual ' handsome casket,' to Anne Elliott, to Fanny Price perhaps . . . but as I write some spirit of compunction disturbs the* ' obiter dicta ' *of a hasty moment. Where is one to draw the line ! Lady Bertram and the Honourable Mrs. Jamieson would surely have been kindred souls, delight-*

ful creatures both with their divergences.   Who will ever forget Lady Bertram's plea for morality, or Mrs. Jamieson's languid replies to Miss Matty's inquiries as to the preparations expected in a gentleman's dressing - room, those answers given in the wearied manner of the Scandinavian prophetess, ' Leave me, leave me to repose.'

But it is all very well to decide who shall and who shall not in turn be a dweller in this favoured spot ! Cranford chooses its own inhabitants, and is everywhere, where people have individuality and kindliness, and where oddities are tolerated, nay, greatly loved for the sake of the individuals.

I am sure Cranford existed in the quarter in Paris where my own early youth was passed.   I can remember it in Kensington also, though we did not quite go the length of putting our cows into gray flannel dressing-gowns, as Miss Betsy Barker did.   Perhaps Cranford did not even stop at Kensington, but may have reached farther afield, taking Chiswick on its way.   Miss Debōrah, as she preferred to be called, is certainly first cousin to Miss Pinkerton ; can either of these ladies have been connected with the unrivalled Miss Seward herself? I do not quite know upon what terms Miss Seward and Dr. Johnson happened to be, but I could imagine the great lexicographer driving them all before him and Miss Pinkerton's turban, or Miss Jenkyns in her little helmet-like bonnet.

Miss Debōrah and Miss Pinkerton belong to an altogether bygone type, but all the rest of the ladies in Cran-

ford are as modern and as much alive as if they had
been born in the 60's.

'I believe the art of telling a story is born with some
people,' writes the author of Cranford ; it was certainly
born with Mrs. Gaskell. My sister and I were once
under the same roof with her in the house of our friends
Mr. and Mrs. George Smith, and the remembrance of her
voice comes back to me, harmoniously flowing on and
on, with spirit and intention, and delightful emphasis, as
we all sat indoors one gusty morning listening to her
ghost stories. They were Scotch ghosts, historical ghosts,
spirited ghosts, with faded uniforms and nice old powdered queues. As I think it over I am suddenly struck
by the immense superiority of the ghosts of my youth to
the present legion of unclean spirits which surround us,
as we are told—wielding teacups, smashing accordions
and banjos, breaking furniture in bits. That morning at
Hampstead, which I recall, was of a different order of
things, spiritual and unseen ; mystery was there, romantic
feeling, some holy terror and emotion, all combined to keep
us gratefully silent and delighted.

II

It is something for us Cockneys to know that Mrs.
Gaskell belongs to London after all, if only as a baby.
Although so much of her life was spent in the North, and
Knutsford was the home of her childhood, and Manchester

that of her married life, yet she was born in Chelsea. She was born in 1810, *in pretty old Lindsay Place, of which the windows—ancient lights even then—still look out upon the river at its turn, as it flows from Cheyne Row, towards the sunset, past Fulham Palace, where the Bishops dwell, and Hampton Court and its histories, out into the country plains beyond.*

Mrs. Gaskell was born in that propitious hour of the great men and women who came into the world in the beginning of this century: may the next hundred years bring to our descendants many more such birthdays ! She belonged to a good stock on either side ; her father came from Berwick upon Tweed, that city built upon the rock ; he was Mr. William Stevenson, a Unitarian minister. There is a tradition that the Stevensons came originally from Norway, and there are old family papers in which the name is spelled Stevensen. Mrs. Gaskell liked to think of her Scandinavian forefathers, and when she went away now and again for little jaunts and expeditions, such as she always enjoyed, she used to laugh and say that the blood of the Vikings her ancestors was rising in her veins. She was always tenderly attached to her father's memory, and proud and fond of him, and he must have been indeed a most interesting and delightful character. A letter lately written to the Athenæum, *evidently by some old friend of the family, gives a quotation from Longman's* Annual Obituary *for* 1830 *and of the notice of Mr. Stevenson's death, beginning thus: 'The literary and 'scientific world has sustained a great loss in the death of*

' *Mr. Stevenson, a man remarkable for the stores of know-*
' *ledge which he possessed, and for the simplicity and*
' *modesty by which his rare attainments were concealed.*'
Among other facts we read that in early life while
preaching at Manchester Mr. Stevenson was also '*Classical*
Tutor in the Manchester Academy, so well known through
the Aikens and Barbaulds. He was afterwards appointed
secretary to Lord Lauderdale, and finally Keeper of the
Records to the Treasury, both of which appointments
brought him up to London.' *He laboured with unremit-*
ting diligence, contributing to the Edinburgh Review, *the*
Westminster, *and Dr. Brewster's* Encyclopedia. ' *He had*
' *the true spirit of a faithful historian, and, contrary to the*
' *practice too prevalent in those days, dived into original*
' *sources of information.*'[1] *Was not this the father, one*
might imagine, for such a daughter? Mr. Stevenson
married, as his first wife, Miss Eliza Holland of Sandle-
bridge. It would not be difficult to name some dozen
families now existing which have set their mark upon the
times, trump cards in the game of life, so to speak, and to
one of these families Mrs. Gaskell's mother belonged.
The poor young lady died very soon after her little girl
was born, and the child was taken away to the care of an
aunt, her mother's sister, who was living at Knutsford
in Cheshire with an only child, a cripple. The whole
story was very melancholy, and one can imagine that
it may have been a somewhat sad and silent home for

[1] *Mr. Stevenson's father—Mrs. Gaskell's grandfather—was a captain*
in the Royal Navy. One can well imagine that some of the sailor's blood
still coursed in the veins of the woman whose spirit was so free and so
adventurous.

a little girl full of life and imagination.   There was an
uncle also dwelling in the same little country town, Dr.
Peter Holland, who was the father of the great physician
Sir Henry Holland, and the grandfather of the present
Lord Knutsford.   Besides their houses in Knuts-
ford the Holland family had a pretty old country house
some two or three miles beyond the town, from whence
Mrs. Gaskell's own mother had come.   The house where
Mrs. Gaskell lived as a little girl with her aunt is on the
Heath, a tall red house, with a wide spreading view, and
with a pretty carved staircase and many light windows
both back and front.

I have heard that Mrs. Gaskell was not always quite
happy in those days,—imaginative children go through
many phases and trials of their own,—in her hours of
childish sorrow and trouble she used to run away from
her aunt's house across the Heath and hide herself in one
of its many green hollows, finding comfort in the silence,
and in the company of birds and insects and natural
things.   But at other times she had delightful games of
play with her cousins in the sweet old family house at
Sandlebridge, where so many Hollands in turn had lived.

The old house stands lonely in a beautiful and tranquil
position, with a waving prospect of fields and shady trees
and hedges, reaching to the hills which rise in the far
distance.   As we stood there we could see Alderley Edge
clean painted against the stormy sky.   Just before reaching
the house the road dips into a green hollow, where stands
a forge which has been there for over two hundred years,
handed down from father to son.   Just beyond the forge

is an old mill, shaded by beautiful trees; we could hear
the peaceful sounds of labour, the clanking blows of the
anvil, the soft monotonous thud of the mill.

Sandlebridge is now given up to a farmer; a pretty
flagged stone path leads up to the front door. There
used to be two brick pediments with balls at the garden
gate. Years ago, so long ago that the great Lord Clive
was only a schoolboy in Knutsford at the time (his
mother was a Gaskell and had connections in the place),
he used to come over to spend his half holidays at Sandlebridge, and his pleasure was to jump across from one stone
ball to the other, to the great danger of his legs and arms.
Here too in later times, as we have said, Mrs. Gaskell
used to come as a little girl, and play with her cousins
and gather flowers from the garden. There was a great
bed of saxifrage, which may still be there, it was always
her favourite flower. The old house is now dismantled,
but one or two things still remain out of its past; among
others are the fine old wooden chimney-pieces in the front
parlour, one within the other,—so it seemed to me,—and
the old shuffleboard. A shuffleboard is an immensely
long table, standing upon legs of shining oak with many
drawers and cupboards underneath. There are hardly
any left anywhere now. They were once used for a game
which consisted in jerking heavy counters from one end
to the other of the shining board, and trying to keep your
own and to throw your enemy's over the side of the table.
As we were looking with interest at all these relics of
bygone times, we heard a sort of chucking noise from the
big inner room or kitchen; it came from a little person

some two or three months old lying in a huge carved oak cradle by the fire, which cradle must have rocked any number of generations to sleep.

Knutsford itself is a little town of many oak beams and solid brick walls; there are so many slanting gables left, and lattices and corners, that the High Street has something the look of a mediæval street. ''Tis an old ancient place,' said the shopwoman, standing by her slanting counter, where Shakespeare himself might have purchased hardware. From the main street several narrow courts and passages lead to the other side of the little town, the aristocratic quarter, where are the old houses with their walled gardens. One of these passages runs right through the Royal George Hotel, itself leading from shadow into the sunshine, where a goat disports itself, and one or two ladies seem always passing with quiet yet rapid steps,—the inhabitants of Knutsford do not saunter. My friend the shopwoman told us she had a beautiful garden at the back of her 'old ancient place'; all the houses in Knutsford have gardens, with parterres beautifully kept, and flowers in abundance. It was autumn, but everything was swept and tidy. Straggling branches, plants overgrown and run to seed do not seem to be known in Knutsford amidst its heathy open spaces. There is something so spirited and fresh and methodical in the place that I can understand how even the flower-beds have a certain self-respect, and grow trim and straight, instead of straggling about in lazy abandon, as mine do at home.

As we entered the Royal George Hotel out of the dark street, we came upon a delightful broadside of shining oak staircase and panelled wainscot; old oak settles and cupboards stood upon the landings. On the walls hung pictures, one was of Lord Beaconsfield, one was a fine print of George IV., and others again of that denuded classic school of art which seems to have taken a last refuge in old English Inns. There were Chippendale cabinets, old bits of china, and above all there were the beautiful oak bannisters to admire. But these handsome staircases, the china, the wood carvings are all about the place, to which the great traffic of the coaches from Liverpool and Manchester brought real prosperity for many years, so that the modest little houses are full of worthy things, of pretty doorways, arched corners, carved landings and mahogany doors, to make the fortune of a dealer in bric-à-brac, only that these are not bric-à-brac, and this is their charm. The staircases and chimney-pieces are their own original selves, the cupboards were made to dwell in their own particular niches, and it is the passing generations who turn and unturn the keys as they go by. Our kind Interpreter at Knutsford patiently led us from one place to another; sometimes we seemed to be in Cranford, greeting our visionary friends; sometimes we were back in Knutsford again, looking at the homes of the people we had known in the fact rather than in the fancy. And just as one sometimes sees traces of another place and time still showing in the streets of some new and busy town, so every here

*and there seemed isolated signs and tokens of the visionary
familiar city as it has been raised by the genius of its
founder.*

III

*Mrs. Gaskell was a very beautiful young woman.   I
heard her described only the other day by a friend who
remembered her in her youth.   She had a well-shaped head,
regular, finely-cut features ; her mien was bright and
dignified, almost joyous, so my informant said, and
among her many other gifts was that of delightful
companionship.   She was very young when she was
married to the Reverend William Gaskell, minister of
the Cross Street Unitarian Chapel in Manchester.   She
was married from her aunt's house at Cranford at
the Parish Church, and not in the beautiful old Unitarian
Chapel, with its ivy-clad walls and its latticed windows,
dating from Oliver Cromwell's time.   In those days
marriages were only solemnised in the Parish Church.*

*The young couple settled in their new home, Mrs.
Gaskell ' co-operated with her husband in his work,' we
are told, ' and was always ready for any useful work of
charity or helpfulness.'*

*Mr. Gaskell was one of those ministers whose con-
gregations are outside as well as inside chapel walls, for
I have heard his name mentioned again and again by
different people, and always with affection and respect.*

For some years after her marriage Mrs. Gaskell lived

*a domestic life, busy with her children, and ordering her
household and training her maids, for which indeed she
had a special gift ; then a terrible sorrow fell upon her,
and we know how she began to write to divert her mind
from brooding upon the loss of her only son.*

In 1847 *she had finished that noble book,* Mary Barton,
that book with ' a sob in it,' as the French critic says.
' Ah ! quelle musique douloureuse dans un sanglot.'

But there is something far beyond a sob in Mary
Barton. *The writer is writing of what she has lived,
not only of what she has read or even looked at as she
passed her way. It is true she read* Adam Smith *and
studied* Social Politics, *but with that admirable blending
of the imaginative and the practical qualities which was
her gift, she knows how to stir the dry skeleton to life and
reach her readers' hearts. Many books and novels dealing
with the poor are touchingly expressed and finely conceived,
but somehow this particular gift of the spirit is wanting ;
we admire the books without being ourselves absorbed by
them. It is the difference in short between the light of
genius and the rays of the prism analysed, calculated,
divided. This power of living in the lives of others and
calling others to share the emotion, does not mean, as
people sometimes imagine, that a writer* copies *textually
from the world before her, I have heard my father say
that no author worth anything, deliberately, and as a rule,
copies the subject before him. And so with Mrs. Gaskell.
Her early impressions were vivid and dear to her, but
her world, though coloured by remembrance and sympathy,*

was peopled by the fresh creations of her vivid imagination, not by stale copies of the people she had known.

Mary Barton *made a great and remarkable sensation. Carlyle, Landor, Miss Edgeworth praised and applauded, and nameless thousands also praised and read the noble outspoken book. 'Individuals may have complained,' so says the biographer, from whom I have so often quoted, 'but the work has unquestionably helped to make the manufacturing world very different from what it was forty years ago.'*

The same intuition which guided her along the pleasant country lanes made her at home in the teeming streets and crowded alleys of Manchester.

A very interesting article by Monsieur Emile Monté-gut, written some thirty years ago, pays a fine tribute to Mrs. Gaskell's striking exposition of the life amidst which so much of her own was passed, to her depth of feeling, to her moderation of statement.

The article also, to my surprise, gives an answer to the little riddle I was trying to solve in my own mind as to the difference between the world of Cranford and that of Miss Austen. Each century possesses a force of its own, says the critic, one particular means of action, to the exclusion of others ; it may be intelligence, it may be passion, it may be determination, each rules in turn.

In the sixteenth century will *prevailed, and the character of the men and the martyrs of that time were in value far beyond their convictions. In the eighteenth century, on the contrary, the ideas were worth more than* the lives.   Books and pamphlets were better than the men who wrote them.   What is the force, says Mr. Montégut, of the age in which we ourselves are living? it is certainly not will, nor is it brilliant intelligence, as in the days of Voltaire.   It is a quality which, for want of a better word, we will call ' the force of sentiment.' . . . ' People,' he continues, ' have little confidence in systems, a man with a hobby is immediately a butt, but a man who is not obliged to be right in order to guard his vanity, has but to describe in a few simple and true sentences some fact, some moral wrong which needs redressing, and see the effect, and the silent help which immediately follows, and for this reason it is that in literature we have seen of late the almost exclusive reign of fiction.' . . .

It is this quality of statement which we find in Mrs. Gaskell's books which distinguishes them from so many which preceded them, and which gives them their influence.   It was because she had written Mary Barton that some deeper echoes reach us in Cranford than are to be found in any of Jane Austen's books, delightful as they are.   Young people read books to learn about their lives which are to come, old people read them to forget the present ; there is yet another class of readers, old and young, who read to find expression to the indefinite unshaped feelings by which they are haunted,—of all these will not each find response in the books of Elizabeth Gaskell, in Ruth, in Cousin Phyllis, in Sylvia's Lovers, in that last fine work which she never finished ?

It must be remembered that Mrs. Gaskell wrote in the

great time of literature, in the earlier part of the century. It remains for readers of this later time to see how nobly she held her own among the masters of her craft. ' She has done what we none of us could do,' said George Sand to Lord Houghton ; ' she has written novels which excite the deepest interest in men of the world, and yet which every girl will be the better for reading.'

We all know what a friend Mrs. Gaskell proved herself to Charlotte Brontë, and what happiness this friendship brought to the author of Jane Eyre. Mrs. Gaskell had the gift of giving out in a very remarkable degree. Miss Brontë, as we all know, was tortured and imprisoned by shyness. ' She does not, and cannot care for me, for she does not know me, how should she,' Miss Brontë says, writing of a child of Mrs. Gaskell, but that child's mother did Charlotte Brontë justice, and guessed by happy intuition at the treasure concealed in the unpretending casket.

Mrs. Gaskell quotes a letter from Miss Brontë in her Life which is very characteristic of them both. ' Do you, who have so many friends, so large a circle of acquaintance, find it easy when you sit down to write to isolate yourself from all those ties and their sweet associations, so as to be your own woman, uninfluenced or swayed by the consciousness of how your work may affect other minds, what blame or what sympathy it may call forth ; does no luminous cloud ever come between you and the severe truth in your own secret or clear-seeing soul ? ' This question is best answered by Mrs. Gaskell's own pages.

Whether or not she found it easy I cannot say, but that she did not 'isolate herself,' but did on the contrary entirely associate her own woman with the work of her life, her readers can best realise. Her great natural gift and genius instinctively led her to the secret of things, to the very soul of her race. She must have felt its life and spirit too keenly indeed for her own happiness at times, but how much has she not added to the sunshine of the world!

Not long ago I found myself in Mrs. Gaskell's old home in Manchester, and the thought of the beautiful books created in those very rooms seemed to give life to the stones and to light up the grim Manchester streets outside. Cranford was written in the house in Plymouth Grove, as were almost all Mrs. Gaskell's books. But when tired or overdone she used often to return to Knutsford for rest and for refreshment. Sometimes in later life she stayed with her cousins, the Miss Hollands, whose traditions she wove into shape, together with the quaint conceits and stories which are still told in Knutsford. It has its customs and oddities now, just as when Mrs. Gaskell was a girl. I am told that the streets are sanded on certain days in pretty patterns all along the pavement ; there are temperance processions in which the immortal sedan chair still figures, and I myself observed that some of the humbler bonnets formed quite an important feature in the scene, while recollections of Miss Matty's successive caps seemed to float across one's mind. It was delightful to hear the people of Knutsford still speak of Mrs. Gaskell, and of the pleasure her visits always brought, and the pleasure she always took in them ; of her long country drives with an old friend, a doctor, going his rounds, twenty and thirty miles at a time ; of her talk and interest in all the details along the way. She loved country things and farming things ; she always kept her cow, even in Manchester ; she understood the practical facts of life as well as its feelings. I have heard of her, tired and ill, starting on a three mile walk on behalf of a poor dependent, so as to make sure that some necessary help was properly administered. There is one thrilling tradition of Knutsford far too melodramatic for our Cranford, where the mere rumour of the housebreaker so alarmed Mr. Mulliner ; this story is that of the highwayman Higgins, who lived in Heath House, and who kept his horses underground concealed in the cellar. The highwayman must have enjoyed his lovely garden and his fine old staircase, when he was not escaping by his secret passage.

I heard of one Knutsford lady the other day, greatly excited by some piece of news,—no highway robbery, but a wedding, I believe. To soothe herself she was obliged to have a dish of toasted cheese prepared, and to send for a friend to play bezique, and share the news and the dainty ; it might have been Miss Barker herself. Another little story amused us greatly, so well was it told, and so characteristic of all times, old and new. One of the young Hollands born in the South was greatly interested in the family traditions, and he came for a holiday to Knutsford to see the old home of his fathers. He looked

*all about Knutsford, and then went on to Sandlebridge
to call on the old farmer there, and asked him many
questions, and begged him to show him all over the place.
And the old farmer kindly welcomed the young man for
his parents' and grandparents' sake, and said, ' O yes,
Master Frank, I'll show you about. I'll show you wonderful things ; I'll show you things will mak' your hair
stan' on end. Coom along o' me.' So they drove and
they drove along the lanes and under the hedgerows, and
all the way the young man wondered what was coming,
until finally the old farmer, who would not say a word
beforehand, stopped his horse and triumphantly pointed to
the bran new red and yellow villas which had been built
on Alderley Edge, where he found such good custom for
his butter and eggs. And these were the wonderful
things.*

*Knutsford likes to associate itself with Cranford in a
desultory visionary sort of way. One house claims Miss
Matty's tea-shop. The owner was standing in the doorway, and he kindly brought us into the little wainscoted
parlour, with the window on the street through which
Aga Jenkyns may have dispensed Miss Matty's stock of
sugar plums ; here too was a pretty carved staircase and
arches belonging to the early Georges ; another most
charming old house, Church House, with the lovely garden
where the children were gathering the apples and the gay
flower beds were skirting the turf walk, might almost
have been the home of Molly Gibson, and its present
mistress said she liked to imagine her peeping out from*

the side window at the old coaches as they clattered through the town. As I sate there drinking my tea I thought I could almost hear Mrs. Gibson herself conversing. 'Spring! Primavera, as the Italians call it,' the lady was saying.

CONTENTS

CRANFORD

Chapter I

Our Society

IN the first place, Cranford is in possession of the Amazons; all the holders of
houses, above a certain rent, are women.
If a married couple come to settle in the
town, somehow the gentleman disappears;
he is either fairly frightened to death by
being the only man in the Cranford even-
ing parties, or he is accounted for by being with his
regiment, his ship, or closely engaged in business all
the week in the great neighbouring commercial town
of Drumble, distant only twenty miles on a railroad.

B

In short, whatever does become of the gentlemen,
they are not at Cranford. What could they do if
they were there? The surgeon has his round of
thirty miles, and sleeps at Cranford; but every man
cannot be a surgeon. For keeping the trim gardens
full of choice flowers without a weed to speck them;
for frightening away little boys who look wistfully at
the said flowers through the railings; for rushing out
at the geese that occasionally venture into the gardens
if the gates are left open; for deciding all questions
of literature and politics without troubling themselves
with unnecessary reasons or arguments; for obtaining
clear and correct knowledge of everybody's affairs in the
parish; for keeping their neat maidservants in admirable order; for kindness (somewhat dictatorial) to the
poor, and real tender good offices to each other whenever they are in distress,—the ladies of Cranford are
quite sufficient. 'A man,' as one of them observed to
me once, 'is *so* in the way in the house!' Although
the ladies of Cranford know all each other's proceedings,
they are exceedingly indifferent to each other's opinions.
Indeed, as each has her own individuality, not to say
eccentricity, pretty strongly developed, nothing is so
easy as verbal retaliation; but, somehow, goodwill
reigns among them to a considerable degree.

The Cranford ladies have only an occasional little
quarrel, spirted out in a few peppery words and angry
jerks of the head; just enough to prevent the even
tenor of their lives from becoming too flat. Their
dress is very independent of fashion; as they observe,
'What does it signify how we dress here at Cranford,
where everybody knows us?' And if they go from
home, their reason is equally cogent, 'What does it

signify how we dress here, where nobody knows us?'
The materials of their clothes are, in general, good and
plain, and most of them are nearly as scrupulous as
Miss Tyler, of cleanly memory; but I will answer for
it, the last gigot, the last tight and scanty petticoat in

"A Magnificent
Family Red silk umbrella."

wear in England, was seen in Cranford—and seen
without a smile.

I can testify to a magnificent family red silk
umbrella, under which a gentle little spinster, left alone
of many brothers and sisters, used to patter to church
on rainy days. Have you any red silk umbrellas in

London ?   We had a tradition of the first that had
ever been seen in Cranford; and the little boys mobbed
it, and called it 'a stick in petticoats.'   It might have
been the very red silk one I have described, held by a
strong father over a troop of little ones ; the poor little
lady—the survivor of all—could scarcely carry it.

Then there were rules and regulations for visiting
and calls ; and they were announced to any young
people, who might be staying in the town, with all the
solemnity with which the old Manx laws were read
once a year on the Tinwald Mount.

'Our friends have sent to inquire how you are after
your journey to-night, my dear' (fifteen miles in a
gentleman's carriage) ; 'they will give you some rest
to-morrow, but the next day, I have no doubt, they
will call ; so be at liberty after twelve—from twelve to
three are our calling-hours.'

Then, after they had called—

'It is the third day ; I daresay your mamma has
told you, my dear, never to let more than three days
elapse between receiving a call and returning it ; and
also, that you are never to stay longer than a quarter
of an hour.'

'But am I to look at my watch ?   How am I to
find out when a quarter of an hour has passed ?'

'You must keep thinking about the time, my dear,
and not allow yourself to forget it in conversation.'

As everybody had this rule in their minds, whether
they received or paid a call, of course no absorbing
subject was ever spoken about.   We kept ourselves to
short sentences of small talk, and were punctual to our
time.

I imagine that a few of the gentlefolks of Cranford

were poor, and had some difficulty in making both
ends meet ; but they were like the Spartans, and concealed their smart under a smiling face.   We none of
us spoke of money, because that subject savoured of
commerce and trade, and though some might be poor,
we were all aristocratic.   The Cranfordians had that
kindly *esprit de corps* which made them overlook all
deficiencies in success when some among them tried
to conceal their poverty.   When Mrs. Forrester, for
instance, gave a party in her baby-house of a dwelling,
and the little maiden disturbed the ladies on the sofa
by a request that she might get the tea-tray out from
underneath, every one took this novel proceeding as the
most natural thing in the world, and talked on about
household forms and ceremonies as if we all believed
that our hostess had a regular servants' hall, second
table, with housekeeper and steward, instead of the one
little charity-school maiden, whose short ruddy arms
could never have been strong enough to carry the tray
upstairs if she had not been assisted in private by her
mistress, who now sat in state, pretending not to know
what cakes were sent up, though she knew, and we
knew, and she knew that we knew, and we knew that
she knew that we knew, she had been busy all the
morning making tea-bread and sponge-cakes.

There were one' or two consequences arising from
this general but unacknowledged poverty, and this very
much acknowledged gentility, which were not amiss, and
which might be introduced into many circles of society
to their great improvement.   For instance, the inhabitants of Cranford kept early hours, and clattered home
in their pattens, under the guidance of a lantern-bearer,
about nine o'clock at night ; and the whole town was

abed and asleep by half-past ten. Moreover, it was considered 'vulgar' (a tremendous word in Cranford) to give anything expensive, in the way of eatable or drinkable, at the evening entertainments. Wafer bread-and-butter and sponge-biscuits were all that the Honourable Mrs. Jamieson gave; and she was sister-in-law to the late Earl of Glenmire, although she did practise such 'elegant economy.'

'Clattered home in their pattens

'Elegant economy!' How naturally one falls back into the phraseology of Cranford! There, economy was always 'elegant,' and money-spending always 'vulgar and ostentatious'; a sort of sour grapism which made us very peaceful and satisfied. I never shall forget the dismay felt when a certain Captain Brown came to live at Cranford, and openly spoke about his being poor—not in a whisper to an intimate friend, the doors and windows being previously closed, but in the public street! in a loud military voice! alleging his poverty as a reason for not taking a particular house. The ladies of Cranford were already rather moaning over the invasion of their territories by a man and a gentleman. He was a half-pay Captain, and had obtained some situation on a neighbouring railroad, which had been vehemently petitioned against by the little town; and if, in addition to his masculine gender, and his con-

nection with the obnoxious railroad, he was so brazen
as to talk of being poor—why, then, indeed, he must be
sent to Coventry.   Death was as true and as common
as poverty ; yet people never spoke about that, loud
out in the streets.   It was a word not to be mentioned
to ears polite.   We had tacitly agreed to ignore that
any with whom we associated on terms of visiting
equality could ever be prevented by poverty from doing
anything that they wished.   If we walked to or from a
party, it was because the night was *so* fine, or the air *so*
refreshing, not because sedan chairs were expensive.   If
we wore prints, instead of summer silks, it was because
we preferred a washing material ; and so on, till we
blinded ourselves to the vulgar fact that we were, all of
us, people of very moderate means.   Of course, then,
we did not know what to make of a man who could
speak of poverty as if it was not a disgrace.   Yet, somehow, Captain Brown made himself respected in Cranford,
and was called upon, in spite of all resolutions to the
contrary.   I was surprised to hear his opinions quoted
as authority at a visit which I paid to Cranford about a
year after he had settled in the town.   My own friends
had been among the bitterest opponents of any proposal
to visit the Captain and his daughters only twelve
months before ; and now he was even admitted in the
tabooed hours before twelve.   True, it was to discover
the cause of a smoking chimney, before the fire was
lighted ; but still Captain Brown walked upstairs, nothing daunted, spoke in a voice too large for the room,
and joked quite in the way of a tame man about the
house.   He had been blind to all the small slights, and
omissions of trivial ceremonies, with which he had been
received.   He had been friendly, though the Cranford

ladies had been cool ; he had answered small sarcastic
compliments in good faith ; and with his manly frank-
ness had overpowered all the shrinking which met him
as a man who was not ashamed to be poor. And, at
last, his excellent masculine common sense, and his
facility in devising expedients to overcome domestic
dilemmas, had gained him an extraordinary place as
authority among the Cranford ladies. He himself went
on in his course, as unaware of his popularity as he had
been of the reverse ; and I am sure he was startled one
day when he found his advice so highly esteemed as to
make some counsel which he had given in jest to be
taken in sober, serious earnest.

It was on this subject : An old lady had an
Alderney cow, which she looked upon as a daughter.
You could not pay the short quarter-of-an-hour call
without being told of the wonderful milk or wonderful
intelligence of this animal. The whole town knew and
kindly regarded Miss Betsy Barker's Alderney ; therefore great was the sympathy and regret when, in an
unguarded moment, the poor cow tumbled into a lime-
pit. She moaned so loudly that she was soon heard
and rescued ; but meanwhile the poor beast had lost
most of her hair, and came out looking naked, cold, and
miserable, in a bare skin. Everybody pitied the animal,
though a few could not restrain their smiles at her droll
appearance. Miss Betsy Barker absolutely cried with
sorrow and dismay ; and it was said she thought of
trying a bath of oil. This remedy, perhaps, was recommended by some one of the number whose advice she
asked ; but the proposal, if ever it was made, was
knocked on the head by Captain Brown's decided ' Get
her a flannel waistcoat and flannel drawers, ma'am, if

you wish to keep her alive.   But my advice is, kill the
poor creature at once.'

Miss Betsy Barker dried her eyes, and thanked the
Captain heartily ; she set to work, and by and by all

' To see the Alderney.'

the town turned out to see the Alderney meekly going
to her pasture, clad in dark gray flannel.   I have
watched her myself many a time.   Do you ever see
cows dressed in gray flannel in London ?

Captain Brown had taken a small house on the out-skirts of the town, where he lived with his two daughters. He must have been upwards of sixty at the time of the first visit I paid to Cranford after I had left it as a residence. But he had a wiry, well-trained, elastic figure, a stiff military throw-back of his head, and a springing step, which made him appear much younger than he was. His eldest daughter looked almost as old as himself, and betrayed the fact that his real was more than his apparent age. Miss Brown must have been forty; she had a sickly, pained, careworn expression on her face, and looked as if the gaiety of youth had long faded out of sight. Even when young she must have been plain and hard-featured. Miss Jessie Brown was ten years younger than her sister, and twenty shades prettier. Her face was round and dimpled. Miss Jenkyns once said, in a passion against Captain Brown (the cause of which I will tell you presently), 'that she thought it was time for Miss Jessie to leave off her dimples, and not always to be trying to look like a child.' It was true there was something childlike in her face; and there will be, I think, till she dies, though she should live to a hundred. Her eyes were large blue wondering eyes, looking straight at you; her nose was unformed and snub, and her lips were red and dewy; she wore her hair, too, in little rows of curls, which heightened this appearance. I do not know whether she was pretty or not; but I liked her face, and so did everybody, and I do not think she could help her dimples. She had something of her father's jauntiness of gait and manner; and any female observer might detect a slight difference in the attire of the two sisters—that of Miss Jessie being about two pounds per

annum more expensive than Miss Brown's. Two
pounds was a large sum in Captain Brown's annual
disbursements.

Such was the impression made upon me by the
Brown family when I first saw them all together in

Sang out loud and joyfully.

Cranford Church. The Captain I had met before—on
the occasion of the smoky chimney, which he had cured
by some simple alteration in the flue. In church, he
held his double eye-glass to his eyes during the Morning
Hymn, and then lifted up his head erect and sang out
loud and joyfully. He made the responses louder than

the clerk—an old man with a piping feeble voice, who, I think, felt aggrieved at the Captain's sonorous bass, and quavered higher and higher in consequence.

'Coming out of church.'

On coming out of church, the brisk Captain paid the most gallant attention to his two daughters. He nodded and smiled to his acquaintances; but he shook hands with none until he had helped Miss Brown to unfurl her umbrella, had relieved her of her prayer-book, and had waited patiently till she, with trembling nervous hands, had taken up her gown to walk through the wet roads.

I wondered what the Cranford ladies did with Captain Brown at their parties. We had often rejoiced, in former days, that there was no gentleman to be attended to, and to find conversation for, at the card-parties. We had congratulated ourselves upon the snug-ness of the evenings ; and, in our love for gentility and distaste of mankind, we had almost persuaded ourselves that to be a man was to be ' vulgar '; so that when I found my friend and hostess, Miss Jenkyns, was going to have a party in my honour, and that Captain and the Miss Browns were invited, I wondered much what would be the course of the evening. Card-tables, with green-baize tops, were set out by daylight, just as usual ; it was the third week in November, so the evenings closed in about four. Candles and clean packs of cards were arranged on each table. The fire was made up ; the neat maidservant had received her last directions ; and there we stood, dressed in our best, each with a candle-lighter in our hands, ready to dart at the candles as soon as the first knock came. Parties in Cranford were solemn festivities, making the ladies feel gravely elated as they sat together in their best dresses. As soon as three had arrived, we sat down to ' Preference,' I being the unlucky fourth. The next four comers were put down immediately to another table ; and presently the tea-trays, which I had seen set out in the storeroom as I passed in the morning, were placed each on the middle of a card-table. The china was delicate egg-shell ; the old-fashioned silver glittered with polishing ; but the eatables were of the slightest description. While the trays were yet on the

tables, Captain and the Miss Browns came in; and I
could see that, somehow or other, the Captain was a
favourite with all the ladies present. Ruffled brows
were smoothed, sharp voices lowered at his approach.
Miss Brown looked ill, and depressed almost to gloom.
Miss Jessie smiled as usual, and seemed nearly as
popular as her father. He immediately and quietly
assumed the man's place in the room; attended to
every one's wants, lessened the pretty maidservant's
labour by waiting on empty cups and bread-and-
butterless ladies; and yet did it all in so easy and
dignified a manner, and so much as if it were a matter
of course for the strong to attend to the weak, that he
was a true man throughout. He played for threepenny
points with as grave an interest as if they had been
pounds; and yet, in all his attention to strangers, he
had an eye on his suffering daughter—for suffering I
was sure she was, though to many eyes she might only
appear to be irritable. Miss Jessie could not play
cards, but she talked to the sitters-out, who, before her
coming, had been rather inclined to be cross. She
sang, too, to an old cracked piano, which I think had
been a spinnet in its youth. Miss Jessie sang 'Jock o'
Hazeldean' a little out of tune; but we were none of
us musical, though Miss Jenkyns beat time, out of time,
by way of appearing to be so.

It was very good of Miss Jenkyns to do this; for I
had seen that, a little before, she had been a good deal
annoyed by Miss Jessie Brown's unguarded admission
(à propos of Shetland wool) that she had an uncle, her
mother's brother, who was a shopkeeper in Edinburgh.
Miss Jenkyns tried to drown this confession by a terrible
cough—for the Honourable Mrs. Jamieson was sitting

at the card-table nearest Miss Jessie, and what would
she say or think if she found out she was in the same
room with a shopkeeper's niece! But Miss Jessie Brown
(who had no tact, as we all agreed the next morning)
would repeat the information, and assure Miss Pole she
could easily get her the identical Shetland wool required,
'through my uncle, who has the best assortment of
Shetland goods of any one in Edinbro'.' It was to take
the taste of this out of our mouths, and the sound of
this out of our ears, that Miss Jenkyns proposed music ;
so I say again, it was very good of her to beat time to
the song.

When the trays reappeared with biscuits and wine,
punctually at a quarter to nine, there was conversation,
comparing of cards, and talking over tricks ; but by
and by Captain Brown sported a bit of literature.

'Have you seen any numbers of *The Pickwick
Papers* ?' said he. (They were then publishing in
parts.) 'Capital thing!'

Now Miss Jenkyns was daughter of a deceased
rector of Cranford ; and, on the strength of a number
of manuscript sermons, and a pretty good library of
divinity, considered herself literary, and looked upon
any conversation about books as a challenge to her.
So she answered and said, 'Yes, she had seen them ;
indeed, she might say she had read them.'

'And what do you think of them ?' exclaimed
Captain Brown. 'Aren't they famously good ?'

So urged, Miss Jenkyns could not but speak.

'I must say, I don't think they are by any means
equal to Dr. Johnson. Still, perhaps, the author is young.
Let him persevere, and who knows what he may become
if he will take the great Doctor for his model.' This

was evidently too much for Captain Brown to take
placidly ; and I saw the words on the tip of his tongue
before Miss Jenkyns had finished her sentence.

'It is quite a different sort of thing, my dear
madam,' he began.

The account of the " swarry."

'I am quite aware of that,' returned she. 'And I
make allowances, Captain Brown.'

'Just allow me to read you a scene out of this
month's number,' pleaded he. 'I had it only this
morning, and I don't think the company can have read
it yet.'

'As you please,' said she, settling herself with an air of resignation. He read the account of the 'swarry' which Sam Weller gave at Bath. Some of us laughed heartily. *I* did not dare, because I was staying in the house. Miss Jenkyns sat in patient gravity. When it was ended, she turned to me, and said, with mild dignity—

'Fetch me *Rasselas*, my dear, out of the book-room.'

When I brought it to her she turned to Captain Brown—

'Now allow *me* to read you a scene, and then the present company can judge between your favourite, Mr. Boz, and Dr. Johnson.'

She read one of the conversations between Rasselas and Imlac, in a high-pitched majestic voice; and when she had ended she said, 'I imagine I am now justified in my preference of Dr. Johnson as a writer of fiction.' The Captain screwed his lips up, and drummed on the table, but he did not speak. She thought she would give a finishing blow or two.

'I consider it vulgar, and below the dignity of literature, to publish in numbers.'

'How was *The Rambler* published, ma'am?' asked Captain Brown, in a low voice, which I think Miss Jenkyns could not have heard.

'Dr. Johnson's style is a model for young beginners. My father recommended it to me when I began to write letters—I have formed my own style upon it; I recommend it to your favourite.'

'I should be very sorry for him to exchange his style for any such pompous writing,' said Captain Brown.

Miss Jenkyns felt this as a personal affront, in a way of which the Captain had not dreamed. Epistolary writing she and her friends considered as her *forte*. Many a copy of many a letter have I seen written and corrected on the slate, before she 'seized the half-hour just previous to post-time to assure' her friends of this or of that; and Dr. Johnson was, as she said, her model in these compositions. She drew herself up with dignity, and only replied to Captain Brown's last remark by saying, with marked emphasis on every syllable, 'I prefer Dr. Johnson to Mr. Boz.'

It is said—I won't vouch for the fact—that Captain Brown was heard to say, *sotto voce*, 'D——n Dr. Johnson!' If he did, he was penitent afterwards, as he showed by going to stand near Miss Jenkyns's armchair, and endeavouring to beguile her into conversation on some more pleasing subject. But she was inexorable. The next day she made the remark I have mentioned about Miss Jessie's dimples.

Chapter II.

IT was impossible to live a month at Cranford and not know the daily habits of each resident; and long before my visit was ended I knew much concerning the whole Brown trio. There was nothing new to be discovered respecting their poverty; for they had spoken simply and openly about that from the very first. They made no mystery of the necessity for their being economical. All that remained to be discovered was the Captain's infinite kindness of heart, and the various modes in which, unconsciously to himself, he manifested it. Some little anecdotes were talked about for some time after they occurred. As we did not read much, and as all the ladies were pretty well suited with servants, there was a dearth of subjects for conversation. We therefore discussed the circumstance of the Captain taking a poor old woman's dinner out of her hands one very slippery Sunday. He had met her returning from the bakehouse as he came from church, and noticed her precarious footing; and, with the grave

'*Carrying her baked mutton and potatoes.*'

dignity with which he did everything, he relieved her of her burden, and steered along the street by her side, carrying her baked mutton and potatoes safely home. This was thought very eccentric; and it was rather expected that he would pay a round of calls, on the Monday morning, to explain and apologise to the

Cranford sense of propriety : but he did no such thing ; and then it was decided that he was ashamed, and was keeping out of sight. In a kindly pity for him we began to say, 'After all, the Sunday morning's occurrence showed great goodness of heart,' and it was resolved that he should be comforted on his next appearance amongst us ; but, lo! he came down upon us, untouched by any sense of shame, speaking loud and bass as ever, his head thrown back, his wig as jaunty and well-curled as usual, and we were obliged to conclude he had forgotten all about Sunday.

Miss Pole and Miss Jessie Brown had set up a kind of intimacy on the strength of the Shetland wool and the new knitting stitches ; so it happened that when I went to visit Miss Pole I saw more of the Browns than I had done while staying with Miss Jenkyns, who had never got over what she called Captain Brown's disparaging remarks upon Dr. Johnson as a writer of light and agreeable fiction. I found that Miss Brown was seriously ill of some lingering incurable complaint, the pain occasioned by which gave the uneasy expression to her face that I had taken for unmitigated crossness. Cross, too, she was at times, when the nervous irritability occasioned by her disease became past endurance. Miss Jessie bore with her at these times, even more patiently than she did with the bitter self-upbraidings by which they were invariably succeeded. Miss Brown used to accuse herself, not merely of hasty and irritable temper, but also of being the cause why her father and sister were obliged to pinch, in order to allow her the small luxuries which were necessaries in her condition. She would so fain have made sacrifices for them, and have lightened their cares, that the original generosity of her

disposition added acerbity to her temper.   All this was
borne by Miss Jessie and her father with more than
placidity—with absolute tenderness.   I forgave Miss
Jessie her singing out of tune, and her juvenility of
dress, when I saw her at home.   I came to perceive

'No one could black his boots
except himself.'

that Captain Brown's dark Brutus wig and padded coat
(alas! too often threadbare) were remnants of the
military smartness of his youth, which he now wore
unconsciously.   He was a man of infinite resources,
gained in his barrack experience.   As he confessed, no
one could black his boots to please him except himself:

but, indeed, he was not above saving the little maid-servant's labours in every way—knowing, most likely, that his daughter's illness made the place a hard one.

He endeavoured to make peace with Miss Jenkyns, soon after the memorable dispute I have named, by a present of a wooden fire-shovel (his own making), having heard her say how much the grating of an iron one annoyed her. She received the present with cool gratitude, and thanked him formally. When he was gone, she bade me put it away in the lumber-room ; feeling, probably, that no present from a man who preferred Mr. Boz to Dr. Johnson could be less jarring than an iron fire-shovel.

Such was the state of things when I left Cranford and went to Drumble. I had, however, several correspondents who kept me *au fait* as to the proceedings of the dear little town. There was Miss Pole, who was becoming as much absorbed in crochet as she had been once in knitting, and the burden of whose letter was something like, ' But don't you forget the white worsted at Flint's ' of the old song ; for at the end of every sentence of news came a fresh direction as to some crochet commission which I was to execute for her. Miss Matilda Jenkyns (who did not mind being called Miss Matty when Miss Jenkyns was not by) wrote nice, kind, rambling letters, now and then venturing into an opinion of her own ; but suddenly pulling herself up, and either begging me not to name what she had said, as Deborah thought differently, and *she* knew, or else putting in a postscript to the effect that, since writing the above, she had been talking over the subject with Deborah, and was quite convinced that, etc.—(here probably followed a recantation of every opinion she

had given in the letter). Then came Miss Jenkyns—
Debōrah, as she liked Miss Matty to call her, her father
having once said that the Hebrew name ought to be so
pronounced. I secretly think she took the Hebrew
prophetess for a model in character; and, indeed, she

Miss Jenkyns

was not unlike the stern prophetess in some ways,
making allowance, of course, for modern customs and
difference in dress. Miss Jenkyns wore a cravat, and
a little bonnet like a jockey-cap, and altogether had the
appearance of a strong-minded woman; although she
would have despised the modern idea of women being

equal to men. Equal, indeed! she knew they were
superior. But to return to her letters. Everything in
them was stately and grand, like herself. I have been
looking them over (dear Miss Jenkyns, how I honoured
her!), and I will give an extract, more especially because
it relates to our friend Captain Brown—

The Honourable Mrs. Jamieson has only just quitted
me; and, in the course of conversation, she communicated to me the intelligence that she had yesterday
received a call from her revered husband's quondam
friend, Lord Mauleverer. You will not easily conjecture
what brought his lordship within the precincts of our
little town. It was to see Captain Brown, with whom,
it appears, his lordship was acquainted in the "plumed
wars," and who had the privilege of averting destruction from his lordship's head, when some great peril was
impending over it, off the misnomered Cape of Good
Hope. You know our friend the Honourable Mrs.
Jamieson's deficiency in the spirit of innocent curiosity;
and you will therefore not be so much surprised when
I tell you she was quite unable to disclose to me the
exact nature of the peril in question. I was anxious, I
confess, to ascertain in what manner Captain Brown,
with his limited establishment, could receive so distinguished a guest; and I discovered that his lordship
retired to rest, and, let us hope, to refreshing slumbers,
at the Angel Hotel; but shared the Brunonian meals
during the two days that he honoured Cranford with
his august presence. Mrs. Johnson, our civil butcher's
wife, informs me that Miss Jessie purchased a leg of
lamb; but, besides this, I can hear of no preparation
whatever to give a suitable reception to so distinguished
a visitor. Perhaps they entertained him with "the feast

of reason and the flow of soul"; and to us, who are acquainted with Captain Brown's sad want of relish for "the pure wells of English undefiled," it may be matter for congratulation that he has had the opportunity of

'*One with whom his lordship held conversation.*'

improving his taste by holding converse with an elegant and refined member of the British aristocracy. But from some mundane failings who is altogether free?'

Miss Pole and Miss Matty wrote to me by the same post. Such a piece of news as Lord Mauleverer's visit was not to be lost on the Cranford letter-writers; they made the most of it. Miss Matty humbly apologised for writing at the same time as her sister, who was so much more capable than she to describe the honour done to Cranford; but, in spite of a little bad spelling, Miss Matty's account gave me the best idea of the commotion occasioned by his lordship's visit, after it had occurred; for, except the people at the Angel, the Browns, Mrs. Jamieson, and a little lad his lordship had sworn at for driving a dirty hoop against the aristocratic legs, I could not hear of any one with whom his lordship had held conversation.

My next visit to Cranford was in the summer. There had been neither births, deaths, nor marriages since I was there last. Everybody lived in the same house, and wore pretty nearly the same well-preserved old-fashioned clothes. The greatest event was, that the Miss Jenkynses had purchased a new carpet for the drawing-room. Oh, the busy work Miss Matty and I had in chasing the sunbeams, as they fell in an afternoon right down on this carpet through the blindless window! We spread newspapers over the places, and sat down to our book or our work; and lo! in a quarter of an hour the sun had moved, and was blazing away on a fresh spot; and down again we went on our knees to alter the position of the newspapers. We were very busy, too, one whole morning, before Miss Jenkyns gave her party, in following her directions, and in cutting out and stitching together pieces of newspaper so as to form little paths to every chair set for the expected visitors, lest their shoes might dirty or defile the purity of the carpet. Do you make paper paths for every guest to walk upon in London?

Captain Brown and Miss Jenkyns were not very cordial to each other. The literary dispute, of which I had seen the beginning. was a 'raw,' the slightest touch on which made them wince. It was the only difference of opinion they had ever had; but that difference was enough. Miss Jenkyns could not refrain from talking *at* Captain Brown; and, though he did not reply, he drummed with his fingers, which action she felt and resented as very disparaging to Dr. Johnson. He was rather ostentatious in his preference of the writings of Mr. Boz; would walk through the streets so absorbed in them that he all but ran against Miss Jenkyns; and though his apologies were earnest and sincere, and though he did not, in fact, do more than startle her and himself, she owned to me she had rather he had knocked her down, if he had only been reading a higher style of literature. The poor, brave Captain! he looked older, and more worn, and his clothes were very threadbare. But he seemed as bright and cheerful as ever, unless he was asked about his daughter's health.

'She suffers a great deal, and she must suffer more; we do what we can to alleviate her pain;—God's will be done!' He took off his hat at these last words. I found, from Miss Matty, that everything had been done, in fact. A medical man, of high repute in that country neighbourhood, had been sent for, and every injunction he had given was attended to, regardless of expense. Miss Matty was sure they denied themselves many things in order to make the invalid comfortable; but they never spoke about it; and as for Miss Jessie!—'I really think she's an angel,' said poor Miss Matty, quite overcome. 'To see her way of bearing with Miss Brown's crossness, and the bright face she puts on after she's been sitting up a whole night and scolded above half of it, is quite beautiful. Yet she looks as neat and as ready to welcome the Captain

at breakfast-time as if she had been asleep in the Queen's
bed all night.   My dear! you could never laugh at her
prim little curls or her pink bows again if you saw her
as I have done.'   I could only feel very penitent, and
greet Miss Jessie with double respect when I met her
next.   She looked faded and pinched; and her lips
began to quiver, as if she was very weak, when she spoke
of her sister.   But she brightened, and sent back the tears
that were glittering in her pretty eyes, as she said—

'But, to be sure, what a town Cranford is for kindness!   I don't suppose any one has a better dinner
than usual cooked, but the best part of all comes in
a little covered basin for my sister.   The poor people
will leave their earliest vegetables at our door for her.
They speak short and gruff, as if they were ashamed
of it; but I am sure it often goes to my heart to see
their thoughtfulness.'   The tears now came back and
overflowed; but after a minute or two she began to
scold herself, and ended by going away the same cheerful Miss Jessie as ever.

'But why does not this Lord Mauleverer do something for the man who saved his life?' said I.

'Why, you see, unless Captain Brown has some
reason for it, he never speaks about being poor; and
he walked along by his lordship looking as happy and
cheerful as a prince; and as they never called attention
to their dinner by apologies, and as Miss Brown was
better that day, and all seemed bright, I daresay his lordship never knew how much care there was in the background.   He did send game in the winter pretty often,
but now he is gone abroad.'

I had often occasion to notice the use that was
made of fragments and small opportunities in Cran-

ford : the rose-leaves that were gathered ere they fell
to make into a pot-pourri for some one who had no
garden ; the little bundles of lavender-flowers sent to
strew the drawers of some town-dweller, or to burn in
the chamber of some invalid.   Things that many would
despise, and actions which it seemed scarcely worth
while to perform, were all attended to in Cranford.
Miss Jenkyns stuck an apple full of cloves, to be
heated and smell pleasantly in Miss Brown's room ;
and as she put in each clove she uttered a Johnsonian
sentence.   Indeed, she never could think of the Browns
without talking Johnson ; and, as they were seldom
absent from her thoughts just then, I heard many a
rolling three-piled sentence.

Captain Brown called one day to thank Miss Jenkyns
for many little kindnesses, which I did not know until
then that she had rendered.   He had suddenly become
like an old man ; his deep bass voice had a quavering
in it, his eyes looked dim, and the lines on his face were
deep.   He did not—could not—speak cheerfully of his
daughter's state, but he talked with manly, pious resignation, and not much.   Twice over he said, 'What
Jessie has been to us, God only knows !' and after the
second time, he got up hastily, shook hands all round
without speaking, and left the room.

That afternoon we perceived little groups in the
street, all listening with faces aghast to some tale or
other.   Miss Jenkyns wondered what could be the
matter for some time before she took the undignified
step of sending Jenny out to inquire.

Jenny came back with a white face of terror.   'Oh,
ma'am ! oh, Miss Jenkyns, ma'am ! Captain Brown is
killed by them nasty cruel railroads !' and she burst

into tears.   She, along with many others, had experienced
the poor Captain's kindness.

'How?—where—where?   Good God!   Jenny, don't
waste time in crying, but tell us something.'   Miss Matty
rushed out into the street at once, and collared the man
who was telling the tale.

'Come in—come
to my sister at once,
—Miss Jenkyns, the
rector's daughter. Oh,
man, man!—say it is
not true,' she cried,
as she brought the
affrighted carter,
sleeking down his
hair, into the draw-
ing-room, where he
stood with his wet
boots on the new
carpet, and no one
regarded it.

'Please, mum, it
is true.   I seed it
myself,' and he shud-
dered at the recollec-

'And he shuddered at the recollection.'

tion.   'The Captain was a-reading some new book as
he was deep in, a-waiting for the down train; and there
was a little lass as wanted to come to its mammy, and
gave its sister the slip, and came toddling across the
line.   And he looked up sudden, at the sound of the
train coming, and seed the child, and he darted on the
line and cotched it up, and his foot slipped, and the
train came over him in no time.   Oh Lord, Lord!

Mum, it's quite true—and they've come over to tell his daughters. The child's safe, though, with only a bang on its shoulder, as he threw it to its mammy. Poor Captain would be glad of that, mum, wouldn't he? God bless him!' The great rough carter puckered up his manly face, and turned away to hide his tears. I turned to Miss Jenkyns. She looked very ill, as if she were going to faint, and signed to me to open the window.

'Matilda, bring me my bonnet. I must go to those girls. God pardon me, if ever I have spoken contemptuously to the Captain!'

Miss Jenkyns arrayed herself to go out, telling Miss Matilda to give the man a glass of wine. While she was away Miss Matty and I huddled over the fire, talking in a low and awestruck voice. I know we cried quietly all the time.

Miss Jenkyns came home in a silent mood, and we durst not ask her many questions. She told us that Miss Jessie had fainted, and that she and Miss Pole had had some difficulty in bringing her round; but that, as soon as she recovered, she begged one of them to go and sit with her sister.

'Mr. Hoggins says she cannot live many days, and she shall be spared this shock,' said Miss Jessie, shivering with feelings to which she dared not give way.

'But how can you manage, my dear?' asked Miss Jenkyns; 'you cannot bear up, she must see your tears.'

'God will help me—I will not give way—she was asleep when the news came; she may be asleep yet. She would be so utterly miserable, not merely at my father's death, but to think of what would become of me; she is so good to me.' She looked up earnestly in their faces with her soft true eyes, and Miss Pole told Miss Jenkyns afterwards she could hardly bear it, knowing, as she did, how Miss Brown treated her sister.

However, it was settled according to Miss Jessie's wish. Miss Brown was to be told her father had been summoned to take a short journey on railway business. They had managed it in some way—Miss Jenkyns could not exactly say how. Miss Pole was to stop with Miss Jessie. Mrs. Jamieson had sent to inquire. And this was all we heard that night; and a sorrowful night it was. The next day a full account of the fatal accident was in the county paper which Miss Jenkyns took in. Her eyes were very weak, she said, and she asked me to read it. When I came to the 'gallant gentleman was deeply engaged in the perusal of a number of *Pickwick*, which he had just received,' Miss Jenkyns shook her head long and solemnly, and then sighed out, ' Poor, dear, infatuated man !'

The corpse was to be taken from the station to the parish church, there to be interred. Miss Jessie had set her heart on following it to the grave ; and no dissuasives could alter her resolve. Her restraint upon herself made her almost obstinate ; she resisted all Miss Pole's entreaties and Miss Jenkyns's advice. At last Miss Jenkyns gave up the point ; and after a silence, which I feared portended some deep displeasure against Miss Jessie, Miss Jenkyns said she should accompany the latter to the funeral.

' It is not fit for you to go alone. It would be against both propriety and humanity were I to allow it.'

Miss Jessie seemed as if she did not half like this arrangement ; but her obstinacy, if she had any, had been exhausted in her determination to go to the interment. She longed, poor thing, I have no doubt, to cry

D

alone over the grave of the dear father to whom she had been all in all, and to give way, for one little half-hour, uninterrupted by sympathy and unobserved by friendship. But it was not to be. That afternoon Miss Jenkyns sent out for a yard of black crape, and employed herself busily in trimming the little black silk bonnet I have spoken about. When it was finished she put it on, and looked at us for approbation—admiration she despised. I was full of sorrow, but, by one of those whimsical thoughts which come unbidden into our heads, in times of deepest grief, I no sooner saw the bonnet than I was reminded of a helmet; and in that hybrid bonnet, half-helmet, half-jockey cap, did Miss Jenkyns attend Captain Brown's funeral, and, I believe, supported Miss Jessie with a tender indulgent firmness which was invaluable, allowing her to weep her passionate fill before they left.

Miss Pole, Miss Matty, and I, meanwhile, attended to Miss Brown : and hard work we found it to relieve her querulous and never-ending complaints. But if we were so weary and dispirited, what must Miss Jessie have been ! Yet she came back almost calm, as if she had gained a new strength. She put off her mourning dress, and came in, looking pale and gentle, thanking us each with a soft long pressure of the hand. She could even smile—a faint, sweet, wintry smile—as if to reassure us of her power to endure : but her look made our eyes fill suddenly with tears, more than if she had cried outright.

It was settled that Miss Pole was to remain with her all the watching livelong night ; and that Miss Matty and I were to return in the morning to relieve them, and give Miss Jessie the opportunity for a few hours of sleep. But when the morning came, Miss Jenkyns appeared at the breakfast-table, equipped in her helmet-bonnet, and ordered Miss Matty to stay at home, as she meant to go and help to nurse. She was evidently in a state of great friendly excitement, which she showed by eating her breakfast standing, and scolding the household all round.

No nursing—no energetic strong-minded woman could help Miss Brown now. There was that in the room as we entered which was stronger than us all, and made us shrink into solemn awestruck helplessness. Miss Brown was dying. We hardly knew her voice, it was so devoid of the complaining tone we had always associated with it. Miss Jessie told me afterwards that it, and her face too, were just what they had been formerly, when her mother's death left her the young anxious head of the family, of whom only Miss Jessie survived.

She was conscious of her sister's presence, though not, I think, of ours. We stood a little behind the curtain : Miss Jessie knelt with her face near her sister's, in order to catch the last soft awful whispers.

'Oh, Jessie! Jessie! How selfish I have been! God forgive me for letting you sacrifice yourself for me as you did! I have so loved you—and yet I have thought only of myself. God forgive me!'

'Hush, love! hush!' said Miss Jessie, sobbing.

'And my father! my dear, dear father! I will not complain now, if God will give me strength to be patient. But, oh, Jessie! tell my father how I longed and yearned to see him at last, and to ask his forgiveness. He can never know now how I loved him—oh! if I might but tell him, before I die! What a life of sorrow his has been, and I have done so little to cheer him!'

A light came into Miss Jessie's face. 'Would it comfort you, dearest, to think that he does know?— would it comfort you, love, to know that his cares, his sorrows——' Her voice quivered, but she steadied it into calmness,—'Mary! he has gone before you to the place where the weary are at rest. He knows now how you loved him.'

A strange look, which was not distress, came over Miss Brown's face. She did not speak for some time, but then we saw her lips form the words, rather than heard the sound—'Father, mother, Harry, Archy;'— then, as if it were a new idea throwing a filmy shadow over her darkened mind—'But you will be alone, Jessie!'

Miss Jessie had been feeling this all during the silence, I think; for the tears rolled down her cheeks like rain at these words, and she could not answer at first. Then she put her hands together tight, and lifted them up, and said—but not to us—

'Though He slay me, yet will I trust in Him.'

In a few moments more Miss Brown lay calm and still—never to sorrow or murmur more.

After this second funeral, Miss Jenkyns insisted that Miss Jessie should come to stay with her rather than go back to the desolate house, which, in fact, we learned from Miss Jessie, must now be given up, as she had not wherewithal to maintain it. She had something above twenty pounds a-year, besides the interest of the money for which the furniture would sell; but she could not live upon that: and so we talked over her qualifications for earning money.

'I can sew neatly,' said she, 'and I like nursing.
I think, too, I could manage a house, if any one would
try me as housekeeper; or I would go into a shop as
saleswoman, if they would have patience with me at
first.'

Miss Jenkyns declared, in an angry voice, that she
should do no such thing; and talked to herself about
'some people having no idea of their rank as a captain's
daughter,' nearly an hour afterwards, when she brought
Miss Jessie up a basin of delicately-made arrow-root,
and stood over her like a dragoon until the last spoon-
ful was finished: then she disappeared. Miss Jessie
began to tell me some more of the plans which had
suggested themselves to her, and insensibly fell into
talking of the days that were past and gone, and interested me so much I neither knew nor heeded how time
passed. We were both startled when Miss Jenkyns
reappeared, and caught us crying. I was afraid lest
she would be displeased, as she often said that crying
hindered digestion, and I knew she wanted Miss Jessie
to get strong; but, instead, she looked queer and excited,
and fidgeted round us without saying anything. At
last she spoke.

'I have been so much startled—no, I've not been
at all startled—don't mind me, my dear Miss Jessie—
I've been very much surprised—in fact, I've had a caller,
whom you knew once, my dear Miss Jessie——'

Miss Jessie went very white, then flushed scarlet, and
looked eagerly at Miss Jenkyns.

'A gentleman, my dear, who wants to know if you
would see him.'

'Is it?—it is not——' stammered out Miss Jessie
—and got no farther.

'This is his card,' said Miss Jenkyns, giving it to Miss Jessie; and while her head was bent over it, Miss Jenkyns went through a series of winks and odd faces

He shook hands with Miss Jessie

to me, and formed her lips into a long sentence, of which, of course, I could not understand a word.

'May he come up?' asked Miss Jenkyns at last.

'Oh yes! certainly!' said Miss Jessie, as much as to say, this is your house, you may show any visitor where you like. She took up some knitting of Miss Matty's and began to be very busy, though I could see how she trembled all over.

Miss Jenkyns rang the bell, and told the servant who answered it to show Major Gordon upstairs ; and, presently, in walked a tall, fine, frank-looking man of forty or upwards. He shook hands with Miss Jessie ; but he could not see her eyes, she kept them so fixed on the ground. Miss Jenkyns asked me if I would come and help her to tie up the preserves in the store-room ; and, though Miss Jessie plucked at my gown, and even looked up at me with begging eye, I durst not refuse to go where Miss Jenkyns asked. Instead of tying up preserves in the store-room, however, we went to talk in the dining-room ; and there Miss Jenkyns told me what Major Gordon had told her ;— how he had served in the same regiment with Captain Brown, and had become acquainted with Miss Jessie, then a sweet-looking blooming girl of eighteen ; how the acquaintance had grown into love on his part, though it had been some years before he had spoken ; how, on becoming possessed, through the will of an uncle, of a good estate in Scotland, he had offered and been refused, though with so much agitation and evi-dent distress that he was sure she was not indifferent to him ; and how he had discovered that the obstacle was the fell disease which was, even then, too surely threatening her sister. She had mentioned that the surgeons foretold intense suffering ; and there was no one but herself to nurse her poor Mary, or cheer and comfort her father during the time of illness. They had had long discussions ; and on her refusal to pledge herself to him as his wife when all should be over, he had grown angry, and broken off entirely, and

gone abroad, believing that she was a cold-hearted
person whom he would do well to forget. He had
been travelling in the East, and was on his return home
when, at Rome, he saw the account of Captain Brown's
death in *Galignani*.

Just then Miss Matty, who had been out all the
morning, and had only lately returned to the house,
burst in with a face of dismay and outraged propriety.

'Oh, goodness me!' she said. 'Deborah, there's a
gentleman sitting in the drawing-room with his arm
round Miss Jessie's waist!' Miss Matty's eyes looked
large with terror.

Miss Jenkyns snubbed her down in an instant.

'The most proper place in the world for his arm
to be in. Go away, Matilda, and mind your own
business.' This from her sister, who had hitherto
been a model of feminine decorum, was a blow for
poor Miss Matty, and with a double shock she left
the room.

The last time I ever saw poor Miss Jenkyns was
many years after this. Mrs. Gordon had kept up a
warm and affectionate intercourse with all at Cranford.
Miss Jenkyns, Miss Matty, and Miss Pole had all been
to visit her, and returned with wonderful accounts of
her house, her husband, her dress, and her looks. For,
with happiness, something of her early bloom returned;
she had been a year or two younger than we had taken
her for. Her eyes were always lovely, and, as Mrs.
Gordon, her dimples were not out of place. At the
time to which I have referred, when I last saw Miss
Jenkyns, that lady was old and feeble, and had lost
something of her strong mind. Little Flora Gordon
was staying with the Misses Jenkyns, and when I came

in she was reading aloud to Miss Jenkyns, who lay feeble and changed on the sofa. Flora put down *The Rambler* when I came in.

'Ah!' said Miss Jenkyns, 'you find me changed, my dear. I can't see as I used to do. If Flora were not here to read to me, I hardly know how I should get through the day. Did you ever read *The Rambler*? It's a wonderful book—wonderful! and the most improving reading for Flora' (which I daresay it would have been if she could have read half the words without spelling, and could have understood the meaning of a third), 'better than that strange old book, with the queer name, poor Captain Brown was killed for reading —that book by Mr. Boz, you know—*Old Poz*; when I was a girl—but that's a long time ago—I acted Lucy in *Old Poz*.' She babbled on long enough for Flora to get a good long spell at *The Christmas Carol,* which Miss Matty had left on the table.

Chapter 3.

A Love Affair of Long Ago.

I thought that probably my connection with Cranford would cease after Miss Jenkyns's death; at least, that it would have to be kept up by correspondence, which bears much the same relation to personal intercourse that the books of dried plants I sometimes see ('Hortus Siccus,' I think they call the thing) do to the living and fresh flowers in the lanes and meadows. I was pleasantly surprised, therefore, by receiving a letter from Miss Pole (who had always come in for a supplementary week after my annual visit to Miss Jenkyns) proposing that I should go and stay with her; and then, in a couple of days after my acceptance, came a note from Miss Matty, in which, in a rather circuitous and very humble manner, she told me how much pleasure I should confer if I could spend a week or two with her, either before or after I had been at Miss Pole's ; ' for,' she said, ' since my dear sister's death I am well aware I have no attractions to offer; it is only to the kindness of my friends that I can owe their company.'

Of course I promised to come to dear Miss Matty as soon as I had ended my visit to Miss Pole ; and the day after my arrival at Cranford I went to see her, much wondering what the house would be like without Miss Jenkyns, and rather dreading the changed aspect of things. Miss Matty began to cry as soon as she saw me. She was evidently nervous from having anticipated my call. I comforted her as well as I could ; and I found the best consolation I could give was the honest praise that came from my heart as I spoke of the deceased. Miss Matty slowly shook her head over each virtue as it was named and attributed to her sister ; and at last she could not restrain the tears which had long been silently flowing, but hid her face behind her handkerchief, and sobbed aloud.

' Dear Miss Matty!' said I, taking her hand—for indeed I did not know in what way to tell her how sorry I was for her, left deserted in the world. She put down her handkerchief, and said—

' My dear, I'd rather you did not call me Matty. *She* did not like it ; but I did many a thing she did not like, I'm afraid—and now she's gone! If you please, my love, will you call me Matilda ?'

I promised faithfully, and began to practise the new name with Miss Pole that very day ; and, by degrees, Miss Matilda's feeling on the subject was known through Cranford, and we all tried to drop the more familiar

name, but with so little success that by and by we gave
up the attempt.

My visit to Miss Pole was very quiet.   Miss Jenkyns
had so long taken the lead in Cranford that, now she
was gone, they hardly knew how to give a party.   The

'*If you please, my love, will you call me Matilda?*'

Honourable Mrs. Jamieson, to whom Miss Jenkyns
herself had always yielded the post of honour, was fat
and inert, and very much at the mercy of her old
servants.   If they chose that she should give a party,
they reminded her of the necessity for so doing ; if not,
she let it alone.   There was all the more time for me

to hear old-world stories from Miss Pole, while she sat knitting, and I making my father's shirts. I always took a quantity of plain sewing to Cranford ; for, as we did not read much, or walk much, I found it a capital time to get through my work. One of Miss Pole's stories related to a shadow of a love affair that was dimly perceived or suspected long years before.

Presently, the time arrived when I was to remove to Miss Matilda's house. I found her timid and anxious about the arrangements for my comfort. Many a time, while I was unpacking, did she come backwards and forwards to stir the fire, which burned all the worse for being so frequently poked.

'Have you drawers enough, dear?' asked she. 'I don't know exactly how my sister used to arrange them. She had capital methods. I am sure she would have trained a servant in a week to make a better fire than this, and Fanny has been with me four months.'

This subject of servants was a standing grievance, and I could not wonder much at it ; for if gentlemen were scarce, and almost unheard of in the 'genteel society' of Cranford, they or their counterparts—handsome young men—abounded in the lower classes. The pretty neat servant-maids had their choice of desirable 'followers' ; and their mistresses, without having the sort of mysterious dread of men and matrimony that Miss Matilda had, might well feel a little anxious lest the heads of their comely maids should be turned by the joiner, or the butcher, or the gardener, who were obliged, by their callings, to come to the house, and who, as ill-luck would have it, were generally handsome and unmarried. Fanny's lovers, if she had any—and Miss Matilda suspected her of so many flirtations that, if she had not been very pretty, I should have doubted her having one—were a constant anxiety to her mistress. She was forbidden, by the articles of her engagement,

to have 'followers'; and though she had answered, innocently enough, doubling up the hem of her apron as she spoke, 'Please, ma'am, I never had more than one at a time,' Miss Matty prohibited that one. But a vision of a man seemed to haunt the kitchen. Fanny assured me that it was all fancy, or else I should have said myself that I had seen a man's coat-tails whisk into the scullery once, when I went on an errand into the store-room at night; and another evening, when,

'So as to throw the shadow on the clock face.'

our watches having stopped, I went to look at the clock, there was a very odd appearance, singularly like a young man squeezed up between the clock and the back of the open kitchen door; and I thought Fanny snatched up the candle very hastily, so as to throw the shadow on the clock face, while she very positively told me the time half an hour too early, as we found out afterwards by the church clock. But I did not add to Miss Matty's anxieties by naming my suspicions, especially as Fanny said to me, the next day, that it was such a queer kitchen for having odd shadows about it, she really was almost afraid to stay; 'for you know, miss,' she added, 'I don't see a creature from six o'clock tea till Missus rings the bell for prayers at ten.'

However, it so fell out that Fanny had to leave; and Miss Matilda begged me to stay and 'settle her' with the new maid; to which I consented, after I had heard from my father that he did not want me at home. The new servant was a rough, honest-looking country girl, who had only lived in a farm place before; but I liked her looks when she came to be hired; and I promised Miss Matilda to put her in the ways of the house. The said ways were religiously such as Miss Matilda thought her sister would approve. Many a domestic rule and regulation had been a subject of plaintive whispered murmur to me during Miss Jenkyns's life; but now that she was gone, I do not think that even I, who was a favourite, durst have suggested an alteration. To give an instance: we constantly adhered to the forms which were observed, at meal times, in 'my father, the rector's house.' Accordingly, we had always wine and dessert; but the decanters were only filled when there was a party, and what remained was seldom touched, though we had two wine glasses apiece every day after dinner, until the next festive occasion arrived, when the state of the remainder wine was examined into in a family council. The dregs were often given to the poor; but occasionally, when a good deal had been left at the last party (five months ago, it might be), it was added to some of a fresh bottle, brought up from the cellar. I fancy poor Captain Brown did not much like wine, for I noticed he never finished his first glass, and most military men take several. Then, as to our dessert, Miss Jenkyns used to gather currants and goose-berries for it herself, which I sometimes thought would have tasted better fresh from the trees ; but then, as Miss Jenkyns observed, there would have been nothing for dessert in summer-time. As it was, we felt very genteel with our two glasses apiece, and a dish of gooseberries at the top, of currants and biscuits at the sides, and two decanters at the bottom. When oranges came in, a curious proceeding was gone through. Miss Jenkyns did not like to cut the fruit ; for, as she ob-served, the juice all ran out nobody knew where ; suck-ing (only I think she used some more recondite word) was in fact the only way of enjoying oranges ; but then there was the unpleasant association with a ceremony frequently gone through by little babies ; and so, after dessert, in orange season, Miss Jenkyns and Miss Matty used to rise up, possess themselves each of an orange in silence, and withdraw to the privacy of their own rooms to indulge in sucking oranges.

I had once or twice tried, on such occasions, to prevail on Miss Matty to stay, and had succeeded in her sister's lifetime. I held up a screen, and did not look, and, as she said, she tried not to make the noise very offensive ; but now that she was left alone, she seemed quite horrified when I begged her to remain with me in the warm dining-parlour, and enjoy her orange as she liked best. And so it was in everything. Miss Jenkyns's rules were made more stringent than ever, because the framer of them was gone where there

could be no appeal. In all things else Miss Matilda
was meek and undecided to a fault. I have heard
Fanny turn her round twenty times in a morning about
dinner, just as the little hussy chose ; and I sometimes
fancied she worked on Miss Matilda's weakness in order
to bewilder her, and to make her feel more in the power
of her clever servant. I determined that I would not
leave her till I had seen what sort of a person Martha
was ; and, if I found her trustworthy, I would tell her
not to trouble her mistress with every little decision.

Martha was blunt and plain-spoken to a fault ; otherwise she was a brisk, well-meaning, but very ignorant
girl. She had not been with us a week before Miss
Matilda and I were astounded one morning by the
receipt of a letter from a cousin of hers, who had been
twenty or thirty years in India, and who had lately, as
we had seen by the 'Army List,' returned to England,
bringing with him an invalid wife who had never been
introduced to her English relations. Major Jenkyns
wrote to propose that he and his wife should spend a
night at Cranford, on his way to Scotland—at the inn,
if it did not suit Miss Matilda to receive them into her
house ; in which case they should hope to be with her
as much as possible during the day. Of course, it *must*
suit her, as she said ; for all Cranford knew that she
had her sister's bedroom at liberty ; but I am sure she
wished the major had stopped in India and forgotten
his cousins out and out.

'Oh! how must I manage?' asked she helplessly.
'If Deborah had been alive she would have known
what to do with a gentleman-visitor. Must I put
razors in his dressing-room ? Dear ! dear ! and I've
got none. Deborah would have had them. And

E

slippers, and coat-brushes?' I suggested that probably
he would bring all these things with him. 'And after
dinner, how am I to know when to get up and leave
him to his wine? Deborah would have done it so
well; she would have been quite in her clement. Will
he want coffee, do you think?' I undertook the
management of the coffee, and told her I would instruct
Martha in the art of waiting—in which, it must be
owned, she was terribly deficient—and that I had no
doubt Major and Mrs. Jenkyns would understand the
quiet mode in which a lady lived by herself in a country
town. But she was sadly fluttered. I made her empty
her decanters and bring up two fresh bottles of wine.
I wished I could have prevented her from being present
at my instructions to Martha, for she frequently cut in
with some fresh direction, muddling the poor girl's mind,
as she stood open-mouthed, listening to us both.

'Hand the vegetables round,' said I (foolishly, I see
now—for it was aiming at more than we could accomplish with quietness and simplicity); and then, seeing
her look bewildered, I added, 'Take the vegetables
round to people, and let them help themselves.'

'And mind you go first to the ladies,' put in Miss
Matilda. 'Always go to the ladies before gentlemen
when you are waiting.'

'I'll do it as you tell me, ma'am,' said Martha;
'but I like lads best.'

We felt very uncomfortable and shocked at this
speech of Martha's, yet I don't think she meant any
harm; and, on the whole, she attended very well to
our directions, except that she 'nudged' the major
when he did not help himself as soon as she expected
to the potatoes, while she was handing them round.

The major and his wife were quiet, unpretending people enough when they did come ; languid, as all East Indians are, I suppose. We were rather dismayed at their bringing two servants with them, a Hindoo body-servant for the major, and a steady elderly maid

'She nudged the Major'

for his wife ; but they slept at the inn, and took off a good deal of the responsibility by attending carefully to their master's and mistress's comfort. Martha, to be sure, had never ended her staring at the East Indian's white turban and brown complexion, and I saw that Miss Matilda shrunk away from him a little as he waited at dinner. Indeed, she asked me, when they were gone, if he did not remind me of Blue Beard ? On the whole, the visit was most satisfactory, and is a subject of conversation even now with Miss Matilda ; at the time it greatly excited Cranford, and even stirred up the apathetic and Honourable Mrs. Jamieson to some expression of interest, when I went to call and thank her for the kind answers she had vouchsafed to Miss Matilda's inquiries as to the arrangement of a gentle-man's dressing-room—answers which, I must confess, she had given in the wearied manner of the Scandinavian prophetess—

Leave me, leave me to repose.

And *now* I come to the love affair.

It seems that Miss Pole had a cousin, once or twice removed, who had offered to Miss Matty long ago. Now this cousin lived four or five miles from Cranford on his own estate ; but his property was not large enough to entitle him to rank higher than a yeoman ; or rather, with something of the 'pride which apes humility,' he had refused to push himself on, as so many of his class had done, into the ranks of the squires. He would not allow himself to be called Thomas Holbrook, *Esq.*; he even sent back letters with this address, telling the postmistress at Cranford that his name was *Mr.* Thomas Holbrook, yeoman. He rejected all domestic innovations ; he would have the house-door stand open in summer and shut in winter, without knocker or bell to summon a servant. The closed fist or the knob of the stick did this office for him if he found the door locked. He despised every refinement which had not its root deep down in humanity. If people were not ill, he saw no necessity for moderating his voice. He spoke the dialect of the country in perfection, and constantly used it in conversation; although Miss Pole (who gave me these particulars) added, that he read aloud more beautifully and with more feeling than any one she had ever heard, except the late rector.

'And how came Miss Matilda not to marry him?' asked I.

'Oh, I don't know. She was willing enough, I think; but you know cousin Thomas would not have been enough of a gentleman for the rector and Miss Jenkyns.'

'Well! but they were not to marry him,' said I impatiently.

'No; but they did not like Miss Matty to marry below her rank. You know she was the rector's daughter, and somehow they are related to Sir Peter Arley: Miss Jenkyns thought a deal of that.'

'Poor Miss Matty!' said I.

'Nay, now, I don't know anything more than that he offered and was refused. Miss Matty might not like him—and Miss Jenkyns might never have said a word—it is only a guess of mine.'

'Has she never seen him since?' I inquired.

'No, I think not. You see Woodley, cousin Thomas's house, lies half-way between Cranford and Misselton; and I know he made Misselton his market-town very soon after he had offered to Miss Matty; and I don't think he has been into Cranford above once or twice since—once, when I was walking with Miss Matty, in High Street, and suddenly she darted from me, and went up Shire Lane. A few minutes after I was startled by meeting cousin Thomas.'

'How old is he?' I asked, after a pause of castle-building.

'He must be about seventy, I think, my dear,' said

'How are you? how are you?'

Miss Pole, blowing up my castle, as if by gunpowder, into small fragments.

Very soon after—at least during my long visit to Miss Matilda—I had the opportunity of seeing Mr. Holbrook; seeing, too, his first encounter with his

former love, after thirty or forty years' separation. I
was helping to decide whether any of the new assortment of coloured silks which they had just received at
the shop would do to match a gray and black mous-
seline-de-laine that wanted a new breadth, when a tall,
thin, Don Quixote-looking old man came into the shop
for some woollen gloves. I had never seen the person
(who was rather striking) before, and I watched him
rather attentively while Miss Matty listened to the
shopman. The stranger wore a blue coat with brass
buttons, drab breeches, and gaiters, and drummed with
his fingers on the counter until he was attended to.
When he answered the shop-boy's question, 'What can
I have the pleasure of showing you to-day, sir?' I saw
Miss Matilda start, and then suddenly sit down; and
instantly I guessed who it was. She had made some
inquiry which had to be carried round to the other
shopman.

'Miss Jenkyns wants the black sarsenet two-and-
twopence the yard;' and Mr. Holbrook had caught
the name, and was across the shop in two strides.

'Matty—Miss Matilda—Miss Jenkyns! God bless
my soul! I should not have known you. How are
you? how are you?' He kept shaking her hand in a
way which proved the warmth of his friendship; but
he repeated so often, as if to himself, 'I should not
have known you!' that any sentimental romance which
I might be inclined to build was quite done away with
by his manner.

However, he kept talking to us all the time we were
in the shop; and then waving the shopman with the
unpurchased gloves on one side, with 'Another time,
sir! another time!' he walked home with us. I am

happy to say my client, Miss Matilda, also left the shop
in an equally bewildered state, not having purchased
either green or red silk.   Mr. Holbrook was evidently
full with honest loud-spoken joy at meeting his old
love again ; he touched on the changes that had taken
place ; he even spoke of Miss Jenkyns as 'Your poor
sister !   Well, well ! we have all our faults ; ' and bade
us good-bye with many a hope that he should soon see
Miss Matty again.   She went straight to her room, and
never came back till our early tea-time, when I thought
she looked as if she had been crying.

Chapter 4.

A Visit to An Old Bachelor.

few days after, a note came from Mr. Holbrook, asking us—impartially asking both of us—in a formal, old-fashioned style, to spend a day at his house—a long June day—for it was June now. He named that he had also invited his cousin, Miss Pole; so that we might join in a fly, which could be put up at his house.

I expected Miss Matty to jump at this invitation; but, no! Miss Pole and I had the greatest difficulty in persuading her to go. She thought it was improper; and was even half annoyed when we utterly ignored the idea of any impropriety in her going with two other

ladies to see her old lover. Then came a more serious
difficulty. She did not think Deborah would have liked
her to go. This took us half a day's good hard talking
to get over ; but, at the first sentence of relenting, I
seized the opportunity, and wrote and despatched an
acceptance in her name—fixing day and hour, that all
might be decided and done with.

The next morning she asked me if I would go down
to the shop with her ; and there, after much hesitation,
we chose out three caps to be sent home and tried on,
that the most becoming might be selected to take with
us on Thursday.

She was in a state of silent agitation all the way to
Woodley. She had evidently never been there before ;
and, although she little dreamt I knew anything of her
early story, I could perceive she was in a tremor at the
thought of seeing the place which might have been her
home, and round which it is probable that many of her
innocent girlish imaginations had clustered. It was a
long drive there, through paved jolting lanes. Miss
Matilda sat bolt upright, and looked wistfully out of the
windows as we drew near the end of our journey. The
aspect of the country was quiet and pastoral. Woodley
stood among fields ; and there was an old-fashioned
garden where roses and currant-bushes touched each
other, and where the feathery asparagus formed a pretty
background to the pinks and gilly-flowers ; there was
no drive up to the door. We got out at a little gate,
and walked up a straight box-edged path.

'My cousin might make a drive, I think,' said Miss
Pole, who was afraid of ear-ache, and had only her
cap on.

'I think it is very pretty,' said Miss Matty, with a

soft plaintiveness in her voice, and almost in a whisper, for just then Mr. Holbrook appeared at the door, rubbing his hands in very effervescence of hospitality.   He looked more like my idea of Don Quixote than ever, and yet the likeness was only external.   His respectable housekeeper stood modestly at the door to bid us welcome ; and, while she led the elder ladies upstairs to a bedroom, I begged to look about the garden.   My request evidently pleased the old gentleman, who took me all round the place, and showed me his six and twenty cows, named after the different letters of the alphabet.   As we went along, he surprised me occasionally by repeating apt and beautiful quotations from the poets, ranging easily from Shakespeare and George Herbert to those of our own day.   He did this as naturally as if he were thinking aloud, and their true and beautiful words were the best expression he could find for what he was thinking or feeling.   To be sure he called Byron ‘ my Lord Byrron,’ and pronounced the name of Goethe strictly in accordance with the English sound of the letters—‘ As Goethe says, “ Ye ever-verdant palaces,” ’ etc.   Altogether, I never met with a man, before or since, who had spent so long a life in a secluded and not impressive country, with ever-increasing delight in the daily and yearly change of season and beauty.

When he and I went in, we found that dinner was nearly ready in the kitchen—for so I suppose the room ought to be called, as there were oak dressers and cupboards all round, all over by the side of the fireplace, and only a small Turkey carpet in the middle of the flag-floor.   The room might have been easily made into a handsome dark oak dining-parlour by removing the oven and a few other appurtenances of a kitchen, which were evidently never used, the real cooking-place being at some distance. The room in which we were expected to sit was a stiffly-furnished, ugly apartment; but that in which we did sit was what Mr. Holbrook called the counting-house, when he paid his labourers their weekly wages at a great desk near the door. The rest of the pretty sitting-room—looking into the orchard, and all covered over with dancing tree-shadows —was filled with books. They lay on the ground, they covered the walls, they strewed the table. He was evidently half-ashamed and half-proud of his extrava- gance in this respect. They were of all kinds—poetry and wild weird tales prevailing. He evidently chose his books in accordance with his own tastes, not because such and such were classical or established favourites.

'Ah!' he said, 'we farmers ought not to have much time for reading; yet somehow one can't help it.'

'What a pretty room!' said Miss Matty, *sotto voce*.

'What a pleasant place!' said I aloud, almost simultaneously.

'Nay! if you like it,' replied he; 'but can you sit on these great black-leather three-cornered chairs? I like it better than the best parlour; but I thought ladies would take that for the smarter place.'

It was the smarter place, but, like most smart things, not at all pretty, or pleasant, or home-like; so, while we were at dinner, the servant-girl dusted and scrubbed the counting-house chairs, and we sat there all the rest of the day.

We had pudding before meat; and I thought Mr. Holbrook was going to make some apology for his old- fashioned ways, for he began——

' I don't know whether you like new-fangled ways.'

' Oh, not at all!' said Miss Matty.

' No more do I,' said he. 'My housekeeper *will* have these in her new fashion ; or else I tell her that, when I was a young man, we used to keep strictly to my father's rule, " No broth, no ball ; no ball, no beef ; " and always began dinner with broth. Then we had suet puddings, boiled in the broth with the beef ; and then the meat itself. If we did not sup our broth, we had no ball, which we liked a deal better ; and the beef came last of all, and only those had it who had done justice to the broth and the ball. Now folks begin with sweet things, and turn their dinners topsy-turvy.'

When the ducks and green peas came, we looked at each other in dismay ; we had only two-pronged black-handled forks. It is true the steel was as bright as silver ; but what were we to do ? Miss Matty picked up her peas, one by one, on the point of the prongs, much as Aminé ate her grains of rice after her previous feast with the Ghoul. Miss Pole sighed over her delicate young peas as she left them on one side of her plate untasted, for they *would* drop between the prongs. I looked at my host : the peas were going wholesale into his capacious mouth, shovelled up by his large round-ended knife. I saw, I imitated, I survived ! My friends, in spite of my precedent, could not muster up courage enough to do an ungenteel thing ; and, if Mr. Holbrook had not been so heartily hungry, he would probably have seen that the good peas went away almost untouched.

After dinner a clay pipe was brought in, and a spittoon ; and, asking us to retire to another room,

where he would soon join us, if we disliked tobacco-
smoke, he presented his pipe to Miss Matty, and requested her to fill the bowl. This was a compliment
to a lady in his youth; but it was rather inappropriate

'Requested her to fill the bowl.'

to propose it as an honour to Miss Matty, who had
been trained by her sister to hold smoking of every
kind in utter abhorrence. But if it was a shock to her
refinement, it was also a gratification to her feelings to

be thus selected; so she daintily stuffed the strong tobacco into the pipe, and then we withdrew.

'It is very pleasant dining with a bachelor,' said Miss Matty softly, as we settled ourselves in the counting-house. 'I only hope it is not improper; so many pleasant things are!'

'What a number of books he has!' said Miss Pole, looking round the room. 'And how dusty they are!'

'I think it must be like one of the great Dr. Johnson's rooms,' said Miss Matty. 'What a superior man your cousin must be!'

'Yes!' said Miss Pole, 'he's a great reader; but I am afraid he has got into very uncouth habits with living alone.'

'Oh! uncouth is too hard a word. I should call him eccentric; very clever people always are!' replied Miss Matty.

When Mr. Holbrook returned, he proposed a walk in the fields; but the two elder ladies were afraid of damp and dirt, and had only very unbecoming calashes to put on over their caps; so they declined, and I was again his companion in a turn which he said he was obliged to take to see after his men. He strode along, either wholly forgetting my existence, or soothed into silence by his pipe—and yet it was not silence exactly. He walked before me, with a stooping gait, his hands clasped behind him; and, as some tree or cloud, or glimpse of distant upland pastures, struck him, he quoted poetry to himself, saying it out loud in a grand sonorous voice, with just the emphasis that true feeling and appreciation give. We came upon an old cedar-tree, which stood at one end of the house—

The cedar spreads his dark-green layers of shade.

'Capital term—"layers!" Wonderful man!' I did not know whether he was speaking to me or not; but I put in an assenting 'wonderful,' although I knew nothing about it, just because I was tired of being forgotten, and of being consequently silent.

He turned sharp round. 'Ay! you may say "wonderful." Why, when I saw the review of his

'*Or glimpse of distant upland pastures.*'

poems in *Blackwood*, I set off within an hour, and walked seven miles to Misselton (for the horses were not in the way) and ordered them. Now, what colour are ash-buds in March?'

Is the man going mad? thought I. He is very like Don Quixote.

'What colour are they, I say?' repeated he vehemently.

'I am sure I don't know, sir,' said I, with the meekness of ignorance.

'I knew you didn't. No more did I—an old fool that I am!—till this young man comes and tells me. Black as ash-buds in March. And I've lived all my life in the country; more shame for me not to know. Black: they are jet-black, madam.' And he went off again, swinging along to the music of some rhyme he had got hold of.

When we came back, nothing would serve him but he must read us the poems he had been speaking of; and Miss Pole encouraged him in his proposal, I thought, because she wished me to hear his beautiful reading, of which she had boasted; but she afterwards said it was because she had got to a difficult part of her crochet, and wanted to count her stitches without having to talk. Whatever he had proposed would have been right to Miss Matty; although she did fall sound asleep within five minutes after he had begun a long poem, called 'Locksley Hall,' and had a comfortable nap, unobserved, till he ended; when the cessation of his voice wakened her up, and she said, feeling that something was expected, and that Miss Pole was counting—

'What a pretty book!'

'Pretty, madam! it's beautiful! Pretty, indeed!'

'Oh yes! I meant beautiful!' said she, fluttered at his disapproval of her word. 'It is so like that beautiful poem of Dr. Johnson's my sister used to read—I forget the name of it; what was it, my dear?' turning to me.

'Which do you mean, ma'am? What was it about?'

'I don't remember what it was about, and I've quite forgotten what the name of it was; but it was written by Dr. Johnson, and was very beautiful, and very like what Mr. Holbrook has just been reading.'

'I don't remember it,' said he reflectively. 'But I don't know Dr. Johnson's poems well. I must read them.'

As we were getting into the fly to return, I heard Mr. Holbrook say he should call on the ladies soon, and inquire how they got home; and this evidently

"He had begun a long poem,

pleased and fluttered Miss Matty at the time he said it; but after we had lost sight of the old house among the trees her sentiments towards the master of it were gradually absorbed into a distressing wonder as to whether Martha had broken her word, and seized on the opportunity of her mistress's absence to have a 'follower.' Martha looked good, and steady, and composed enough, as she came to help us out; she was always careful of Miss Matty, and to-night she made use of this unlucky speech—

'Eh! dear ma'am, to think of your going out in an evening in such a thin shawl! It's no better than muslin. At your age, ma'am, you should be careful.'

'My age!' said Miss Matty, almost speaking crossly, for her, for she was usually gentle—'my age! Why, how old do you think I am, that you talk about my age?'

'Well, ma'am, I should say you were not far short of sixty: but folks' looks is often against them—and I'm sure I meant no harm.'

'Martha, I'm not yet fifty-two!' said Miss Matty, with grave emphasis; for probably the remembrance of her youth had come very vividly before her this day, and she was annoyed at finding that golden time so far away in the past.

But she never spoke of any former and more intimate acquaintance with Mr. Holbrook. She had probably met with so little sympathy in her early love that she had shut it up close in her heart; and it was only by a sort of watching, which I could hardly avoid since Miss Pole's confidence, that I saw how faithful her poor heart had been in its sorrow and its silence.

She gave me some good reason for wearing her best cap every day, and sat near the window, in spite of her rheumatism, in order to see, without being seen, down into the street.

He came. He put his open palms upon his knees, which were far apart, as he sat with his head bent down, whistling, after we had replied to his inquiries about our safe return. Suddenly he jumped up—

'Well, madam! have you any commands for Paris? I am going there in a week or two.'

'To Paris!' we both exclaimed.

'Yes, madam! I've never been there, and always had a wish to go; and I think if I don't go soon, I mayn't go at all; so as soon as the hay is got in I shall go, before harvest time.'

'Here are the poems for you.

We were so much astonished that we had no commissions.

Just as he was going out of the room, he turned back, with his favourite exclamation—

'God bless my soul, madam! but I nearly forgot half my errand. Here are the poems for you you admired so much the other evening at my house.' He tugged away at a parcel in his coat-pocket. 'Good-bye, miss,' said he; 'good-bye, Matty! take care of yourself.' And he was gone. But he had given her a book, and he had called her Matty, just as he used to do thirty years ago.

'I wish he would not go to Paris,' said Miss Matilda anxiously. 'I don't believe frogs will agree with him; he used to have to be very careful what he ate, which was curious in so strong-looking a young man.'

Soon after this I took my leave, giving many an injunction to Martha to look after her mistress, and to let me know if she thought that Miss Matilda was not so well; in which case I would volunteer a visit to my old friend, without noticing Martha's intelligence to her.

Accordingly I received a line or two from Martha every now and then; and, about November, I had a note to say her mistress was 'very low and sadly off her food'; and the account made me so uneasy that, although Martha did not decidedly summon me, I packed up my things and went.

I received a warm welcome, in spite of the little flurry produced by my impromptu visit, for I had only been able to give a day's notice. Miss Matilda looked miserably ill; and I prepared to comfort and cosset her.

I went down to have a private talk with Martha.

'How long has your mistress been so poorly?' I asked, as I stood by the kitchen fire.

'Well, I think it's better than a fortnight; it is, I know; it was one Tuesday, after Miss Pole had been, that she went into this moping way. I thought she was tired, and it would go off with a night's rest; but no! she has gone on and on ever since, till I thought it my duty to write to you, ma'am.'

'You did quite right, Martha. It is a comfort to think she has so faithful a servant about her. And I hope you find your place comfortable?'

'Well, ma'am, missus is very kind, and there's plenty to eat and drink, and no more work but what I can do easily,—but——' Martha hesitated.

'But what, Martha?'

'Why, it seems so hard of missus not to let me have any followers; there's such lots of young fellows in the town; and many a one has as much as offered to keep company with me; and I may never be in such a likely place again, and it's like wasting an opportunity. Many a girl as I know would have 'em unbeknownst to missus; but I've given my word, and I'll stick to it; or else this is just the house for missus never to be the wiser if they did come: and it's such a capable kitchen—there's such good dark corners in it—I'd be bound to hide any one. I counted up last Sunday night—for I'll not deny I was crying because I had to shut the door in Jem Hearn's face, and he's a steady young man, fit for any girl; only I had given missus my word.' Martha was all but crying again; and I had little comfort to give her, for I knew, from old experience, of the horror with which both the Miss Jenkynses looked upon 'followers'; and in Miss Matty's present nervous state this dread was not likely to be lessened.

I went to see Miss Pole the next day, and took her completely by surprise, for she had not been to see Miss Matilda for two days.

'And now I must go back with you, my dear, for I promised to let her know how Thomas Holbrook went on ; and, I'm sorry to say, his housekeeper has sent me word to-day that he hasn't long to live. Poor Thomas! that journey to Paris was quite too much for him. His housekeeper says he has hardly ever been round his fields since, but just sits with his hands on his knees in the counting-house, not reading or anything, but only saying what a wonderful city Paris was ! Paris has much to answer for if it's killed my cousin Thomas, for a better man never lived.'

'Does Miss Matilda know of his illness ? ' asked I— a new light as to the cause of her indisposition dawning upon me.

'Dear! to be sure, yes ! Has not she told you ? I let her know a fortnight ago, or more, when first I heard of it. How odd she shouldn't have told you ! '

Not at all, I thought ; but I did not say anything. I felt almost guilty of having spied too curiously into that tender heart, and I was not going to speak of its secrets — hidden, Miss Matty believed, from all the world. I ushered Miss Pole into Miss Matilda's little drawing-room, and then left them alone. But I was not surprised when Martha came to my bedroom door, to ask me to go down to dinner alone, for that missus had one of her bad headaches. She came into the drawing-room at tea-time, but it was evidently an effort to her ; and, as if to make up for some reproachful feeling against her late sister, Miss Jenkyns, which had been troubling her all the afternoon, and for which she now felt penitent, she kept telling me how good and how clever Deborah was in her youth ; how she used to settle what gowns they were to wear at all the parties (faint, ghostly ideas of grim parties, far away in the distance, when Miss Matty and Miss Pole were young!) ; and how Deborah and her mother had started the benefit society for the poor, and taught girls cooking and plain sewing; and how Deborah had once danced with a lord ; and how she used to visit at Sir Peter Arley's, and try to remodel the quiet rectory establishment on the plans of Arley Hall, where they kept thirty servants ; and how she had nursed Miss Matty through a long, long illness, of which I had never heard before, but which I now dated in my own mind as following the dismissal of the suit of Mr. Holbrook. So we talked softly and quietly of old times through the long November evening.

The next day Miss Pole brought us word that Mr. Holbrook was dead. Miss Matty heard the news in silence ; in fact, from the account of the previous day, it was only what we had to expect. Miss Pole kept calling upon us for some expression of regret, by asking if it was not sad that he was gone, and saying—

'To think of that pleasant day last June, when he seemed so well ! And he might have lived this dozen years if he had not gone to that wicked Paris, where they are always having revolutions.'

She paused for some demonstration on our part. I saw Miss Matty could not speak, she was trembling so nervously ; so I said what I really felt : and after a call of some duration—all the time of which I have no doubt Miss Pole thought Miss Matty received the news very calmly—our visitor took her leave.

Miss Matty made a strong effort to conceal her feelings—a concealment she practised even with me, for she has never alluded to Mr. Holbrook again,

although the book he gave her lies with her Bible on
the little table by her bedside. She did not think I
heard her when she asked the little milliner of Cranford
to make her caps something like the Honourable Mrs.
Jamieson's, or that I noticed the reply—

'But she wears widows' caps, ma'am ?'

"God forbid that I should grieve any young hearts."

'Oh ? I only meant something in that style ; not
widows', of course, but rather like Mrs. Jamieson's.'

This effort at concealment was the beginning of the
tremulous motion of head and hands which I have seen
ever since in Miss Matty.

The evening of the day on which we heard of Mr. Holbrook's death, Miss Matilda was very silent and thoughtful; after prayers she called Martha back, and then she stood, uncertain what to say.

'Martha!' she said at last, 'you are young'—and then she made so long a pause that Martha, to remind her of her half-finished sentence, dropped a curtsey, and said—

'Yes, please, ma'am; two and twenty last third of October, please, ma'am.'

'And perhaps, Martha, you may some time meet with a young man you like, and who likes you. I did say you were not to have followers; but if you meet with such a young man, and tell me, and I find he is respectable, I have no objection to his coming to see you once a week. God forbid!' said she in a low voice, 'that I should grieve any young hearts.' She spoke as if she were providing for some distant contingency, and was rather startled when Martha made her ready eager answer.

'Please, ma'am, there's Jem Hearn, and he's a joiner making three-and-sixpence a day, and six foot one in his stocking feet, please, ma'am; and if you'll ask about him to-morrow morning, every one will give him a character for steadiness; and he'll be glad enough to come to-morrow night, I'll be bound.'

Though Miss Matty was startled, she submitted to Fate and Love.

Chapter 5.

Old Letters.

I have often noticed that almost every one has his own individual small economies—careful habits of saving fractions of pennies in some one peculiar direction — any disturbance of which annoys him more than spending shillings or pounds on some real extravagance. An old gentleman of my acquaintance, who took the intelligence of the failure of a Joint-Stock Bank, in which some of his money was invested, with stoical mildness, worried his family all through a long summer's day, because one of them had torn (instead of cutting) out the written leaves of his now useless bank-book; of course the corresponding pages at the other end came out as well, and this little unnecessary waste of paper (his private economy) chafed him more than all the loss of his money. Envelopes fretted his soul terribly when they first came in; the only way in which he could reconcile himself to such waste of his cherished article was by patiently turning inside out all that were sent to him, and so making them serve again. Even now, though tamed by age, I see him casting wistful glances at his daughters when they send a whole inside of a half-sheet of note-paper, with the three lines of acceptance to an invitation, written on only one of the sides. I am not above owning that I have this human weakness myself. String is my foible. My pockets get full of little hanks of it, picked up and twisted together, ready for uses that never come. I am seriously annoyed if any one cuts the string of a parcel instead of patiently and faithfully undoing it fold by fold. How people can bring themselves to use india-rubber rings, which are a sort of deification of string, as lightly as they do, I cannot imagine. To me an india-rubber ring is a precious treasure. I have one which is not new—one that I picked up off the floor nearly six years ago. I have really tried to use it, but my heart failed me, and I could not commit the extravagance.

Small pieces of butter grieve others. They cannot attend to conversation because of the annoyance occasioned by the habit which some people have of invariably taking more butter than they want. Have you not seen the anxious look (almost mesmeric) which such persons fix on the article? They would feel it a relief if they might bury it out of their sight by popping it into their own mouths and swallowing it down ; and they are really made happy if the person on whose plate it lies unused suddenly breaks off a piece of toast (which he does not want at all) and eats up his butter. They think that this is not waste.

Now Miss Matty Jenkyns was chary of candles.

We had many devices to use as few as possible. In the winter afternoons she would sit knitting for two or three hours—she could do this in the dark, or by fire-light—and when I asked if I might not ring for candles to finish stitching my wristbands, she told me to 'keep blind man's holiday.' They were usually brought in with tea ; but we only burnt one at a time. As we lived in constant preparation for a friend who might come in any evening (but who never did), it required some contrivance to keep our two candles of the same length, ready to be lighted, and to look as if we burnt two always. The candles took it in turns ; and, what-ever we might be talking about or doing, Miss Matty's eyes were habitually fixed upon the candle, ready to jump up and extinguish it and to light the other before they had become too uneven in length to be restored to equality in the course of the evening.

One night, I remember this candle economy par-ticularly annoyed me. I had been very much tired of my compulsory 'blind man's holiday,' especially as Miss Matty had fallen asleep, and I did not like to stir the fire and run the risk of awakening her ; so I could not even sit on the rug, and scorch myself with sewing by fire-light, according to my usual custom. I fancied Miss Matty must be dreaming of her early life ; for she spoke one or two words in her uneasy sleep bearing reference to persons who were dead long before. When Martha brought in the lighted candle and tea, Miss Matty started into wakefulness, with a strange be-wildered look around, as if we were not the people she expected to see about her. There was a little sad expression that shadowed her face as she recognised me ; but immediately afterwards she tried to give me

her usual smile. All through tea-time her talk ran
upon the days of her childhood and youth. Perhaps
this reminded her of the desirableness of looking over
all the old family letters, and destroying such as ought
not to be allowed to fall into the hands of strangers ;

'*When Martha brought in the lighted candle and tea.*

for she had often spoken of the necessity of this task,
but had always shrunk from it, with a timid dread of
something painful. To-night, however, she rose up
after tea and went for them—in the dark ; for she
piqued herself on the precise neatness of all her chamber
arrangements, and used to look uneasily at me when I

lighted a bed-candle to go to another room for anything.
When she returned there was a faint pleasant smell of
Tonquin beans in the room.   I had always noticed this
scent about any of the things which had belonged to
her mother ; and many of the letters were addressed to
her—yellow bundles of love-letters, sixty or seventy
years old.

Miss Matty undid the packet with a sigh ; but she
stifled it directly, as if it were hardly right to regret the
flight of time, or of life either.   We agreed to look
them over separately, each taking a different letter out
of the same bundle and describing its contents to the
other before destroying it.   I never knew what sad
work the reading of old letters was before that evening,
though I could hardly tell why.   The letters were as
happy as letters could be—at least those early letters
were.   There was in them a vivid and intense sense of
the present time, which seemed so strong and full, as if
it could never pass away, and as if the warm living
hearts that so expressed themselves could never die, and
be as nothing to the sunny earth.   I should have felt
less melancholy, I believe, if the letters had been more
so.   I saw the tears stealing down the well-worn furrows
of Miss Matty's cheeks, and her spectacles often wanted
wiping.   I trusted at last that she would light the other
candle, for my own eyes were rather dim, and I wanted
more light to see the pale faded ink ; but no, even
through her tears, she saw and remembered her little
economical ways.

The earliest set of letters were two bundles tied
together, and ticketed (in Miss Jenkyns's handwriting),
' Letters interchanged between my ever-honoured father
and my dearly-beloved mother, prior to their marriage,

in July 1774.' I should guess that the rector of Cranford was about twenty-seven years of age when he wrote those letters; and Miss Matty told me that her mother was just eighteen at the time of her wedding. With my idea of the rector, derived from a picture in the dining-parlour, stiff and stately, in a huge full-bottomed wig, with gown, cassock, and bands, and his hand upon a copy of the only sermon he ever published—it was strange to read these letters. They were full of eager passionate ardour; short homely sentences, right fresh from the heart (very different from the grand Latinised, Johnsonian style of the printed sermon, preached before some judge at assize time). His letters were a curious contrast to those of his girl-bride. She was evidently rather annoyed at his demands upon her for expressions of love, and could not quite understand what he meant by repeating the same thing over in so many different ways; but what she was quite clear about was a longing for a white 'Paduasoy'—whatever that might be; and six or seven letters were principally occupied in asking her lover to use his influence with her parents (who evidently kept her in good order) to obtain this or that article of dress, more especially the white 'Paduasoy.' He cared nothing how she was dressed; she was always lovely enough for him, as he took pains to assure her, when she begged him to express in his answers a predilection for particular pieces of finery, in order that she might show what he said to her parents. But at length he seemed to find out that she would not be married till she had a 'trousseau' to her mind; and then he sent her a letter, which had evidently accompanied a whole boxful of finery, and in which he requested that she might

be dressed in everything her heart desired. This was
the first letter, ticketed in a frail, delicate hand, 'From
my dearest John.' Shortly afterwards they were married,
I suppose, from the intermission in their correspondence.

preached before some Judge

'We must burn them, I think,' said Miss Matty,
looking doubtfully at me. 'No one will care for them
when I am gone.' And one by one she dropped them
into the middle of the fire, watching each blaze up, die
out, and rise away, in faint, white, ghostly semblance,
up the chimney, before she gave another to the same
fate. The room was light enough now; but I, like

her, was fascinated into watching the destruction of
those letters, into which the honest warmth of a manly
heart had been poured forth.

The next letter, likewise docketed by Miss Jenkyns,
was endorsed, 'Letter of pious congratulation and
exhortation from my venerable grandfather to my
beloved mother, on occasion of my own birth. Also
some practical remarks on the desirability of keeping
warm the extremities of infants, from my excellent
grandmother.'

The first part was, indeed, a severe and forcible
picture of the responsibilities of mothers, and a warning
against the evils that were in the world, and lying in
ghastly wait for the little baby of two days old. His
wife did not write, said the old gentleman, because he
had forbidden it, she being indisposed with a sprained
ankle, which (he said) quite incapacitated her from
holding a pen. However, at the foot of the page was
a small 'T.O.,' and on turning it over, sure enough, there
was a letter to 'my dear, dearest Molly,' begging her,
when she left her room, whatever she did, to go *up*
stairs before going *down* : and telling her to wrap her
baby's feet up in flannel, and keep it warm by the fire,
although it was summer, for babies were so tender.

It was pretty to see from the letters, which were
evidently exchanged with some frequency between the
young mother and the grandmother, how the girlish
vanity was being weeded out of her heart by love for
her baby. The white 'Paduasoy' figured again in the
letters, with almost as much vigour as before. In one,
it was being made into a christening cloak for the baby.
It decked it when it went with its parents to spend a
day or two at Arley Hall. It added to its charms

when it was 'the prettiest little baby that ever was seen. Dear mother, I wish you could see her ! Without any parshality, I do think she will grow up a regular bewty !' I thought of Miss Jenkyns, gray, withered, and wrinkled, and I wondered if her mother had known her in the courts of heaven ; and then I knew that she had, and that they stood there in angelic guise.

There was a great gap before any of the rector's letters appeared. And then his wife had changed her mode of endorsement. It was no longer from 'My dearest John' ; it was from 'My honoured Husband.' The letters were written on occasion of the publication of the same Sermon which was represented in the picture. The preaching before 'My Lord Judge,' and the 'publishing by request,' was evidently the culminating point—the event of his life. It had been necessary for him to go up to London to superintend it through the press. Many friends had to be called upon, and consulted, before he could decide on any printer fit for so onerous a task ; and at length it was arranged that J. and J. Rivingtons were to have the honourable responsibility. The worthy rector seemed to be strung up by the occasion to a high literary pitch, for he could hardly write a letter to his wife without cropping out into Latin. I remember the end of one of his letters ran thus : 'I shall ever hold the virtuous qualities of my Molly in remembrance, *dum memor ipse mei, dum spiritus regit artus*,' which, considering that the English of his correspondent was sometimes at fault in grammar, and often in spelling, might be taken as a proof of how much he 'idealised his Molly' ; and, as Miss Jenkyns used to say, 'People talk a great deal about idealising nowadays, whatever that may mean.' But this was nothing to a fit of writing classical poetry which soon seized him, in which his Molly figured away as 'Maria.' The letter containing the *carmen* was endorsed by her, 'Hebrew verses sent me by my honoured husband. I thowt to have had a letter about killing the pig, but must wait. Mem., to send the poetry to Sir Peter Arley, as my husband desires.' And in a post-scriptum note in his handwriting it was stated that the Ode had appeared in the *Gentleman's Magazine*, December 1782.

Her letters back to her husband (treasured as fondly by him as if they had been *M. T. Ciceronis Epistolæ*) were more satisfactory to an absent husband and father than his could ever have been to her. She told him how Deborah sewed her seam very neatly every day, and read to her in the books he had set her ; how she was a very 'forrard,' good child, but *would* ask questions her mother could not answer, but how she did not let herself down by saying she did not know, but took to stirring the fire, or sending the 'forrard' child on an errand. Matty was now the mother's darling, and promised (like her sister at her age) to be a great beauty. I was reading this aloud to Miss Matty, who smiled and sighed a little at the hope, so fondly expressed, that 'little Matty might not be vain, even if she were a bewty.'

'I had very pretty hair, my dear,' said Miss Matilda ; 'and not a bad mouth.' And I saw her soon afterwards adjust her cap and draw herself up.

But to return to Mrs. Jenkyns's letters. She told her husband about the poor in the parish ; what homely domestic medicines she had administered ; what kitchen physic she had sent. She had evidently held his dis-pleasure as a rod in pickle over the heads of all the

ne'er-do-wells. She asked for his directions about the
cows and pigs; and did not always obtain them, as I
have shown before.

The kind old grandmother was dead when a little
boy was born, soon after the publication of the Sermon;
but there was another letter of exhortation from the
grandfather, more stringent and admonitory than ever,
now that there was a boy to be guarded from the snares
of the world. He described all the various sins into
which men might fall, until I wondered how any man
ever came to a natural death. The gallows seemed as if
it must have been the termination of the lives of most
of the grandfather's friends and acquaintance; and I
was not surprised at the way in which he spoke of this
life being 'a vale of tears.'

It seemed curious that I should never have heard of
this brother before; but I concluded that he had died
young, or else surely his name would have been alluded
to by his sisters.

By and by we came to packets of Miss Jenkyns's
letters. These Miss Matty did regret to burn. She
said all the others had been only interesting to those
who loved the writers, and that it seemed as if it would
have hurt her to allow them to fall into the hands of
strangers, who had not known her dear mother, and
how good she was, although she did not always spell
quite in the modern fashion; but Deborah's letters
were so very superior! Any one might profit by
reading them. It was a long time since she had read
Mrs. Chapone, but she knew she used to think that
Deborah could have said the same things quite as well;
and as for Mrs. Carter! people thought a deal of her
letters, just because she had written *Epictetus*, but she

was quite sure Deborah would never have made use of such a common expression as ' I canna be fashed!'

Miss Matty did grudge burning these letters, it was evident. She would not let them be carelessly passed over with any quiet reading, and skipping, to myself.

A Post Boy.

She took them from me, and even lighted the second candle in order to read them aloud with a proper emphasis, and without stumbling over the big words. Oh dear! how I wanted facts instead of reflections, before those letters were concluded! They lasted us two nights; and I won't deny that I made use of the time to think of many other things, and yet I was always at my post at the end of each sentence.

The rector's letters, and those of his wife and mother-in-law, had all been tolerably short and pithy, written in a straight hand, with the lines very close together. Sometimes the whole letter was contained on a mere scrap of paper. The paper was very yellow, and the ink very brown ; some of the sheets were (as Miss Matty made me observe) the old original post, with the stamp in the corner representing a post-boy riding for life and twanging his horn. The letters of Mrs. Jenkyns and her mother were fastened with a great round red wafer ; for it was before Miss Edgeworth's *Patronage* had banished wafers from polite society. It was evident, from the tenor of what was said, that franks were in great request, and were even used as a means of paying debts by needy members of Parliament. The rector sealed his espistles with an immense coat of arms, and showed by the care with which he had performed this ceremony that he expected they should be cut open, not broken by any thoughtless or impatient hand. Now, Miss Jenkyns's letters were of a later date in form and writing. She wrote on the square sheet which we have learned to call old-fashioned. Her hand was admirably calculated, together with her use of many-syllabled words, to fill up a sheet, and then came the pride and delight of crossing. Poor Miss Matty got sadly puzzled with this, for the words gathered size like snowballs, and towards the end of her letter Miss Jenkyns used to become quite sesquipedalian. In one to her father, slightly theological and controversial in its tone, she had spoken of Herod, Tetrarch of Idumea. Miss Matty read it 'Herod,

Petrarch of Etruria,' and was just as well pleased as if
she had been right.

I can't quite remember the date, but I think it was
in 1805 that Miss Jenkyns wrote the longest series of
letters—on occasion of her absence on a visit to some
friends near Newcastle-upon-Tyne. These friends were

'*Turning out of the volunteers.*'

intimate with the commandant of the garrison there,
and heard from him of all the preparations that were
being made to repel the invasion of Buonaparte, which
some people imagined might take place at the mouth
of the Tyne. Miss Jenkyns was evidently very much
alarmed ; and the first part of her letters was often

written in pretty intelligible English, conveying particulars of the preparations which were made in the family with whom she was residing against the dreaded event; the bundles of clothes that were packed up ready for a flight to Alston Moor (a wild hilly piece of ground between Northumberland and Cumberland); the signal that was to be given for this flight, and for the simultaneous turning out of the volunteers under arms—which said signal was to consist (if I remember rightly) in ringing the church bells in a particular and ominous manner. One day, when Miss Jenkyns and her hosts were at a dinner party in Newcastle, this warning summons was actually given (not a very wise proceeding, if there be any truth in the moral attached to the fable of the Boy and the Wolf; but so it was), and Miss Jenkyns, hardly recovered from her fright, wrote the next day to describe the sound, the breathless shock, the hurry and alarm; and then, taking breath, she added, 'How trivial, my dear father, do all our apprehensions of the last evening appear, at the present moment, to calm and inquiring minds!' And here Miss Matty broke in with—

'But, indeed, my dear, they were not at all trivial or trifling at the time. I know I used to wake up in the night many a time and think I heard the tramp of the French entering Cranford. Many people talked of hiding themselves in the salt mines—and meat would have kept capitally down there, only perhaps we should have been thirsty. And my father preached a whole set of sermons on the occasion; one set in the mornings, all about David and Goliath, to spirit up the people to fighting with spades or bricks, if need were; and the other set in the afternoons, proving that

Napoleon (that was another name for Bony, as we used
to call him) was all the same as an Apollyon and
Abaddon.   I remember my father rather thought he
should be asked to print this last set ; but the parish
had, perhaps, had enough of them with hearing.'

Peter Marmaduke Arley Jenkyns ('poor Peter !' as
Miss Matty began to call him) was at school at Shrewsbury by this time.   The rector took up his pen, and
rubbed up his Latin once more, to correspond with his
boy.   It was very clear that the lad's were what are
called show letters.   They were of a highly mental
description, giving an account of his studies, and his
intellectual hopes of various kinds, with an occasional
quotation from the classics ; but, now and then, the
animal nature broke out in such a little sentence as
this, evidently written in a trembling hurry, after the
letter had been inspected : 'Mother dear, do send me a
cake, and put plenty of citron in.'   The 'mother dear'
probably answered her boy in the form of cakes and
'goody,' for there were none of her letters among this
set ; but a whole collection of the rector's, to whom the
Latin in his boy's letters was like a trumpet to the
old war-horse.   I do not know much about Latin,
certainly, and it is, perhaps, an ornamental language,
but not very useful, I think—at least to judge from the
bits I remember out of the rector's letters.   One was,
'You have not got that town in your map of Ireland ;
but *Bonus Bernardus non videt omnia*, as the Proverbia
say.'   Presently it became very evident that 'poor
Peter' got himself into many scrapes.   There were
letters of stilted penitence to his father, for some
wrong-doing ; and, among them all was a badly-written,
badly-sealed, badly-directed, blotted note—'My dear,

dear, dear, dearest mother, I will be a better boy; I will, indeed; but don't, please, be ill for me; I am not worth it; but I will be good, darling mother.'

Miss Matty could not speak for crying, after she had read this note. She gave it to me in silence, and then got up and took it to her sacred recesses in her own room, for fear, by any chance, it might get burnt. 'Poor Peter!' she said; 'he was always in scrapes; he was too easy. They led him wrong, and then left him in the lurch. But he was too fond of mischief. He could never resist a joke. Poor Peter!'

Chapter 6.

Poor Peter

Poor *Peter's* career lay before him rather pleasantly mapped out by kind friends, but *Bonus Bernardus non videt omnia*, in this map too. He was to win honours at Shrewsbury School, and carry them thick to Cambridge, and after that, a living awaited him, the gift of his godfather, Sir Peter Arley. Poor Peter! his lot in life was very different to what his friends had hoped and planned. Miss Matty told me all about it, and I think it was a relief to her when she had done so.

He was the darling of his mother, who seemed to dote on all her children, though she was, perhaps, a little afraid of Deborah's superior acquirements. Deborah was the favourite of her father, and when Peter disappointed him she became his pride. The sole honour Peter brought away from Shrewsbury was the reputation of being the best good fellow that ever was, and of being the captain of the school in the art of practical joking. His father was disappointed, but set about remedying the matter in a manly way. He could not afford to send Peter to read with any tutor, but he could read with him himself ; and Miss Matty told me much of the awful preparations in the way of dictionaries and lexicons that were made in her father's study the morning Peter began.

'My poor mother!' said she. 'I remember how she used to stand in the hall, just near enough the study-door, to catch the tone of my father's voice. I could tell in a moment if all was going right, by her face. And it did go right for a long time.'

'What went wrong at last?' said I. 'That tiresome Latin, I daresay.'

'No! it was not the Latin. Peter was in high favour with my father, for he worked up well for him. But he seemed to think that the Cranford people might be joked about, and made fun of, and they did not like it ; nobody does. He was always hoaxing them ; "hoaxing" is not a pretty word, my dear, and I hope you won't tell your father I used it, for I should not like him to think that I was not choice in my language, after living with such a woman as Deborah. And be sure you never use it yourself. I don't know how it slipped out of my mouth, except it was that I was thinking of poor Peter, and it was always his expression. But he was a very gentlemanly boy in many things. He was like dear Captain Brown in always being ready to help any old person or a child. Still, he did like joking and making fun ; and he seemed to think the old ladies in Cranford would believe anything. There were many old ladies living here then ; we are principally ladies now, I know, but we are not so old as the ladies used to be when I was a girl. I could laugh to think of some of Peter's jokes. No, my dear, I won't tell you of them, because they might not shock you as they ought to do, and they were very shocking. He even took in my father once, by dressing himself up as a lady that was passing through the town and wished to see the Rector of Cranford, "who had published that admirable Assize Sermon." Peter said he was awfully frightened himself when he saw how my father took it all in, and even offered to copy out all his Napoleon Buonaparte sermons for her—him, I mean—no, her, for Peter was a lady then. He told me he was more terrified than he ever was before, all the time my father was speaking. He did not think my father would have believed him; and yet if he had not, it would have been a sad thing for Peter. As it was, he was none so glad of it, for my father kept him hard at work copying out all those twelve Buonaparte sermons for the lady —that was for Peter himself, you know. He was the lady. And once when he wanted to go fishing, Peter said, "Confound the woman!"—very bad language, my dear, but Peter was not always so guarded as he should have been; my father was so angry with him, it nearly frightened me out of my wits: and yet I could hardly keep from laughing at the little curtseys Peter kept making, quite slyly, whenever my father spoke of the lady's excellent taste and sound discrimination.'

'Did Miss Jenkyns know of these tricks?' said I.

'Oh no! Deborah would have been too much shocked. No, no one knew but me. I wish I had always known of Peter's plans; but sometimes he did not tell me. He used to say the old ladies in the town wanted something to talk about; but I don't think

they did.   They had the *St. James's Chronicle* three
times a week, just as we have now, and we have plenty
to say; and I remember the clacking noise there
always was when some of the ladies got together.

'*The little curtseys.*'

But, probably, schoolboys talk more than ladies.   At
last there was a terrible, sad thing happened.'   Miss
Matty got up, went to the door, and opened it; no
one was there.   She rang the bell for Martha, and

when Martha came, her mistress told her to go for eggs
to a farm at the other end of the town.

'I will lock the door after you, Martha. You are
not afraid to go, are you?'

'No, ma'am, not at all; Jem Hearn will be only too
proud to go with me.'

Miss Matty drew herself up, and as soon as we
were alone, she wished that Martha had more maidenly
reserve.

'We'll put out the candle, my dear. We can
talk just as well by firelight, you know. There!
Well, you see, Deborah had gone from home for a
fortnight or so; it was a very still, quiet day, I
remember, overhead; and the lilacs were all in flower,
so I suppose it was spring. My father had gone out
to see some sick people in the parish; I recollect seeing
him leave the house with his wig and shovel-hat and
cane. What possessed our poor Peter I don't know;
he had the sweetest temper, and yet he always seemed
to like to plague Deborah. She never laughed at his
jokes, and thought him ungenteel, and not careful
enough about improving his mind; and that vexed
him.

'Well! he went to her room, it seems, and dressed
himself in her old gown, and shawl, and bonnet; just
the things she used to wear in Cranford, and was
known by everywhere; and he made the pillow into a
little—you are sure you locked the door, my dear, for
I should not like any one to hear—into—into—a little
baby, with white long clothes. It was only, as he told
me afterwards, to make something to talk about in the
town; he never thought of it as affecting Deborah.
and he went and walked up and down in the Filbert

walk—just half-hidden by the rails, and half-seen ; and
he cuddled his pillow, just like a baby, and talked to it
all the nonsense people do. Oh dear ! and my father
came stepping stately up the street, as he always did ;
and what should he see but a little black crowd
of people—I daresay as many as twenty—all peeping
through his garden rails. So he thought, at first, they
were only looking at a new rhododendron that was in
full bloom, and that he was very proud of ; and he
walked slower, that they might have more time to admire.
And he wondered if he could make out a sermon from
the occasion, and thought, perhaps, there was some
relation between the rhododendrons and the lilies of
the field. My poor father ! When he came nearer, he
began to wonder that they did not see him ; but their
heads were all so close together, peeping and peeping !
My father was amongst them, meaning, he said, to ask
them to walk into the garden with him, and admire
the beautiful vegetable production, when—oh, my dear !
I tremble to think of it—he looked through the rails
himself, and saw—I don't know what he thought he
saw, but old Clare told me his face went quite gray-
white with anger, and his eyes blazed out under his
frowning black brows ; and he spoke out—oh, so
terribly !—and bade them all stop where they were—
not one of them to go, not one to stir a step ; and,
swift as light, he was in at the garden door, and down
the Filbert walk, and seized hold of poor Peter, and
tore his clothes off his back—bonnet, shawl, gown, and
all—and threw the pillow among the people over the
railings : and then he was very, very angry indeed, and
before all the people he lifted up his cane and flogged
Peter !

H

'My dear, that boy's trick, on that sunny day, when
all seemed going straight and well, broke my mother's

" Have you done enough, Sir?'

heart, and changed my father for life. It did, indeed.
Old Clare said, Peter looked as white as my father;

and stood as still as a statue to be flogged ; and my
father struck hard ! When my father stopped to take
breath, Peter said, " Have you done enough, sir ? " quite
hoarsely, and still standing quite quiet. I don't know
what my father said—or if he said anything. But old
Clare said, Peter turned to where the people outside
the railing were, and made them a low bow, as grand
and as grave as any gentleman ; and then walked
slowly into the house. I was in the store-room helping
my mother to make cowslip wine. I cannot abide the
wine now, nor the scent of the flowers ; they turn me
sick and faint, as they did that day, when Peter came
in, looking as haughty as any man—indeed, looking
like a man, not like a boy. " Mother ! " he said, " I
am come to say, God bless you for ever." I saw his
lips quiver as he spoke ; and I think he durst not say
anything more loving, for the purpose that was in his
heart. She looked at him rather frightened, and wondering, and asked him what was to do. He did not smile
or speak, but put his arms round her and kissed her as
if he did not know how to leave off ; and before she
could speak again, he was gone. We talked it over, and
could not understand it, and she bade me go and seek
my father, and ask what it was all about. I found him
walking up and down, looking very highly displeased.

' " Tell your mother I have flogged Peter, and that
he richly deserved it."

' I durst not ask any more questions. When I told
my mother, she sat down, quite faint, for a minute. I
remember, a few days after, I saw the poor, withered
cowslip flowers thrown out to the leaf heap, to decay
and die there. There was no making of cowslip-wine
that year at the rectory—nor, indeed, ever after.

'Presently my mother went to my father. I know I thought of Queen Esther and King Ahasuerus; for my mother was very pretty and delicate-looking, and my father looked as terrible as King Ahasuerus. Some time after they came out together; and then my mother told me what had happened, and that she was going up to Peter's room at my father's desire—though she was not to tell Peter this—to talk the matter over with him. But no Peter was there. We looked over the house; no Peter was there! Even my father, who had not liked to join in the search at first, helped us before long. The rectory was a very old house—steps up into a room, steps down into a room, all through. At first, my mother went calling low and soft, as if to reassure the poor boy, "Peter! Peter, dear! it's only me;" but, by and by, as the servants came back from the errands my father had sent them, in different directions, to find where Peter was—as we found he was not in the garden, nor the hayloft, nor anywhere about—my mother's cry grew louder and wilder, "Peter! Peter, my darling! where are you?" for then she felt and understood that that long kiss meant some sad kind of "good-bye." The afternoon went on—my mother never resting, but seeking again and again in every possible place that had been looked into twenty times before, nay, that she had looked into over and over again herself. My father sat with his head in his hands, not speaking except when his messengers came in, bringing no tidings; then he lifted up his face, so strong and sad, and told them to go again in some new direction. My mother kept passing from room to room, in and out of the house, moving noiselessly, but never ceasing. Neither she nor my father durst leave the

house, which was the meeting-place for all the
messengers.   At last (and it was nearly dark) my
father rose up.   He took hold of my mother's arm as
she came with wild, sad pace through one door, and
quickly towards another.   She started at the touch of
his hand, for she had forgotten all in the world but
Peter.

'" Molly!" said he, "I did not think all this would
happen." He looked into her face for comfort——her
poor face, all wild and white; for neither she nor my
father had dared to acknowledge——much less act upon
——the terror that was in their hearts, lest Peter should
have made away with himself.   My father saw no
conscious look in his wife's hot, dreary eyes, and he
missed the sympathy that she had always been ready
to give him——strong man as he was, and at the dumb
despair in her face his tears began to flow.   But when
she saw this, a gentle sorrow came over her countenance,
and she said, "Dearest John! don't cry; come with me,
and we'll find him," almost as cheerfully as if she knew
where he was.   And she took my father's great hand
in her little soft one and led him along, the tears
dropping as he walked on that same unceasing, weary
walk, from room to room, through house and garden.

'Oh, how I wished for Deborah!   I had no time
for crying, for now all seemed to depend on me.   I
wrote for Deborah to come home.   I sent a message
privately to that same Mr. Holbrook's house——poor Mr.
Holbrook!——you know who I mean.   I don't mean I
sent a message to him, but I sent one that I could
trust to know if Peter was at his house.   For at one
time Mr. Holbrook was an occasional visitor at the
rectory——you know he was Miss Pole's cousin——and he

had been very kind to Peter, and taught him how to fish—he was very kind to everybody, and I thought Peter might have gone off there. But Mr. Holbrook was from home, and Peter had never been seen. It was night now ; but the doors were all wide open, and my father and mother walked on and on ; it was more than an hour since he had joined her, and I don't believe they had ever spoken all that time. I was getting the parlour fire lighted, and one of the servants was preparing tea, for I wanted them to have something to eat and drink and warm them, when Old Clare asked to speak to me.

'"I have borrowed the nets from the weir, Miss Matty. Shall we drag the ponds to-night, or wait for the morning ?"

'I remember staring in his face to gather his meaning ; and when I did, I laughed out loud. The horror of that new thought—our bright, darling Peter, cold, and stark, and dead ! I remember the ring of my own laugh now.

'The next day Deborah was at home before I was myself again. She would not have been so weak as to give way as I had done ; but my screams (my horrible laughter had ended in crying) had roused my sweet dear mother, whose poor wandering wits were called back and collected as soon as a child needed her care. She and Deborah sat by my bedside ; I knew by the looks of each that there had been no news of Peter—no awful, ghastly news, which was what I most had dreaded in my dull state between sleeping and waking.

'The same result of all the searching had brought something of the same relief to my mother, to whom, I

am sure, the thought that Peter might even then be
hanging dead in some of the familiar home places had
caused that never-ending walk of yesterday.   Her soft
eyes never were the same again after that ; they had
always a restless, craving look, as if seeking for what
they could not find.   Oh ! it was an awful time ; coming down like a thunderbolt on the still sunny day
when the lilacs were all in bloom.'

'Where was Mr. Peter ?' said I.

'He had made his way to Liverpool ; and there
was war then ; and some of the king's ships lay off the
mouth of the Mersey ; and they were only too glad to
have a fine likely boy such as him (five foot nine he
was) come to offer himself.   The captain wrote to my
father, and Peter wrote to my mother.   Stay ! those
letters will be somewhere here.'

We lighted the candle, and found the captain's letter
and Peter's too.   And we also found a little simple
begging letter from Mrs. Jenkyns to Peter, addressed
to him at the house of an old schoolfellow, whither she
fancied he might have gone.   They had returned it
unopened ; and unopened it had remained ever since,
having been inadvertently put by among the other
letters of that time.   This is it—

'MY DEAREST PETER—You did not think we should
be so sorry as we are, I know, or you would never have
gone away.   You are too good.   Your father sits and
sighs till my heart aches to hear him.   He cannot hold
up his head for grief ; and yet he only did what he
thought was right.   Perhaps he has been too severe, and
perhaps I have not been kind enough ; but God knows
how we love you, my dear only boy.   Don looks so

sorry you are gone.   Come back, and make us happy,
who love you so much.   I *know* you will come back.'

But Peter did not come back.   That spring day
was the last time he ever saw his mother's face.   The
writer of the letter—the last—the only person who had
ever seen what was written in it, was dead long ago;
and I, a stranger, not born at the time when this occurrence took place, was the one to open it.

The captain's letter summoned the father and
mother to Liverpool instantly, if they wished to see
their boy; and, by some of the wild chances of life,
the captain's letter had been detained somewhere,
somehow.

Miss Matty went on, 'And it was race-time, and all
the post-horses at Cranford were gone to the races;
but my father and mother set off in our own gig—and
oh! my dear, they were too late—the ship was gone!
And now read Peter's letter to my mother!'

It was full of love, and sorrow, and pride in his new
profession, and a sore sense of his disgrace in the eyes
of the people at Cranford; but ending with a passionate
entreaty that she would come and see him before he
left the Mersey: 'Mother! we may go into battle.   I
hope we shall, and lick those French; but I must see
you again before that time.'

'And she was too late,' said Miss Matty; 'too late!'

We sat in silence, pondering on the full meaning of
those sad, sad words.   At length I asked Miss Matty
to tell me how her mother bore it.

'Oh!' she said, 'she was patience itself.   She had
never been strong, and this weakened her terribly.   My
father used to sit looking at her: far more sad than

she was. He seemed as if he could look at nothing else when she was by; and he was so humble—so very gentle now. He would, perhaps, speak in his old way —laying down the law, as it were—and then, in a minute or two, he would come round and put his hand on our shoulders, and ask us in a low voice if he had said anything to hurt us. I did not wonder at his speaking so to Deborah, for she was so clever; but I could not bear to hear him talking so to me.

'But, you see, he saw what we did not—that it was killing my mother. Yes! killing her (put out the candle, my dear; I can talk better in the dark), for she was but a frail woman, and ill fitted to stand the fright and shock she had gone through; and she would smile at him and comfort him, not in words, but in her looks and tones, which were always cheerful when he was there. And she would speak of how she thought Peter stood a good chance of being admiral very soon—he was so brave and clever; and how she thought of seeing him in his navy uniform, and what sort of hats admirals wore; and how much more fit he was to be a sailor than a clergyman; and all in that way, just to make my father think she was quite glad of what came of that unlucky morning's work, and the flogging which was always in his mind, as we all knew. But oh, my dear! the bitter, bitter crying she had when she was alone; and at last, as she grew weaker, she could not keep her tears in when Deborah or me was by, and would give us message after message for Peter (his ship had gone to the Mediterranean, or somewhere down there, and then he was ordered off to India, and there was no overland route then); but she still said that no one knew where their death lay in wait, and

that we were not to think hers was near. We did not
think it, but we knew it, as we saw her fading away.

'Well, my dear, it's very foolish of me, I know,
when in all likelihood I am so near seeing her again.

'And only think, love! the very day after her death
—for she did not live quite a twelvemonth after Peter
went away—the very day after—came a parcel for her
from India—from her poor boy. It was a large, soft,
white India shawl, with just a little narrow border all
round ; just what my mother would have liked.

'We thought it might rouse my father, for he had
sat with her hand in his all night long ; so Deborah
took it in to him, and Peter's letter to her, and all. At
first, he took no notice ; and we tried to make a kind
of light careless talk about the shawl, opening it out
and admiring it. Then, suddenly, he got up, and
spoke : "She shall be buried in it," he said ; "Peter
shall have that comfort ; and she would have liked it."

'Well, perhaps it was not reasonable, but what could
we do or say ? One gives people in grief their own
way. He took it up and felt it : "It is just such a
shawl as she wished for when she was married, and her
mother did not give it her. I did not know of it till
after, or she should have had it—she should ; but she
shall have it now."

'My mother looked so lovely in her death ! She
was always pretty, and now she looked fair, and waxen,
and young—younger than Deborah, as she stood
trembling and shivering by her. We decked her in the
long soft folds ; she lay smiling, as if pleased ; and
people came—all Cranford came—to beg to see her,
for they had loved her dearly, as well they might ; and
the countrywomen brought posies ; old Clare's wife

brought some white violets, and begged they might lie on her breast.

'Deborah said to me, the day of my mother's funeral, that if she had a hundred offers she never would marry and leave my father. It was not very likely she would have so many—I don't know that she had one; but it was not less to her credit to say so. She was such a daughter to my father as I think there never was before or since. His eyes failed him, and she read book after book, and wrote, and copied, and was always at his service in any parish business. She could do many more things than my poor mother could; she even once wrote a letter to the bishop for my father. But he missed my mother sorely; the whole parish noticed it. Not that he was less active; I think he was more so, and more patient in helping every one. I did all I could to set Deborah at liberty to be with him; for I knew I was good for little, and that my best work in the world was to do odd jobs quietly, and set others at liberty. But my father was a changed man.'

'Did Mr. Peter ever come home?'

'Yes, once. He came home a lieutenant; he did not get to be admiral. And he and my father were such friends! My father took him into every house in the parish, he was so proud of him. He never walked out without Peter's arm to lean upon. Deborah used to smile (I don't think we ever laughed again after my mother's death), and say she was quite put in a corner. Not but what my father always wanted her when there was letter-writing or reading to be done, or anything to be settled.'

'And then?' said I, after a pause.

'He and my father were such friends!'

'Then Peter went to sea again; and, by and by,
my father died, blessing us both, and thanking Deborah

for all she had been to him; and, of course, our
circumstances were changed; and, instead of living at
the rectory, and keeping three maids and a man, we
had to come to this small house, and be content with a
servant-of-all-work; but, as Deborah used to say, we
have always lived genteelly, even if circumstances have
compelled us to simplicity.   Poor Deborah!'

'And Mr. Peter?' asked I.

'Oh, there was some great war in India—I forget
what they call it—and we have never heard of Peter
since then.   I believe he is dead myself; and it sometimes fidgets me that we have never put on mourning
for him.   And then again, when I sit by myself, and
all the house is still, I think I hear his step coming up
the street, and my heart begins to flutter and beat;
but the sound always goes past—and Peter never
comes.'

'That's Martha back?   No! *I*'ll go, my dear;   I
can always find my way in the dark, you know.   And
a blow of fresh air at the door will do my head good,
and it's rather got a trick of aching.'

So she pattered off.   I had lighted the candle, to
give the room a cheerful appearance against her return.

'Was it Martha?' asked I.

'Yes.   And I am rather uncomfortable, for I heard
such a strange noise, just as I was opening the door.'

'Where?' I asked, for her eyes were round with
affright.

'In the street—just outside—it sounded like——

'Talking?' I put in, as she hesitated a little.

'No! kissing——'

Visiting.

ne morning, as Miss Matty and I sat at our work—it was before twelve o'clock, and Miss Matty had not changed the cap with yellow ribbons that had been Miss Jenkyns's best, and which Miss Matty was now wearing out in private, putting on the one made in imitation of Mrs. Jamieson's at all times when she expected to be seen—Martha came up, and asked if Miss Betty Barker might speak to her mistress. Miss Matty assented, and quickly disappeared to change the yellow ribbons, while Miss Barker came upstairs; but, as she had forgotten her spectacles, and was rather flurried by the unusual time of the visit, I was not surprised to see her return with one cap on the top of the other. She was quite unconscious of it herself, and looked at us with bland satisfaction. Nor do I think Miss Barker perceived it; for, putting aside the little circumstance that she was not so young as she had been, she was very much absorbed in her errand, which

'With bland satisfaction.'

she delivered herself of with an oppressive modesty that found vent in endless apologies.

Miss Betty Barker was the daughter of the old clerk

at Cranford who had officiated in Mr. Jenkyns's time.
She and her sister had had pretty good situations as
ladies' maids, and had saved money enough to set up a
milliner's shop, which had been patronised by the ladies
in the neighbourhood. Lady Arley, for instance, would
occasionally give Miss Barkers the pattern of an old
cap of hers, which they immediately copied and
circulated among the *élite* of Cranford. I say the *élite*,
for Miss Barkers had caught the trick of the place, and
piqued themselves upon their ' aristocratic connection.'
They would not sell their caps and ribbons to any one
without a pedigree. Many a farmer's wife or daughter
turned away huffed from Miss Barkers' select millinery,
and went rather to the universal shop, where the profits
of brown soap and moist sugar enabled the proprietor
to go straight to (Paris, he said, until he found his
customers too patriotic and John Bullish to wear what
the Mounseers wore) London, where, as he often told
his customers, Queen Adelaide had appeared, only the
very week before, in a cap exactly like the one he
showed them, trimmed with yellow and blue ribbons,
and had been complimented by King William on the
becoming nature of her head-dress.

Miss Barkers, who confined themselves to truth, and
did not approve of miscellaneous customers, throve
notwithstanding. They were self-denying, good people.
Many a time have I seen the eldest of them (she that
had been maid to Mrs. Jamieson) carrying out some
delicate mess to a poor person. They only aped their
betters in having ' nothing to do ' with the class immediately below theirs. And when Miss Barker died,
their profits and income were found to be such that
Miss Betty was justified in shutting up shop and retiring

from business.   She also (as I think I have before said)
set up her cow; a mark of respectability in Cranford
almost as decided as setting up a gig is among some
people.   She dressed finer than any lady in Cranford;
and we did not wonder at it; for it was understood
that she was wearing out all the bonnets and caps and
outrageous ribbons which had once formed her stock-
in-trade.   It was five or six years since she had given
up shop, so in any other place than Cranford her dress
might have been considered *passée*.

And now Miss Betty Barker had called to invite
Miss Matty to tea at her house on the following
Tuesday.   She gave me also an impromptu invitation,
as I happened to be a visitor—though I could see she
had a little fear lest, since my father had gone to live
in Drumble, he might have engaged in that 'horrid
cotton trade,' and so dragged his family down out of
'aristocratic society.'   She prefaced this invitation with
so many apologies that she quite excited my curiosity.
'Her presumption' was to be excused.   What had she
been doing?   She seemed so overpowered by it, I
could only think that she had been writing to Queen
Adelaide to ask for a receipt for washing lace; but the
act which she so characterised was only an invitation
she had carried to her sister's former mistress, Mrs.
Jamieson.   'Her former occupation considered, could
Miss Matty excuse the liberty?'   Ah! thought I, she
has found out that double cap, and is going to rectify
Miss Matty's head-dress.   No! it was simply to extend
her invitation to Miss Matty and to me.   Miss Matty
bowed acceptance; and I wondered that, in the graceful
action, she did not feel the unusual weight and extraordinary height of her head-dress.   But I do not think

she did, for she recovered her balance, and went on talking to Miss Betty in a kind, condescending manner, very different from the fidgety way she would have had if she had suspected how singular her appearance was.

'Mrs. Jamieson is coming, I think you said?' asked Miss Matty.

'Yes. Mrs. Jamieson most kindly and condescend-ingly said she would be happy to come. One little stipulation she made, that she should bring Carlo. I told her that if I had a weakness, it was for dogs.'

'And Miss Pole?' questioned Miss Matty, who was thinking of her pool at Preference, in which Carlo would not be available as a partner.

'I am going to ask Miss Pole. Of course, I could not think of asking her until I had asked you, madam —the rector's daughter, madam. Believe me, I do not forget the situation my father held under yours.'

'And Mrs. Forrester, of course?'

'And Mrs. Forrester. I thought, in fact, of going to her before I went to Miss Pole. Although her circumstances are changed, madam, she was born a Tyrrell, and we can never forget her alliance to the Bigges, of Bigelow Hall.'

Miss Matty cared much more for the little circum-stance of her being a very good card-player.

'Mrs. Fitz-Adam—I suppose——'

'No, madam. I must draw a line somewhere. Mrs. Jamieson would not, I think, like to meet Mrs. Fitz-Adam. I have the greatest respect for Mrs. Fitz-Adam —but I cannot think her fit society for such ladies as Mrs. Jamieson and Miss Matilda Jenkyns.'

Miss Betty Barker bowed low to Miss Matty, and pursed up her mouth. She looked at me with sidelong dignity, as much as to say, although a retired milliner, she was no democrat, and understood the difference of ranks.

'May I beg you to come as near half-past six, to my little dwelling, as possible, Miss Matilda? Mrs. Jamieson dines at five, but has kindly promised not to delay her visit beyond that time—half-past six.' And with a swimming curtsey Miss Betty Barker took her leave.

My prophetic soul foretold a visit that afternoon from Miss Pole, who usually came to call on Miss Matilda after any event—or indeed in sight of any event—to talk it over with her.

'Miss Betty told me it was to be a choice and select few,' said Miss Pole, as she and Miss Matty compared notes.

'Yes, so she said. Not even Mrs. Fitz-Adam.'

Now Mrs. Fitz-Adam was the widowed sister of the Cranford surgeon, whom I have named before. Their parents were respectable farmers, content with their station. The name of these good people was Hoggins. Mr. Hoggins was the Cranford doctor now; we disliked the name and considered it coarse; but, as Miss Jenkyns said, if he changed it to Piggins it would not be much better. We had hoped to discover a relationship between him and that Marchioness of Exeter whose name was Molly Hoggins; but the man, careless of his own interests, utterly ignored and denied any such relationship, although, as dear Miss Jenkyns had said, he had a sister called Mary, and the same Christian names were very apt to run in families.

Soon after Miss Mary Hoggins married Mr. Fitz-Adam she disappeared from the neighbourhood for many years. She did not move in a sphere in Cranford society sufficiently high to make any of us care to know

what Mr. Fitz-Adam was.   He died and was gathered
to his fathers without our ever having thought about
him at all.   And then Mrs. Fitz-Adam reappeared in
Cranford ('as bold as a lion,' Miss Pole said), a well-to-
do widow, dressed in rustling black silk, so soon after
her husband's death that poor Miss Jenkyns was
justified in the remark she made, that 'bombazine
would have shown a deeper sense of her loss.'

I remember the convocation of ladies who assembled
to decide whether or not Mrs. Fitz-Adam should be
called upon by the old blue-blooded inhabitants of
Cranford.   She had taken a large rambling house,
which had been usually considered to confer a patent
of gentility upon its tenant, because, once upon a time,
seventy or eighty years before, the spinster daughter
of an earl had resided in it.   I am not sure if the in-
habiting this house was not also believed to convey
some unusual power of intellect ; for the earl's daughter,
Lady Jane, had a sister, Lady Anne, who had married
a general officer in the time of the American war, and
this general officer had written one or two comedies,
which were still acted on the London boards, and which,
when we saw them advertised, made us all draw up,
and feel that Drury Lane was paying a very pretty
compliment to Cranford.   Still, it was not at all a
settled thing that Mrs. Fitz-Adam was to be visited,
when dear Miss Jenkyns died ; and, with her, something
of the clear knowledge of the strict code of gentility
went out too.   As Miss Pole observed, 'As most of the
ladies of good family in Cranford were elderly spinsters,
or widows without children, if we did not relax a little,
and become less exclusive, by and by we should have
no society at all.'

Mrs. Forrester continued on the same side.

' She had always understood that Fitz meant some-thing aristocratic ; there was Fitz-Roy—she thought that some of the King's children had been called Fitz-Roy ; and there was Fitz-Clarence now—they were the children of dear good King William the Fourth.   Fitz-Adam !—it was a pretty name, and she thought it very probably meant " Child of Adam."   No one, who had not some good blood in their veins, would dare to be called Fitz ; there was a deal in a name—she had had a cousin who spelt his name with two little ffs—ffoulkes —and he always looked down upon capital letters, and said they belonged to lately-invented families.   She had been afraid he would die a bachelor, he was so very choice.   When he met with a Mrs. ffarringdon, at a watering-place, he took to her immediately ; and a very pretty genteel woman she was—a widow, with a very good fortune ; and " my cousin," Mr. ffoulkes, married her ; and it was all owing to her two little ffs.'

Mrs. Fitz-Adam did not stand a chance of meeting with a Mr. Fitz-anything in Cranford, so that could not have been her motive for settling there.   Miss Matty thought it might have been the hope of being admitted into the society of the place, which would certainly be a very agreeable rise for *ci-devant* Miss Hoggins ; and if this had been her hope it would be cruel to disappoint her.

So everybody called upon Mrs. Fitz-Adam—every-body but Mrs. Jamieson, who used to show how honourable she was by never seeing Mrs. Fitz-Adam when they met at the Cranford parties.   There would be only eight or ten ladies in the room, and Mrs. Fitz-Adam was the largest of all, and she invariably used to stand up when Mrs. Jamieson came in, and curtsey

very low to her whenever she turned in her direction—
so low, in fact, that I think Mrs. Jamieson must have

Mrs. ffarringdon and Mr. ffoulkes.

looked at the wall above her, for she never moved a
muscle of her face, no more than if she had not seen
her.   Still Mrs. Fitz-Adam persevered.

   The spring evenings were getting bright and long

when three or four ladies in calashes met at Miss
Barker's door.   Do you know what a calash is?   It
is a covering worn over caps, not unlike the heads
fastened on old-fashioned gigs ; but sometimes it is not
quite so large.   This kind of headgear always made
an awful impression on the children in Cranford ; and
now two or three left off their play in the quiet, sunny,
little street, and gathered in wondering silence round
Miss Pole, Miss Matty, and myself.   We were silent
too, so that we could hear loud suppressed whispers
inside Miss Barker's house : ' Wait, Peggy ! wait till I've
run upstairs and washed my hands.   When I cough,
open the door ; I'll not be a minute.'

And, true enough, it was not a minute before we
heard a noise, between a sneeze and a crow ; on which
the door flew open.   Behind it stood a round-eyed
maiden, all aghast at the honourable company of
calashes, who marched in without a word.   She
recovered presence of mind enough to usher us into a
small room, which had been the shop, but was now
converted into a temporary dressing-room.   There we
unpinned and shook ourselves, and arranged our features
before the glass into a sweet and gracious company-
face ; and then, bowing backwards with ' After you,
ma'am,' we allowed Mrs. Forrester to take precedence
up the narrow staircase that led to Miss Barker's
drawing-room.   There she sat, as stately and composed
as though we had never heard that odd-sounding
cough, from which her throat must have been even then
sore and rough.   Kind, gentle, shabbily-dressed Mrs.
Forrester was immediately conducted to the second
place of honour—a seat arranged something like Prince
Albert's near the Queen's—good, but not so good.

The place of pre-eminence was, of course, reserved for the Honourable Mrs. Jamieson, who presently came panting up the stairs—Carlo rushing round her on her progress, as if he meant to trip her up.

And now Miss Betty Barker was a proud and happy woman! She stirred the fire, and shut the door, and sat as near to it as she could, quite on the edge of her chair. When Peggy came in, tottering under the weight of the tea-tray, I noticed that Miss Barker was sadly afraid lest Peggy should not keep her distance sufficiently. She and her mistress were on very familiar terms in their every-day intercourse, and Peggy wanted now to make several little confidences to her, which Miss Barker was on thorns to hear, but which she thought it her duty, as a lady, to repress. So she turned away from all Peggy's asides and signs; but she made one or two very malapropos answers to what was said; and at last, seized with a bright idea, she exclaimed, 'Poor, sweet Carlo! I'm forgetting him. Come downstairs with me, poor ittie doggie, and it shall have its tea, it shall!'

In a few minutes she returned, bland and benignant as before: but I thought she had forgotten to give the 'poor ittie doggie' anything to eat, judging by the avidity with which he swallowed down chance pieces of cake. The tea-tray was abundantly loaded — I was pleased to see it, I was so hungry; but I was afraid the ladies present might think it vulgarly heaped up. I know they would have done at their own houses; but somehow the heaps disappeared here. I saw Mrs. Jamieson eating seed-cake, slowly and considerately, as she did everything; and I was rather surprised, for I knew she had told us, on the occasion of her last party, that she never had it in her house, it reminded her so much of scented soap. She always gave us Savoy biscuits. However, Mrs. Jamieson was kindly indulgent to Miss Barker's want of knowledge of the customs of high life ; and, to spare her feelings, ate three large pieces of seed-cake, with a placid, ruminating expression of countenance, not unlike a cow's.

After tea there was some little demur and difficulty. We were six in number ; four could play at Preference, and for the other two there was Cribbage. But all, except myself (I was rather afraid of the Cranford ladies at cards, for it was the most earnest and serious business they ever engaged in), were anxious to be of the 'pool.' Even Miss Barker, while declaring she did not know Spadille from Manille, was evidently hankering to take a hand. The dilemma was soon put an end to by a singular kind of noise. If a Baron's daughter-in-law could ever be supposed to snore, I should have said Mrs. Jamieson did so then ; for, overcome by the heat of the room, and inclined to doze by nature, the temptation of that very comfortable arm-chair had been too much for her, and Mrs. Jamieson was nodding. Once or twice she opened her eyes with an effort, and calmly but unconsciously smiled upon us ; but, by and by, even her benevolence was not equal to this exertion, and she was sound asleep.

'It is very gratifying to me,' whispered Miss Barker at the card-table to her three opponents, whom, notwithstanding her ignorance of the game, she was 'basting' most unmercifully — 'very gratifying indeed, to see how completely Mrs. Jamieson feels at home in my poor little dwelling ; she could not have paid me a greater compliment.'

Miss Barker provided me with some literature in the shape of three or four handsomely-bound fashion-books ten or twelve years old, observing, as she put a little table and a candle for my especial benefit, that she knew young people liked to look at pictures. Carlo lay and snorted, and started at his mistress's feet. He, too, was quite at home.

'Hush, ladies! if you please, hush!'

The card-table was an animated scene to watch; four ladies heads, with niddle-noddling caps, all nearly meeting over the middle of the table in their eagerness to whisper quick enough and loud enough: and every now and then came Miss Barker's 'Hush, ladies! if you please, hush! Mrs. Jamieson is asleep.'

It was very difficult to steer clear between Mrs. Forrester's deafness and Mrs. Jamieson's sleepiness. But Miss Barker managed her arduous task well. She repeated the whisper to Mrs. Forrester, distorting her face considerably, in order to show, by the motions of her lips, what was said ; and then she smiled kindly all round at us, and murmured to herself, 'Very gratifying indeed ; I wish my poor sister had been alive to see this day.'

Presently the door was thrown wide open; Carlo started to his feet, with a loud snapping bark, and Mrs. Jamieson awoke ; or, perhaps, she had not been asleep —as she said almost directly, the room had been so light she had been glad to keep her eyes shut, but had been listening with great interest to all our amusing and agreeable conversation. Peggy came in once more, red with importance. Another tray ! 'Oh, gentility !' thought I, 'can you endure this last shock ?' For Miss Barker had ordered (nay, I doubt not, prepared, although she did say, 'Why! Peggy, what have you brought us ?' and looked pleasantly surprised at the unexpected pleasure) all sorts of good things for supper —scalloped oysters, potted lobsters, jelly, a dish called 'little Cupids' (which was in great favour with the Cranford ladies, although too expensive to be given, except on solemn and state occasions — macaroons sopped in brandy, I should have called it, if I had not known its more refined and classical name). In short, we were evidently to be feasted with all that was sweetest and best ; and we thought it better to submit graciously, even at the cost of our gentility—which never ate suppers in general, but which, like most non-supper-eaters, was particularly hungry on all special occasions.

Miss Barker, in her former sphere, had, I daresay, been made acquainted with the beverage they call cherry-brandy. We none of us had ever seen such a

thing, and rather shrank back when she proffered it us
—'just a little, leetle glass, ladies; after the oysters
and lobsters, you know.   Shell-fish are sometimes
thought not very wholesome.'   We all shook our heads
like female mandarins; but, at last, Mrs. Jamieson
suffered herself to be persuaded, and we followed her
lead.   It was not exactly unpalatable, though so hot
and so strong that we thought ourselves bound to give
evidence that we were not accustomed to such things
by coughing terribly—almost as strangely as Miss
Barker had done, before we were admitted by Peggy.

'It's very strong,' said Miss Pole, as she put down
her empty glass; 'I do believe there's spirit in it.'

'Only a little drop — just necessary to make it
keep,' said Miss Barker.   'You know we put brandy-
paper over preserves to make them keep.   I often feel
tipsy myself from eating damson tart.'

I question whether damson tart would have opened
Mrs. Jamieson's heart as the cherry-brandy did; but
she told us of a coming event, respecting which she had
been quite silent till that moment.

'My sister-in-law, Lady Glenmire, is coming to stay
with me.'

There was a chorus of 'Indeed!' and then a pause.
Each one rapidly reviewed her wardrobe, as to its
fitness to appear in the presence of a Baron's widow;
for, of course, a series of small festivals were always
held in Cranford on the arrival of a visitor at any of
our friends' houses.   We felt very pleasantly excited
on the present occasion.

Not long after this the maids and the lanterns were
announced.   Mrs. Jamieson had the sedan chair, which
had squeezed itself into Miss Barker's narrow lobby

with some difficulty, and most literally 'stopped the way.' It required some skilful manœuvring on the part of the old chairmen (shoemakers by day, but when summoned to carry the sedan dressed up in a strange old livery—long greatcoats, with small capes, coeval with the sedan, and similar to the dress of the class in Hogarth's pictures) to edge, and back, and try at it again, and finally to succeed in carrying their burden out of Miss Barker's front door. Then we heard their quick pit-a-pat along the quiet little street as we put on our calashes and pinned up our gowns ; Miss Barker hovering about us with offers of help, which, if she had not remembered her former occupation, and wished us to forget it, would have been much more pressing.

Pit-a-Pat.

Chapter 8

"Your Ladyship".

arly the next morning—directly after twelve —Miss Pole made her appearance at Miss Matty's. Some very trifling piece of business was alleged as a reason for the call; but there was evidently something behind. At last out it came.

'By the way, you'll think I'm strangely ignorant; but, do you really know, I am puzzled how we ought to address Lady Glenmire. Do you say " Your Ladyship," where you would say " you " to a common person ? I have been puzzling all morning ; and are we to say " My Lady," instead of " Ma'am " ? Now you knew Lady Arley—will you kindly tell me the most correct way of speaking to the Peerage ? '

Poor Miss Matty! she took off her spectacles and she put them on again——but how Lady Arley was addressed, she could not remember.

'It is so long ago,' she said. 'Dear! dear! how stupid I am! I don't think I ever saw her more than twice. I know we used to call Sir Peter, "Sir Peter" ——but he came much oftener to see us than Lady Arley did. Deborah would have known in a minute. "My lady"——"your ladyship." It sounds very strange, and as if it was not natural. I never thought of it before; but, now you have named it, I am all in a puzzle.'

It was very certain Miss Pole would obtain no wise decision from Miss Matty, who got more bewildered every moment, and more perplexed as to etiquettes of address.

'Well, I really think,' said Miss Pole, 'I had better just go and tell Mrs. Forrester about our little difficulty. One sometimes grows nervous; and yet one would not have Lady Glenmire think we were quite ignorant of the etiquettes of high life in Cranford.'

'And will you just step in here, dear Miss Pole, as you come back, please, and tell me what you decide upon? Whatever you and Mrs. Forrester fix upon, will be quite right, I'm sure. "Lady Arley," "Sir Peter,"' said Miss Matty to herself, trying to recall the old forms of words.

'Who is Lady Glenmire?' asked I.

'Oh, she's the widow of Mr. Jamieson—that's Mrs. Jamieson's late husband, you know—widow of his eldest brother. Mrs. Jamieson was a Miss Walker, daughter of Governor Walker. "Your ladyship." My dear, if they fix on that way of speaking, you must just let me

practise a little on you first, for I shall feel so foolish
and hot saying it the first time to Lady Glenmire.'

It was really a relief to Miss Matty when Mrs.
Jamieson came on a very unpolite errand. I notice
that apathetic people have more quiet impertinence
than others; and Mrs. Jamieson came now to insinuate
pretty plainly that she did not particularly wish that
the Cranford ladies should call upon her sister-in-law.
I can hardly say how she made this clear; for I grew
very indignant and warm, while with slow deliberation
she was explaining her wishes to Miss Matty, who, a
true lady herself, could hardly understand the feeling
which made Mrs. Jamieson wish to appear to her noble
sister-in-law as if she only visited 'county' families.
Miss Matty remained puzzled and perplexed long after
I had found out the object of Mrs. Jamieson's visit.

When she did understand the drift of the honourable
lady's call, it was pretty to see with what quiet dignity
she received the intimation thus uncourteously given.
She was not in the least hurt—she was of too gentle a
spirit for that; nor was she exactly conscious of dis-
approving of Mrs. Jamieson's conduct; but there was
something of this feeling in her mind, I am sure, which
made her pass from the subject to others in a less
flurried and more composed manner than usual. Mrs.
Jamieson was, indeed, the more flurried of the two, and
I could see she was glad to take her leave.

A little while afterwards Miss Pole returned, red
and indignant. 'Well! to be sure! You've had Mrs.
Jamieson here, I find from Martha; and we are not to
call on Lady Glenmire. Yes! I met Mrs. Jamieson,
half-way between here and Mrs. Forrester's, and she
told me; she took me so by surprise, I had nothing to

say. I wish I had thought of something very sharp and sarcastic; I daresay I shall to-night. And Lady Glenmire is but the widow of a Scotch baron after all! I went on to look at Mrs. Forrester's Peerage, to see who this lady was, that is to be kept under a glass case: widow of a Scotch peer—never sat in the House of Lords—and as poor as Job, I daresay; and she—fifth daughter of some Mr. Campbell or other. You are the daughter of a rector, at any rate, and related to the Arleys; and Sir Peter might have been Viscount Arley, every one says.'

Miss Matty tried to soothe Miss Pole, but in vain. That lady, usually so kind and good-humoured, was now in a full flow of anger.

'And I went and ordered a cap this morning, to be quite ready,' said she, at last letting out the secret which gave sting to Mrs. Jamieson's intimation. 'Mrs. Jamieson shall see if it is so easy to get me to make fourth at a pool when she has none of her fine Scotch relations with her!'

In coming out of church, the first Sunday on which Lady Glenmire appeared in Cranford, we sedulously talked together, and turned our backs on Mrs. Jamieson and her guest. If we might not call on her, we would not even look at her, though we were dying with curiosity to know what she was like. We had the comfort of questioning Martha in the afternoon. Martha did not belong to a sphere of society whose observation could be an implied compliment to Lady Glenmire, and Martha had made good use of her eyes.

'Well, ma'am! is it the little lady with Mrs. Jamieson, you mean? I thought you would like more to know how young Mrs. Smith was dressed, her being a bride.' (Mrs. Smith was the butcher's wife.)

Miss Pole said, 'Good gracious me! as if we cared

We
sedulously talked
together

about a Mrs. Smith;' but was silent as Martha resumed
her speech.

'The little lady in Mrs. Jamieson's pew had on,

ma'am, rather an old black silk, and a shepherd's plaid
cloak, ma'am, and very bright black eyes she had,
ma'am, and a pleasant, sharp face ; not over young,
ma'am, but yet, I should guess, younger than Mrs.
Jamieson herself. She looked up and down the church,
like a bird, and nipped up her petticoats, when she came
out, as quick and sharp as ever I see. I'll tell you
what, ma'am, she's more like Mrs. Deacon, at the
" Coach and Horses," nor any one.'

'Hush, Martha!' said Miss Matty, 'that's not
respectful.'

'Isn't it, ma'am ?   I beg pardon, I'm sure ; but Jem
Hearn said so as well.   He said, she was just such a
sharp stirring sort of a body——'

'Lady,' said Miss Pole.

'Lady—as Mrs. Deacon.'

Another Sunday passed away, and we still averted
our eyes from Mrs. Jamieson and her guest, and made
remarks to ourselves that we thought were very severe
—almost too much so. Miss Matty was evidently
uneasy at our sarcastic manner of speaking.

Perhaps by this time Lady Glenmire had found out
that Mrs. Jamieson's was not the gayest, liveliest house
in the world ; perhaps Mrs. Jamieson had found out
that most of the county families were in London, and
that those who remained in the country were not so
alive as they might have been to the circumstance of
Lady Glenmire being in their neighbourhood. Great
events spring out of small causes ; so I will not pretend to say what induced Mrs. Jamieson to alter her
determination of excluding the Cranford ladies, and
send notes of invitation all round for a small party on
the following Tuesday. Mr. Mulliner himself brought

them round.   He *would* always ignore the fact of there
being a back-door to any house, and gave a louder rat-
tat than his mistress, Mrs. Jamieson.   He had three
little notes, which he carried in a large basket, in order

Mr. Mulliner.

to impress his mistress with an idea of their great
weight, though they might easily have gone into his
waistcoat pocket.

Miss Matty and I quietly decided we would have a
previous engagement at home : it was the evening on

which Miss Matty usually made candle-lighters of all the notes and letters of the week; for on Mondays her accounts were always made straight—not a penny owing from the week before; so, by a natural arrangement, making candle-lighters fell upon a Tuesday evening, and gave us a legitimate excuse for declining Mrs. Jamieson's invitation. But before our answer was written, in came Miss Pole, with an open note in her hand.

'So!' she said. 'Ah! I see you have got your note too. Better late than never. I could have told my Lady Glenmire she would be glad enough of our society before a fortnight was over.'

'Yes,' said Miss Matty, 'we're asked for Tuesday evening. And perhaps you would just kindly bring your work across and drink tea with us that night. It is my usual regular time for looking over the last week's bills, and notes, and letters, and making candle-lighters of them; but that does not seem quite reason enough for saying I have a previous engagement at home, though I meant to make it do. Now, if you would come, my conscience would be quite at ease, and luckily the note is not written yet.'

I saw Miss Pole's countenance change while Miss Matty was speaking.

'Don't you mean to go then?' asked she.

'Oh no!' said Miss Matty quietly. 'You don't either, I suppose?'

'I don't know,' replied Miss Pole. 'Yes, I think I do,' said she rather briskly; and on seeing Miss Matty looked surprised, she added, 'You see, one would not like Mrs. Jamieson to think that anything she could do, or say, was of consequence enough to give offence; it

would be a kind of letting down of ourselves, that I, for
one, should not like.   It would be too flattering to Mrs.
Jamieson if we allowed her to suppose that what she
had said affected us a week, nay, ten days afterwards.'

'Well! I suppose it is wrong to be hurt and annoyed
so long about anything; and, perhaps, after all, she did
not mean to vex us.   But I must say I could not have
brought myself to say the things Mrs. Jamieson did
about our not calling.   I really don't think I shall go.'

'Oh, come! Miss Matty, you must go; you know
our friend Mrs. Jamieson is much more phlegmatic than
most people, and does not enter into the little delicacies
of feeling which you possess in so remarkable a degree.'

'I thought you possessed them too, that day Mrs.
Jamieson called to tell us not to go,' said Miss Matty
innocently.

But Miss Pole, in addition to her delicacies of
feeling, possessed a very smart cap, which she was
anxious to show to an admiring world; and so she
seemed to forget all her angry words uttered not a
fortnight before, and to be ready to act on what she
called the great Christian principle of 'Forgive and
forget'; and she lectured dear Miss Matty so long on
this head that she absolutely ended by assuring her it
was her duty, as a deceased rector's daughter, to buy a
new cap and go to the party at Mrs. Jamieson's.   So
'we were most happy to accept,' instead of 'regretting
that we were obliged to decline.'

The expenditure on dress in Cranford was principally
in that one article referred to.   If the heads were
buried in smart new caps, the ladies were like ostriches,
and cared not what became of their bodies.   Old
gowns, white and venerable collars, any number of

brooches, up and down and everywhere (some with dogs' eyes painted in them ; some that were like small picture-frames with mausoleums and weeping-willows

Miss Pole and the brooches.

neatly executed in hair inside ; some, again, with miniatures of ladies and gentlemen sweetly smiling out of a nest of stiff muslin), old brooches for a permanent ornament, and new caps to suit the fashion of the day —the ladies of Cranford always dressed with chaste elegance and propriety, as Miss Barker once prettily expressed it.

And with three new caps, and a greater array of brooches than had ever been seen together at one time since Cranford was a town, did Mrs. Forrester, and Miss Matty, and Miss Pole appear on that memorable Tuesday evening. I counted seven brooches myself on Miss Pole's dress. Two were fixed negligently in her cap (one was a butterfly made of Scotch pebbles, which a vivid imagination might believe to be the real insect); one fastened her net neckerchief; one her collar; one ornamented the front of her gown, midway between her throat and waist; and another adorned the point of her stomacher. Where the seventh was I have forgotten, but it was somewhere about her, I am sure.

But I am getting on too fast, in describing the dresses of the company. I should first relate the gathering on the way to Mrs. Jamieson's. That lady lived in a large house just outside the town. A road which had known what it was to be a street ran right before the house, which opened out upon it without any intervening garden or court. Whatever the sun was about, he never shone on the front of that house. To be sure, the living rooms were at the back, looking on to a pleasant garden; the front windows only belonged to kitchens and housekeepers' rooms and pantries, and in one of them Mr. Mulliner was reported to sit. Indeed, looking askance, we often saw the back of a head covered with hair-powder, which also extended itself over his coat-collar down to his very waist; and this imposing back was always engaged in reading the *St. James's Chronicle*, opened wide, which, in some degree, accounted for the length of time the said newspaper was in reaching us—equal subscribers with Mrs. Jamieson, though, in right of her honourableness, she always had the reading of it first. This very Tuesday, the delay in forwarding the last number had been particularly aggravating; just when both Miss Pole and Miss Matty, the former more especially, had been wanting to see it, in order to coach up the court news ready for the evening's interview with the aristocracy. Miss Pole told us she had absolutely taken time by the forelock, and been dressed by five o'clock, in order to be ready if the *St. James's Chronicle* should come in at the last moment—the very *St. James's Chronicle* which the powdered head was tranquilly and composedly reading as we passed the accustomed window this evening.

'The impudence of the man!' said Miss Pole, in a low indignant whisper. 'I should like to ask him whether his mistress pays her quarter-share for his exclusive use.'

We looked at her in admiration of the courage of her thought; for Mr. Mulliner was an object of great awe to all of us. He seemed never to have forgotten his condescension in coming to live at Cranford. Miss Jenkyns, at times, had stood forth as the undaunted champion of her sex, and spoken to him on terms of equality; but even Miss Jenkyns could get no higher. In his pleasantest and most gracious moods he looked like a sulky cockatoo. He did not speak except in gruff monosyllables. He would wait in the hall when we begged him not to wait, and then look deeply offended because we had kept him there, while, with trembling hasty hands we prepared ourselves for appearing in company.

Miss Pole ventured on a small joke as we went upstairs, intended, though addressed to us, to afford Mr. Mulliner some slight amusement. We all smiled, in order to seem as if we felt at our ease, and timidly looked for Mr. Mulliner's sympathy. Not a muscle of that wooden face had relaxed ; and we were grave in an instant.

Mrs. Jamieson's drawing-room was cheerful ; the evening sun came streaming into it, and the large square window was clustered round with flowers. The furniture was white and gold ; not the later style, Louis Quatorze, I think they call it, all shells and twirls ; no, Mrs. Jamieson's chairs and tables had not a curve or bend about them. The chair and table legs diminished as they neared the ground, and were straight and square in all their corners. The chairs were all a-row against the walls, with the exception of four or five, which stood in a circle round the fire. They were railed with white bars across the back, and nobbed with gold ; neither the railings nor the nobs invited to ease. There was a japanned table devoted to literature, on which lay a Bible, a Peerage, and a Prayer-Book. There was another square Pembroke table dedicated to the Fine Arts, on which were a kaleidoscope, conversation-cards, puzzle-cards (tied together to an interminable length with faded pink satin ribbon), and a box painted in fond imitation of the drawings which decorate tea-chests. Carlo lay on the worsted-worked rug, and ungraciously barked at us as we entered. Mrs. Jamieson stood up, giving us each a torpid smile of welcome, and looking helplessly beyond us at Mr. Mulliner, as if she hoped he would place us in chairs, for, if he did not, she never could. I suppose he

thought we could find our way to the circle round the
fire, which reminded me of Stonehenge, I don't know
why. Lady Glenmire came to the rescue of our
hostess, and, somehow or other, we found ourselves for
the first time placed agreeably, and not formally, in
Mrs. Jamieson's house. Lady Glenmire, now we had
time to look at her, proved to be a bright little woman
of middle age, who had been very pretty in the days of
her youth, and who was even yet very pleasant-looking.
I saw Miss Pole appraising her dress in the first five
minutes, and I take her word when she said the next
day—

'My dear! ten pounds would have purchased every
stitch she had on—lace and all.'

It was pleasant to suspect that a peeress could be
poor, and partly reconciled us to the fact that her
husband had never sat in the House of Lords; which,
when we first heard of it, seemed a kind of swindling
us out of our respect on false pretences; a sort of 'A
Lord and No Lord' business.

We were all very silent at first. We were thinking
what we could talk about, that should be high enough
to interest My Lady. There had been a rise in the
price of sugar, which, as preserving-time was near, was
a piece of intelligence to all our housekeeping hearts,
and would have been the natural topic if Lady Glenmire had not been by. But we were not sure if the
peerage ate preserves—much less knew how they were
made. At last, Miss Pole, who had always a great deal
of courage and *savoir faire*, spoke to Lady Glenmire,
who on her part had seemed just as much puzzled to
know how to break the silence as we were.

'Has your ladyship been to Court lately?' asked

she ; and then gave a little glance round at us, half
timid and half triumphant, as much as to say, 'See
how judiciously I have chosen a subject befitting the
rank of the stranger.'

'I never was there in my life,' said Lady Glenmire,
with a broad Scotch accent, but in a very sweet voice.
And then, as if she had been too abrupt, she added :
'We very seldom went to London—only twice, in fact,
during all my married life ; and before I was married
my father had far too large a family' (fifth daughter of
Mr. Campbell was in all our minds, I am sure) 'to take
us often from our home, even to Edinburgh. Ye'll
have been in Edinburgh, maybe?' said she, suddenly
brightening up with the hope of a common interest.
We had none of us been there ; but Miss Pole had an
uncle who once had passed a night there, which was
very pleasant.

Mrs. Jamieson, meanwhile, was absorbed in wonder
why Mr. Mulliner did not bring the tea ; and at length
the wonder oozed out of her mouth.

'I had better ring the bell, my dear, had not I?'
said Lady Glenmire briskly.

'No—I think not—Mulliner does not like to be
hurried.'

We should have liked our tea, for we dined at an
earlier hour than Mrs. Jamieson. I suspect Mr. Mulliner
had to finish the *St. James's Chronicle* before he chose
to trouble himself about tea. His mistress fidgeted
and fidgeted, and kept saying, 'I can't think why
Mulliner does not bring tea. I can't think what he
can be about.' And Lady Glenmire at last grew quite
impatient, but it was a pretty kind of impatience after
all ; and she rang the bell rather sharply, on receiving

a half-permission from her sister-in-law to do so. Mr.
Mulliner appeared in dignified surprise. 'Oh!' said
Mrs. Jamieson, 'Lady Glenmire rang the bell; I
believe it was for tea.'

"In dignified surprise"

In a few minutes tea was brought. Very delicate
was the china, very old the plate, very thin the bread
and butter, and very small the lumps of sugar. Sugar
was evidently Mrs. Jamieson's favourite economy. I
question if the little filigree sugar-tongs, made some-

thing like scissors, could have opened themselves wide
enough to take up an honest, vulgar, good-sized piece ;
and when I tried to seize two little minnikin pieces at
once, so as not to be detected in too many returns to
the sugar-basin, they absolutely dropped one, with a
little sharp clatter, quite in a malicious and unnatural
manner.   But before this happened, we had had a
slight disappointment.   In the little silver jug was
cream, in the larger one was milk.   As soon as Mr.
Mulliner came in, Carlo began to beg, which was a
thing our manners forbade us to do, though I am sure
we were just as hungry ; and Mrs. Jamieson said she
was certain we would excuse her if she gave her poor
dumb Carlo his tea first.   She accordingly mixed a
saucerful for him, and put it down for him to lap ; and
then she told us how intelligent and sensible the dear
little fellow was ; he knew cream quite well, and
constantly refused tea with only milk in it ; so the
milk was left for us ; but we silently thought we were
quite as intelligent and sensible as Carlo, and felt as if
insult were added to injury when we were called upon
to admire the gratitude evinced by his wagging his
tail for the cream which should have been ours.

After tea we thawed down into common life-subjects.
We were thankful to Lady Glenmire for having proposed
some more bread and butter, and this mutual want
made us better acquainted with her than we should
ever have been with talking about the Court, though
Miss Pole did say she had hoped to know how the
dear Queen was from some one who had seen her.

The friendship begun over bread and butter extended
on to cards.   Lady Glenmire played Preference to
admiration, and was a complete authority as to Ombre

and Quadrille. Even Miss Pole quite forgot to say
'my lady,' and 'your ladyship,' and said 'Basto!
ma'am'; 'you have Spadille, I believe,' just as quietly
as if we had never held the great Cranford parliament
on the subject of the proper mode of addressing a
peeress.

As a proof of how thoroughly we had forgotten that
we were in the presence of one who might have sat
down to tea with a coronet instead of a cap on her
head, Mrs. Forrester related a curious little fact to Lady
Glenmire—an anecdote known to the circle of her intimate friends, but of which even Mrs. Jamieson was not
aware. It related to some fine old lace, the sole relic
of better days, which Lady Glenmire was admiring on
Mrs. Forrester's collar.

'Yes,' said that lady, 'such lace cannot be got now
for either love or money; made by the nuns abroad,
they tell me. They say that they can't make it now,
even there. But perhaps they can now they've passed
the Catholic Emancipation Bill. I should not wonder.
But, in the meantime, I treasure up my lace very much.
I daren't even trust the washing of it to my maid' (the
little charity school-girl I have named before, but who
sounded well as 'my maid'). 'I always wash it myself.
And once it had a narrow escape. Of course, your
ladyship knows that such lace must never be starched
or ironed. Some people wash it in sugar and water,
and some in coffee, to make it the right yellow colour;
but I myself have a very good receipt for washing it in
milk, which stiffens it enough, and gives it a very good
creamy colour. Well, ma'am, I had tacked it together
(and the beauty of this fine lace is that, when it is wet,
it goes into a very little space), and put it to soak in

milk, when, unfortunately, I left the room; on my return I found pussy on the table, looking very like a thief, but gulping very uncomfortably, as if she was half-choked with something she wanted to swallow and could not. And, would you believe it? At first I pitied her, and said "Poor pussy! poor pussy!" till, all at once, I looked and saw the cup of milk empty—cleaned out! "You naughty cat!" said I; and I believe I was provoked enough to give her a slap, which did no good, but only helped the lace down—just as one slaps a choking child on the back. I could have cried, I was so vexed; but I determined I would not give the lace up without a struggle for it. I hoped the lace might disagree with her, at any rate; but it would have been too much for Job, if he had seen, as I did, that cat come in, quite placid and purring, not a quarter of an hour after, and almost expecting to be stroked. "No, pussy!" said I, "if you have any conscience you ought not to expect that!" And then a thought struck me; and I rang the bell for my maid, and sent her to Mr. Hoggins, with my compliments, and would he be kind enough to lend me one of his top-boots for an hour? I did not think there was anything odd in the message; but Jenny said the young men in the surgery laughed as if they would be ill at my wanting a top-boot. When it came, Jenny and I put pussy in, with her fore-feet straight down, so that they were fastened, and could not scratch, and we gave her a teaspoonful of currant-jelly in which (your ladyship must excuse me) I had mixed some tartar emetic. I shall never forget how anxious I was for the next half-hour. I took pussy to my own room, and spread a clean towel on the floor. I could have kissed her when she returned the lace to sight, very much as it had gone down. Jenny had boiling water ready, and we soaked it and soaked it, and spread it on a lavender-bush in the sun before I could touch it again, even to put it in milk. But now your ladyship would never guess that it had been in pussy's inside.'

We found out, in the course of the evening, that Lady Glenmire was going to pay Mrs. Jamieson a long visit, as she had given up her apartments in Edinburgh, and had no ties to take her back there in a hurry. On the whole, we were rather glad to hear this, for she had made a pleasant impression upon us ; and it was also very comfortable to find, from things which dropped out in the course of conversation, that, in addition to many other genteel qualities, she was far removed from the ' vulgarity of wealth.'

' Don't you find it very unpleasant walking ? ' asked Mrs. Jamieson, as our respective servants were announced. It was a pretty regular question from Mrs. Jamieson, who had her own carriage in the coach-house, and always went out in a sedan-chair to the very shortest distances. The answers were nearly as much a matter of course.

' Oh dear, no ! it is so pleasant and still at night ! ' ' Such a refreshment after the excitement of a party ! ' ' The stars are so beautiful ! '   This last was from Miss Matty.

' Are you fond of astronomy ? ' Lady Glenmire asked.

' Not very,' replied Miss Matty, rather confused at the moment to remember which was astronomy and which was astrology—but the answer was true under either circumstance, for she read, and was slightly

L

alarmed at Francis Moore's astrological predictions; and, as to astronomy, in a private and confidential conversation, she had told me she never could believe that the earth was moving constantly, and that she would not believe it if she could, it made her feel so tired and dizzy whenever she thought about it.

In our pattens we picked our way home with extra care that night, so refined and delicate were our perceptions after drinking tea with 'my lady.'

Chapter IX.

Soon after the events of which I gave an account in my last paper, I was summoned home by my father's illness ; and for a time I forgot, in anxiety about him, to wonder how my dear friends at Cranford were getting on, or how Lady Glenmire could reconcile herself to the dulness of the long visit which she was still paying to her sister-in-law, Mrs. Jamieson. When my father grew a little stronger I accompanied him to the seaside, so that altogether I seemed banished from Cranford, and was deprived of the opportunity of hearing any chance intelligence of the dear little town for the greater part of that year.

Late in November—when we had returned home again, and my father was once more in good health—I received a letter from Miss Matty ; and a very mysterious letter it was. She began many sentences without ending them, running them one into another, in much the same confused sort of way in which written words run together on blotting-paper. All I could make out was that, if my father was better (which she hoped he was), and would take warning and wear a greatcoat from Michaelmas to Lady-day, if turbans were in fashion, could I tell her? Such a piece of gaiety was going to happen as had not been seen or known of since Wombwell's lions came, when one of them ate a little child's arm; and she was, perhaps, too old to care about dress, but a new cap she must have; and, having heard that turbans were worn, and some of the county families likely to come, she would like to look tidy, if I would bring her a cap from the milliner I employed; and oh, dear! how careless of her to forget that she wrote to beg I would come and pay her a visit next Tuesday; when she hoped to have something to offer me in the way of amusement, which she would not now more particularly describe, only sea-green was her favourite colour. So she ended her letter; but in a P.S. she added, she thought she might as well tell me what was the peculiar attraction to Cranford just now; Signor Brunoni was going to exhibit his wonderful magic in the Cranford Assembly Rooms on Wednesday and Friday evening in the following week.

I was very glad to accept the invitation from my dear Miss Matty, independently of the conjuror, and most particularly anxious to prevent her from disfiguring her small, gentle, mousey face with a great Saracen's head turban; and, accordingly, I bought her a pretty, neat, middle-aged cap, which, however, was rather a disappointment to her when, on my arrival, she followed me into my bedroom, ostensibly to poke the fire, but in reality, I do believe, to see if the sea-green turban was not inside the cap-box with which I had travelled. It was in vain that I twirled the cap round on my hand to exhibit back and side-fronts : her heart had been set upon a turban, and all she could do was to say, with resignation in her look and voice—

'I am sure you did your best, my dear. It is just like the caps all the ladies in Cranford are wearing, and they have had theirs for a year, I daresay. I should have liked something newer, I confess—something more like the turbans Miss Betty Barker tells me Queen Adelaide wears ; but it is very pretty, my dear. And I daresay lavender will wear better than sea-green. Well, after all, what is dress, that we should care about it ! You'll tell me if you want anything, my dear. Here is the bell. I suppose turbans have not got down to Drumble yet ? '

So saying, the dear old lady gently bemoaned herself out of the room, leaving me to dress for the evening, when, as she informed me, she expected Miss Pole and Mrs. Forrester, and she hoped I should not feel myself too much tired to join the party. Of course I should not ; and I made some haste to unpack and arrange my dress ; but, with all my speed, I heard the arrivals and the buzz of conversation in the next room before I was ready. Just as I opened the door, I caught the words, 'I was foolish to expect anything very genteel out of the Drumble shops ; poor girl ! she did her best, I've no doubt.' But, for all that, I had rather that she blamed Drumble and me than disfigured herself with a turban.

Miss Pole was always the person, in the trio of Cranford ladies now assembled, to have had adventures. She was in the habit of spending the morning in rambling from shop to shop, not to purchase anything (except an occasional reel of cotton, or a piece of tape), but to see the new articles and report upon them, and to collect all the stray pieces of intelligence in the town. She had a way, too, of demurely popping hither and thither into all sorts of places to gratify her curiosity on any point—a way which, if she had not looked so very genteel and prim, might have been considered impertinent. And now, by the expressive way in which she cleared her throat, and waited for all minor subjects (such as caps and turbans) to be cleared off the course, we knew she had something very particular to relate, when the due pause came—and I defy any people, possessed of common modesty, to keep up a conversation long, where one among them sits up aloft in silence, looking down upon all the things they chance to say as trivial and contemptible compared to what they could disclose, if properly entreated. Miss Pole began—

'As I was stepping out of Gordon's shop to-day, I chanced to go into the "George" (my Betty has a second-cousin who is chambermaid there, and I thought Betty would like to hear how she was), and, not seeing any one about, I strolled up the staircase, and found myself in the passage leading to the Assembly Room (you and I remember the Assembly Room, I am sure, Miss Matty! and the menuets de la cour!); so I went on, not thinking of what I was about, when, all at once, I perceived that I was in the middle of the preparations for to-morrow night—the room being divided with great clothes-maids, over which Crosby's men were tacking red flannel ; very dark and odd it seemed ; it quite bewildered me, and I was going on behind the

'Making such a graceful bow.'

screens, in my absence of mind, when a gentleman (quite the gentleman, I can assure you) stepped forwards and asked if I had any business he could arrange for me. He spoke such pretty broken English,

I could not help thinking of Thaddeus of Warsaw, and
the Hungarian Brothers, and Santo Sebastiani; and
while I was busy picturing his past life to myself, he
had bowed me out of the room. But wait a minute!
You have not heard half my story yet! I was going
downstairs, when who should I meet but Betty's
second-cousin. So, of course, I stopped to speak to
her for Betty's sake; and she told me that I had really
seen the conjuror—the gentleman who spoke broken
English was Signor Brunoni himself. Just at this
moment he passed us on the stairs, making such a
graceful bow! in reply to which I dropped a curtsey
—all foreigners have such polite manners, one catches
something of it. But, when he had gone downstairs,
I bethought me that I had dropped my glove in the
Assembly Room (it was safe in my muff all the time,
but I never found it till afterwards); so I went back,
and, just as I was creeping up the passage left on one
side of the great screen that goes nearly across the
room, who should I see but the very same gentleman
that had met me before, and passed me on the stairs,
coming now forwards from the inner part of the room,
to which there is no entrance—you remember, Miss
Matty—and just repeating, in his pretty broken
English, the inquiry if I had any business there—I
don't mean that he put it quite so bluntly, but he
seemed very determined that I should not pass the
screen—so, of course, I explained about my glove,
which, curiously enough, I found at that very moment.'

Miss Pole, then, had seen the conjuror—the real,
live conjuror! and numerous were the questions we
all asked her. 'Had he a beard?' 'Was he young,
or old?' 'Fair, or dark?' 'Did he look'—(unable

to shape my question prudently, I put it in another form)—' How did he look ? '   In short, Miss Pole was the heroine of the evening, owing to her morning's encounter.   If she was not the rose (that is to say, the conjuror), she had been near it.

Conjuration, sleight of hand, magic, witchcraft, were the subjects of the evening.   Miss Pole was slightly sceptical, and inclined to think there might be a scientific solution found for even the proceedings of the Witch of Endor.   Mrs. Forrester believed every-thing, from ghosts to death-watches.   Miss Matty ranged between the two—always convinced by the last speaker.   I think she was naturally more inclined to Mrs. Forrester's side, but a desire of proving herself a worthy sister to Miss Jenkyns kept her equally balanced —Miss Jenkyns, who would never allow a servant to call the little rolls of tallow that formed themselves round candles ' winding-sheets,' but insisted on their being spoken of as ' roley-poleys ! '   A sister of hers to be superstitious !   It would never do.

After tea, I was despatched downstairs into the dining-parlour for that volume of the old Encyclopædia which contained the nouns beginning with C, in order that Miss Pole might prime herself with scientific explanations for the tricks of the following evening. It spoilt the pool at Preference which Miss Matty and Mrs. Forrester had been looking forward to, for Miss Pole became so much absorbed in her subject, and the plates by which it was illustrated, that we felt it would be cruel to disturb her otherwise than by one or two well-timed yawns, which I threw in now and then, for I was really touched by the meek way in which the two ladies were bearing their disappointment.   But

Miss Pole only read the more zealously, imparting to
us no more interesting information than this—

'Ah! I see; I comprehend perfectly.   A represents
the ball.   Put A between B and D—no! between C
and F, and turn the second joint of the third finger of
your left hand over the wrist of your right H.   Very
clear indeed!   My dear Mrs. Forrester, conjuring and
witchchraft is a mere affair of the alphabet.   Do let
me read you this one passage?'

Mrs. Forrester implored Miss Pole to spare her,
saying, from a child upwards, she never could understand being read aloud to; and I dropped the pack of
cards, which I had been shuffling very audibly, and by
this discreet movement I obliged Miss Pole to perceive
that Preference was to have been the order of the
evening, and to propose, rather unwillingly, that the
pool should commence.   The pleasant brightness that
stole over the other two ladies' faces on this!   Miss
Matty had one or two twinges of self-reproach for
having interrupted Miss Pole in her studies: and did
not remember her cards well, or give her full attention
to the game, until she had soothed her conscience by
offering to lend the volume of the Encyclopædia to Miss
Pole, who accepted it thankfully, and said Betty should
take it home when she came with the lantern.

The next evening we were all in a little gentle
flutter at the idea of the gaiety before us.   Miss Matty
went up to dress betimes, and hurried me until I was
ready, when we found we had an hour and a half to
wait before the 'doors opened at seven precisely.'   And
we had only twenty yards to go!   However, as Miss
Matty said, it would not do to get too much absorbed
in anything and forget the time; so she thought we

had better sit quietly, without lighting the candles, till
five minutes to seven. So Miss Matty dozed, and I
knitted.

At length we set off; and at the door, under the
carriage-way at the 'George,' we met Mrs. Forrester
and Miss Pole : the latter was discussing the subject of
the evening with more vehemence than ever, and
throwing A's and B's at our heads like hailstones. She
had even copied one or two of the 'receipts'—as she
called them—for the different tricks, on backs of letters,
ready to explain and to detect Signor Brunoni's arts.

We went into the cloak-room adjoining the Assembly
Room ; Miss Matty gave a sigh or two to her departed
youth, and the remembrance of the last time she had
been there, as she adjusted her pretty new cap before
the strange, quaint old mirror in the cloak-room. The
Assembly Room had been added to the inn, about a
hundred years before, by the different county families,
who met together there once a month during the winter
to dance and play at cards. Many a county beauty
had first swum through the minuet that she afterwards
danced before Queen Charlotte in this very room. It
was said that one of the Gunnings had graced the
apartment with her beauty ; it was certain that a rich
and beautiful widow, Lady Williams, had here been
smitten with the noble figure of a young artist, who was
staying with some family in the neighbourhood for
professional purposes, and accompanied his patrons to
the Cranford Assembly. And a pretty bargain poor
Lady Williams had of her handsome husband, if all
tales were true. Now, no beauty blushed and dimpled
along the sides of the Cranford Assembly Room ; no
handsome artist won hearts by his bow, *chapeau bras* in

hand ; the old room was dingy ; the salmon-coloured
paint had faded into a drab ; great pieces of plaster had
chipped off from the white wreaths and festoons on its
walls ; but still a mouldy odour of aristocracy lingered

'Walk mincingly up the room.

about the place, and a dusty recollection of the days
that were gone made Miss Matty and Mrs. Forrester
bridle up as they entered, and walk mincingly up the
room, as if there were a number of genteel observers,
instead of two little boys with a stick of toffy between
them with which to beguile the time.

We stopped short at the second front row ; I could hardly understand why, until I heard Miss Pole ask a stray waiter if any of the county families were expected ; and when he shook his head, and believed not, Mrs. Forrester and Miss Matty moved forwards, and our party represented a conversational square. The front row was soon augmented and enriched by Lady Glenmire and Mrs. Jamieson. We six occupied the two front rows, and our aristocratic seclusion was respected by the groups of shopkeepers who strayed in from time to time and huddled together on the back benches. At least I conjectured so, from the noise they made, and the sonorous bumps they gave in sitting down ; but when, in weariness of the obstinate green curtain that would not draw up, but would stare at me with two odd eyes, seen through holes, as in the old tapestry story, I would fain have looked round at the merry chattering people behind me, Miss Pole clutched my arm, and begged me not to turn, for 'it was not the thing.' What 'the thing' was, I never could find out, but it must have been something eminently dull and tiresome. However, we all sat eyes right, square front, gazing at the tantalising curtain, and hardly speaking intelligibly, we were so afraid of being caught in the vulgarity of making any noise in a place of public amusement. Mrs. Jamieson was the most fortunate, for she fell asleep.

At length the eyes disappeared—the curtain quivered —one side went up before the other, which stuck fast ; it was dropped again, and, with a fresh effort, and a vigorous pull from some unseen hand, it flew up, revealing to our sight a magnificent gentleman in the Turkish costume, seated before a little table, gazing at us (I

should have said with the same eyes that I had last
seen through the hole in the curtain) with calm and
condescending dignity, 'like a being of another sphere,'
as I heard a sentimental voice ejaculate behind me.

'That's not Signor Brunoni!' said Miss Pole decidedly; and so audibly that I am sure he heard, for
he glanced down over his flowing beard at our party
with an air of mute reproach. 'Signor Brunoni had no
beard—but perhaps he'll come soon.' So she lulled
herself into patience. Meanwhile, Miss Matty had
reconnoitred through her eye-glass, wiped it, and looked
again. Then she turned round, and said to me, in a
kind, mild, sorrowful tone—

'You see, my dear, turbans *are* worn.'

But we had no time for more conversation. The
Grand Turk, as Miss Pole chose to call him, arose and
announced himself as Signor Brunoni.

'I don't believe him!' exclaimed Miss Pole, in a de-
fiant manner. He looked at her again, with the same
dignified upbraiding in his countenance. 'I don't!'
she repeated more positively than ever. 'Signor Brunoni had not got that muffy sort of thing about his chin,
but looked like a close-shaved Christian gentleman.'

Miss Pole's energetic speeches had the good effect
of wakening up Mrs. Jamieson, who opened her eyes
wide, in sign of the deepest attention—a proceeding
which silenced Miss Pole and encouraged the Grand
Turk to proceed, which he did in very broken English
—so broken that there was no cohesion between the
parts of his sentences; a fact which he himself perceived
at last, and so left off speaking and proceeded to action.

Now we *were* astonished. How he did his tricks I
could not imagine; no, not even when Miss Pole pulled

out her pieces of paper and began reading aloud—or
at least in a very audible whisper—the separate
'receipts' for the most common of his tricks. If ever
I saw a man frown and look enraged, I saw the Grand
Turk frown at Miss Pole ; but, as she said, what could
be expected but unchristian looks from a Mussulman ?
If Miss Pole were sceptical, and more engrossed with
her receipts and diagrams than with his tricks, Miss
Matty and Mrs. Forrester were mystified and perplexed
to the highest degree. Mrs. Jamieson kept taking
her spectacles off and wiping them, as if she thought
it was something defective in them which made the
legerdemain ; and Lady Glenmire, who had seen many
curious sights in Edinburgh, was very much struck
with the tricks, and would not at all agree with Miss
Pole, who declared that anybody could do them with a
little practice, and that she would, herself, undertake to
do all he did, with two hours given to study the
Encyclopædia and make her third finger flexible.

At last Miss Matty and Mrs. Forrester became
perfectly awe-stricken. They whispered together. I
sat just behind them, so I could not help hearing what
they were saying. Miss Matty asked Mrs. Forrester
'if she thought it was quite right to have come to see
such things ? She could not help fearing they were
lending encouragement to something that was not
quite——' A little shake of the head filled up the
blank. Mrs. Forrester replied that the same thought
had crossed her mind ; she, too, was feeling very uncomfortable, it was so very strange. She was quite certain that it was her pocket-handkerchief which was in
that loaf just now ; and it had been in her own hand not
five minutes before. She wondered who had furnished

the bread ?   She was sure it could not be Dakin,
because he was the churchwarden.   Suddenly Miss
Matty half-turned towards me—

   'Will you look, my dear—you are a stranger in the
town, and it won't give rise to unpleasant reports—will

'The Church smiling approval.

you just look round and see if the rector is here?   If
he is, I think we may conclude that this wonderful man
is sanctioned by the Church, and that will be a great
relief to my mind.'

   I looked, and I saw the tall, thin, dry, dusty rector,
sitting surrounded by National School boys, guarded by
troops of his own sex from any approach of the many

Cranford spinsters. His kind face was all agape with broad smiles, and the boys around him were in chinks of laughing. I told Miss Matty that the Church was smiling approval, which set her mind at ease.

I have never named Mr. Hayter, the rector, because I, as a well-to-do and happy young woman, never came in contact with him. He was an old bachelor, but as afraid of matrimonial reports getting abroad about him as any girl of eighteen : and he would rush into a shop, or drive down an entry, sooner than encounter any of the Cranford ladies in the street ; and, as for the Preference parties, I did not wonder at his not accepting invitations to them. To tell the truth, I always suspected Miss Pole of having given very vigorous chase to Mr. Hayter when he first came to Cranford ; and not the less, because now she appeared to share so vividly in his dread lest her name should ever be coupled with his. He found all his interests among the poor and helpless ; he had treated the National School boys this very night to the performance ; and virtue was for once its own reward, for they guarded him right and left, and clung round him as if he had been the queen-bee and they the swarm. He felt so safe in their environment that he could even afford to give our party a bow as we filed out. Miss Pole ignored his presence, and pretended to be absorbed in convincing us that we had been cheated, and had not seen Signor Brunoni after all.

CHAPTER X

The Panic

think a series of circumstances dated from Signor Brunoni's visit to Cranford, which seemed at the time connected in our minds with him, though I don't know that he had anything really to do with them. All at once all sorts of uncomfortable rumours got afloat in the town. There were one or two robberies—real *bonâ fide* robberies; men had up before the magistrates and committed for trial—and that seemed to make us all afraid of being robbed; and for a long time, at Miss Matty's, I know, we used to make a regular expedition all round the kitchens and cellars every night, Miss Matty leading the way, armed with the poker, I following with the hearth-brush, and Martha carrying the shovel and fire-irons with which to sound the alarm; and by the accidental hitting together of them she often frightened us so much that we bolted ourselves up, all three together, in the back-kitchen, or store-room,

or wherever we happened to be, till, when our affright
was over, we recollected ourselves, and set out afresh
with double valiance.   By day we heard strange stories
from the shopkeepers and cottagers, of carts that went
about in the dead of night, drawn by horses shod with

' A regular expedition.'

felt, and guarded by men in dark clothes, going round
the town, no doubt in search of some unwatched house
or some unfastened door.

Miss Pole, who affected great bravery herself, was
the principal person to collect and arrange these reports
so as to make them assume their most fearful aspect.

But we discovered that she had begged one of Mr. Hoggins's worn-out hats to hang up in her lobby, and we (at least I) had doubts as to whether she really would enjoy the little adventure of having her house broken into, as she protested she should. Miss Matty made no secret of being an arrant coward, but she went regularly through her housekeeper's duty of inspection —only the hour for this became earlier and earlier, till at last we went the rounds at half-past six, and Miss Matty adjourned to bed soon after seven, 'in order to get the night over the sooner.'

Cranford had so long piqued itself on being an honest and moral town that it had grown to fancy itself too genteel and well-bred to be otherwise, and felt the stain upon its character at this time doubly. But we comforted ourselves with the assurance which we gave to each other that the robberies could never have been committed by any Cranford person ; it must have been a stranger or strangers who brought this disgrace upon the town, and occasioned as many precautions as if we were living among the Red Indians or the French.

This last comparison of our nightly state of defence and fortification was made by Mrs. Forrester, whose father had served under General Burgoyne in the American war, and whose husband had fought the French in Spain. She indeed inclined to the idea that, in some way, the French were connected with the small thefts, which were ascertained facts, and the burglaries and highway robberies, which were rumours. She had been deeply impressed with the idea of French spies at some time in her life ; and the notion could never be fairly eradicated, but sprang up again from time to time. And now her theory was this : The

Cranford people respected themselves too much, and were too grateful to the aristocracy who were so kind as to live near the town, ever to disgrace their bringing up by being dishonest or immoral ; therefore, we must believe that the robbers were strangers—if strangers, why not foreigners ?—if foreigners, who so likely as the French ? Signor Brunoni spoke broken English like a Frenchman ; and, though he wore a turban like a Turk, Mrs. Forrester had seen a print of Madame de Staël with a turban on, and another of Mr. Denon in just such a dress as that in which the conjuror had made his appearance, showing clearly that the French, as well as the Turks, wore turbans. There could be no doubt Signor Brunoni was a Frenchman—a French spy come to discover the weak and undefended places of England, and doubtless he had his accomplices. For her part, she, Mrs. Forrester, had always had her own opinion of Miss Pole's adventure at the 'George Inn'—seeing two men where only one was believed to be. French people had ways and means which, she was thankful to say, the English knew nothing about ; and she had never felt quite easy in her mind about going to see that conjuror—it was rather too much like a forbidden thing, though the rector was there. In short, Mrs. Forrester grew more excited than we had ever known her before, and, being an officer's daughter and widow, we looked up to her opinion, of course.

Really I do not know how much was true or false in the reports which flew about like wildfire just at this time ; but it seemed to me then that there was every reason to believe that at Mardon (a small town about eight miles from Cranford) houses and shops were entered by holes made in the walls, the bricks being

silently carried away in the dead of the night, and all
done so quietly that no sound was heard either in or out
of the house.   Miss Matty gave it up in despair when she
heard of this.   'What was the use,' said she, 'of locks
and bolts, and bells to the windows, and going round
the house every night?   That last trick was fit for a
conjuror.   Now she did believe that Signor Brunoni
was at the bottom of it.'

One afternoon, about five o'clock, we were startled
by a hasty knock at the door.   Miss Matty bade me
run and tell Martha on no account to open the door
till she (Miss Matty) had reconnoitred through the
window; and she armed herself with a footstool to
drop down on the head of the visitor, in case he should
show a face covered with black crape, as he looked up
in answer to her inquiry of who was there.   But it was
nobody but Miss Pole and Betty.   The former came
upstairs, carrying a little hand-basket, and she was
evidently in a state of great agitation.

'Take care of that!' said she to me, as I offered to
relieve her of her basket.   'It's my plate.   I am sure
there is a plan to rob my house to-night.   I am come
to throw myself on your hospitality, Miss Matty.
Betty is going to sleep with her cousin at the "George."
I can sit up here all night if you will allow me; but
my house is so far from any neighbours, and I don't
believe we could be heard if we screamed ever so!'

'But,' said Miss Matty, 'what has alarmed you so
much?   Have you seen any men lurking about the
house?'

'Oh yes!' answered Miss Pole.   'Two very bad-
looking men have gone three times past the house,
very slowly; and an Irish beggar-woman came not

half-an-hour ago, and all but forced herself in past
Betty, saying her children were starving, and she must
speak to the mistress. You see, she said "mistress,"
though there was a hat hanging up in the hall, and it

'Armed with a footstool.'

would have been more natural to have said "master."
But Betty shut the door in her face, and came up to
me, and we got the spoons together, and sat in the
parlour-window watching till we saw Thomas Jones
going from his work, when we called to him and asked
him to take care of us into the town.'

We might have triumphed over Miss Pole, who had professed such bravery until she was frightened ; but we were too glad to perceive that she shared in the weaknesses of humanity to exult over her ; and I gave up my room to her very willingly, and shared Miss Matty's bed for the night.   But before we retired, the two ladies rummaged up, out of the recesses of their memory, such horrid stories of robbery and murder that I quite quaked in my shoes.   Miss Pole was evidently anxious to prove that such terrible events had occurred within her experience that she was justified in her sudden panic ; and Miss Matty did not like to be outdone, and capped every story with one yet more horrible, till it reminded me, oddly enough, of an old story I had read somewhere, of a nightingale and a musician, who strove one against the other which could produce the most admirable music, till poor Philomel dropped down dead.

One of the stories that haunted me for a long time afterwards was of a girl who was left in charge of a great house in Cumberland on some particular fair-day, when the other servants all went off to the gaieties. The family were away in London, and a pedlar came by, and asked to leave his large and heavy pack in the kitchen, saying he would call for it again at night ; and the girl (a gamekeeper's daughter), roaming about in search of amusement, chanced to hit upon a gun hanging up in the hall, and took it down to look at the chasing ; and it went off through the open kitchen door, hit the pack, and a slow dark thread of blood came oozing out.   (How Miss Pole enjoyed this part of the story, dwelling on each word as if she loved it !) She rather hurried over the further account of the girl's bravery, and I have but a confused idea that, somehow, she baffled the robbers with Italian irons, heated red-hot, and then restored to blackness by being dipped in grease.

We parted for the night with an awe-stricken wonder as to what we should hear of in the morning —and, on my part, with a vehement desire for the night to be over and gone: I was so afraid lest the robbers should have seen, from some dark lurking-place, that Miss Pole had carried off her plate, and thus have a double motive for attacking our house.

But until Lady Glenmire came to call next day we heard of nothing unusual. The kitchen fire-irons were in exactly the same position against the back door as when Martha and I had skilfully piled them up, like spillikins, ready to fall with an awful clatter if only a cat had touched the outside panels. I had wondered what we should all do if thus awakened and alarmed, and had proposed to Miss Matty that we should cover up our faces under the bed-clothes, so that there should be no danger of the robbers thinking that we could identify them; but Miss Matty, who was trembling very much, scouted this idea, and said we owed it to society to apprehend them, and that she should certainly do her best to lay hold of them and lock them up in the garret till morning.

When Lady Glenmire came, we almost felt jealous of her. Mrs. Jamieson's house had really been attacked; at least there were men's footsteps to be seen on the flower borders, underneath the kitchen windows, 'where nae men should be;' and Carlo had barked all through the night as if strangers were abroad. Mrs. Jamieson had been awakened by Lady Glenmire,

and they had rung the bell which communicated with
Mr. Mulliner's room in the third story, and when his
nightcapped head had appeared over the banisters, in
answer to the summons, they had told him of their
alarm, and the reasons for it; whereupon he retreated
into his bedroom, and locked the door (for fear of

'Called out valiantly.'

draughts, as he informed them in the morning), and
opened the window, and called out valiantly to say, if
the supposed robbers would come to him he would
fight them; but, as Lady Glenmire observed, that was
but poor comfort, since they would have to pass by
Mrs. Jamieson's room and her own before they could
reach him, and must be of a very pugnacious disposition
indeed if they neglected the opportunities of robbery

presented by the unguarded lower stories, to go up to a garret, and there force a door in order to get at the champion of the house. Lady Glenmire, after waiting and listening for some time in the drawing-room, had proposed to Mrs. Jamieson that they should go to bed ; but that lady said she should not feel comfortable unless she sat up and watched ; and, accordingly, she packed herself warmly up on the sofa, where she was found by the housemaid, when she came into the room at six o'clock, fast asleep ; but Lady Glenmire went to bed, and kept awake all night.

When Miss Pole heard of this, she nodded her head in great satisfaction. She had been sure we should hear of something happening in Cranford that night ; and we had heard. It was clear enough they had first proposed to attack her house ; but when they saw that she and Betty were on their guard, and had carried off the plate, they had changed their tactics and gone to Mrs. Jamieson's, and no one knew what might have happened if Carlo had not barked, like a good dog as he was !

Poor Carlo ! his barking days were nearly over. Whether the gang who infested the neighbourhood were afraid of him, or whether they were revengeful enough, for the way in which he had baffled them on the night in question, to poison him ; or whether, as some among the more uneducated people thought, he died of apoplexy, brought on by too much feeding and too little exercise ; at any rate, it is certain that, two days after this eventful night, Carlo was found dead, with his poor little legs stretched out stiff in the attitude of running, as if by such unusual exertion he could escape the sure pursuer, Death.

We were all sorry for Carlo, the old familiar friend who had snapped at us for so many years ; and the mysterious mode of his death made us very uncomfortable.   Could Signor Brunoni be at the bottom of this ? He had apparently killed a canary with only a word of command ; his will seemed of deadly force ; who knew but what he might yet be lingering in the neighbourhood willing all sorts of awful things !

We whispered these fancies among ourselves in the evenings ; but in the mornings our courage came back with the daylight, and in a week's time we had got over the shock of Carlo's death ; all but Mrs. Jamieson. She, poor thing, felt it as she had felt no event since her husband's death ; indeed Miss Pole said, that, as the Honourable Mr. Jamieson drank a good deal, and occasioned her much uneasiness, it was possible that Carlo's death might be the greater affliction.   But there was always a tinge of cynicism in Miss Pole's remarks. However, one thing was clear and certain—it was necessary for Mrs. Jamieson to have some change of scene ; and Mr. Mulliner was very impressive on this point, shaking his head whenever we inquired after his mistress, and speaking of her loss of appetite and bad nights very ominously ; and with justice too, for if she had two characteristics in her natural state of health they were a facility of eating and sleeping.   If she could neither eat nor sleep, she must be indeed out of spirits and out of health.

Lady Glenmire (who had evidently taken very kindly to Cranford) did not like the idea of Mrs. Jamieson's going to Cheltenham, and more than once insinuated pretty plainly that it was Mr. Mulliner's doing, who had been much alarmed on the occasion of the house being attacked, and since had said, more than once, that he felt it a very responsible charge to have to defend so many women. Be that as it might, Mrs. Jamieson went to Cheltenham, escorted by Mr. Mulliner ;

'Speaking very ominously.'

and Lady Glenmire remained in possession of the house, her ostensible office being to take care that the maid-servants did not pick up followers. She made a very pleasant-looking dragon ; and, as soon as it was arranged for her stay in Cranford, she found out that Mrs. Jamieson's visit to Cheltenham was just the best

thing in the world.   She had let her house in Edinburgh, and was for the time houseless, so the charge of
her sister-in-law's comfortable abode was very convenient
and acceptable.

Miss Pole was very much inclined to instal herself
as a heroine, because of the decided steps she had
taken in flying from the two men and one woman, whom
she entitled 'that murderous gang.'   She described their
appearance in glowing colours, and I noticed that every
time she went over the story some fresh trait of
villany was added to their appearance.   One was tall
—he grew to be gigantic in height before we had done
with him ; he of course had black hair—and by and
by it hung in elf-locks over his forehead and down his
back.   The other was short and broad—and a hump
sprouted out on his shoulder before we heard the last
of him ; he had red hair—which deepened into carroty ;
and she was almost sure he had a cast in the eye—a
decided squint.   As for the woman, her eyes glared,
and she was masculine looking—a perfect virago ; most
probably a man dressed in woman's clothes : afterwards,
we heard of a beard on her chin, and a manly voice and
a stride.

If Miss Pole was delighted to recount the events of
that afternoon to all inquirers, others were not so proud
of their adventures in the robbery line.   Mr. Hoggins,
the surgeon, had been attacked at his own door by two
ruffians, who were concealed in the shadow of the
porch, and so effectually silenced him that he was
robbed in the interval between ringing his bell and the
servant's answering it.   Miss Pole was sure it would
turn out that this robbery had been committed by 'her
men,' and went the very day she heard the report to

have her teeth examined, and to question Mr. Hoggins.
She came to us afterwards; so we heard what she had
heard, straight and direct from the source, while we
were yet in the excitement and flutter of the agitation

'*To have her teeth examined.*'

caused by the first intelligence; for the event had only
occurred the night before.

'Well!' said Miss Pole, sitting down with the
decision of a person who has made up her mind as to
the nature of life and the world (and such people never
tread lightly, or seat themselves without a bump), 'well,
Miss Matty! men will be men. Every mother's son of
them wishes to be considered Samson and Solomon

rolled into one—too strong ever to be beaten or discomfited—too wise ever to be outwitted. If you will notice, they have always foreseen events, though they never tell one for one's warning before the events happen. My father was a man, and I know the sex pretty well.'

She had talked herself out of breath, and we should have been very glad to fill up the necessary pause as chorus, but we did not exactly know what to say, or which man had suggested this diatribe against the sex; so we only joined in generally, with a grave shake of the head, and a soft murmur of ' They are very incomprehensible, certainly!'

' Now, only think,' said she. ' There, I have undergone the risk of having one of my remaining teeth drawn (for one is terribly at the mercy of any surgeon-dentist; and I, for one, always speak them fair till I have got my mouth out of their clutches), and, after all, Mr. Hoggins is too much of a man to own that he was robbed last night.'

' Not robbed!' exclaimed the chorus.

' Don't tell me!' Miss Pole exclaimed, angry that we could be for a moment imposed upon. ' I believe he was robbed, just as Betty told me, and he is ashamed to own it; and, to be sure, it was very silly of him to be robbed just at his own door; I daresay he feels that such a thing won't raise him in the eyes of Cranford society, and is anxious to conceal it—but he need not have tried to impose upon me by saying I must have heard an exaggerated account of some petty theft of a neck of mutton, which, it seems, was stolen out of the safe in his yard last week; he had the impertinence to add, he believed that that was taken by the cat. I have no doubt, if I could get at the bottom of it, it was that Irishman dressed up in woman's clothes, who came spying about my house, with the story about the starving children.'

After we had duly condemned the want of candour which Mr. Hoggins had evinced, and abused men in general, taking him for the representative and type, we got round to the subject about which we had been talking when Miss Pole came in ; namely, how far, in the present disturbed state of the country, we could venture to accept an invitation which Miss Matty had just received from Mrs. Forrester, to come as usual and keep the anniversary of her wedding-day by drinking tea with her at five o'clock, and playing a quiet pool afterwards. Mrs. Forrester had said that she asked us with some diffidence, because the roads were, she feared, very unsafe. But she suggested that perhaps one of us would not object to take the sedan, and that the others, by walking briskly, might keep up with the long trot of the chairmen, and so we might all arrive safely at Over Place, a suburb of the town. (No ; that is too large an expression : a small cluster of houses separated from Cranford by about two hundred yards of a dark and lonely lane.) There was no doubt but that a similar note was awaiting Miss Pole at home ; so her call was a very fortunate affair, as it enabled us to consult together. . . . We would all much rather have declined this invitation ; but we felt that it would not be quite kind to Mrs. Forrester, who would otherwise be left to a solitary retrospect of her not very happy or fortunate life. Miss Matty and Miss Pole had been visitors on this occasion for many years, and now they gallantly determined to nail their colours to the mast,

and to go through Darkness-lane rather than fail in
loyalty to their friend.

But when the evening came, Miss Matty (for it was
she who was voted into the chair, as she had a cold)
before being shut down in the sedan, like jack-in-a-box

'*Implored the chairman.*'

implored the chairman, whatever might befall, not to
run away and leave her fastened up there, to be
murdered; and even after they had promised, I saw
her tighten her features into the stern determination of
a martyr, and she gave me a melancholy and ominous
shake of the head through the glass. However, we

got there safely, only rather out of breath, for it was who could trot hardest through Darkness-lane, and I am afraid poor Miss Matty was sadly jolted.

Mrs. Forrester had made extra preparations, in acknowledgment of our exertion in coming to see her through such dangers. The usual forms of genteel ignorance as to what her servants might send up were all gone through ; and harmony and Preference seemed likely to be the order of the evening, but for an interesting conversation that began I don't know how, but which had relation, of course, to the robbers who infested the neighbourhood of Cranford.

Having braved the dangers of Darkness-lane, and thus having a little stock of reputation for courage to fall back upon ; and also, I dare say, desirous of proving ourselves superior to men (*videlicet* Mr. Hoggins) in the article of candour, we began to relate our individual fears, and the private precautions we each of us took. I owned that my pet apprehension was eyes——eyes looking at me, and watching me, glittering out from some dull, flat, wooden surface ; and that if I dared to go up to my looking-glass when I was panic-stricken, I should certainly turn it round, with its back towards me, for fear of seeing eyes behind me looking out of the darkness. I saw Miss Matty nerving herself up for a confession ; and at last out it came. She owned that, ever since she had been a girl, she had dreaded being caught by her last leg, just as she was getting into bed, by some one concealed under it. She said, when she was younger and more active, she used to take a flying leap from a distance, and so bring both her legs up safely into bed at once ; but that this had always annoyed Deborah, who

piqued herself upon getting into bed gracefully, and
she had given it up in consequence. But now the old
terror would often come over her, especially since Miss
Pole's house had been attacked (we had got quite to
believe in the fact of the attack having taken place),
and yet it was very unpleasant to think of looking
under a bed, and seeing a man concealed, with a great,
fierce face staring out at you ; so she had bethought
herself of something—perhaps I had noticed that she
had told Martha to buy her a penny ball, such as
children play with—and now she rolled this ball under
the bed every night ; if it came out on the other side,
well and good ; if not she always took care to have
her hand on the bell-rope, and meant to call out John
and Harry, just as if she expected men-servants to
answer her ring.

We all applauded this ingenious contrivance, and
Miss Matty sank back into satisfied silence, with a look
at Mrs. Forrester as if to ask for *her* private weakness.

Mrs. Forrester looked askance at Miss Pole, and
tried to change the subject a little by telling us that
she had borrowed a boy from one of the neighbouring
cottages and promised his parents a hundredweight of
coals at Christmas, and his supper every evening, for
the loan of him at nights. She had instructed him in
his possible duties when he first came ; and, finding
him sensible, she had given him the Major's sword (the
Major was her late husband), and desired him to put it
very carefully behind his pillow at night, turning the
edge towards the head of the pillow. He was a sharp
lad, she was sure ; for, spying out the Major's cocked
hat, he had said, if he might have that to wear, he was
sure he could frighten two Englishmen, or four French-

men, any day.   But she had impressed upon him anew
that he was to lose no time in putting on hats or anything else ; but, if he heard any noise, he was to run at

He was a sharp lad

it with his drawn sword.   On my suggesting that some
accident might occur from such slaughterous and indis-
criminate directions, and that he might rush on Jenny
getting up to wash, and have spitted her before he had
discovered that she was not a Frenchman, Mrs. Forrester

said she did not think that that was likely, for he was
a very sound sleeper, and generally had to be well
shaken or cold-pigged in a morning before they could
rouse him. She sometimes thought such dead sleep
must be owing to the hearty suppers the poor lad ate,
for he was half-starved at home, and she told Jenny to
see that he got a good meal at night.

Still this was no confession of Mrs. Forrester's
peculiar timidity, and we urged her to tell us what
she thought would frighten her more than anything.
She paused, and stirred the fire, and snuffed the
candles, and then she said, in a sounding whisper—

'Ghosts!'

She looked at Miss Pole, as much as to say she
had declared it, and would stand by it. Such a look
was a challenge in itself. Miss Pole came down upon
her with indigestion, spectral illusions, optical delusions,
and a great deal out of Dr. Ferrier and Dr. Hibbert
besides. Miss Matty had rather a leaning to ghosts,
as I have mentioned before, and what little she did say
was all on Mrs. Forrester's side, who, emboldened by
sympathy, protested that ghosts were a part of her
religion; that surely she, the widow of a Major in the
army, knew what to be frightened at, and what not;
in short, I never saw Mrs. Forrester so warm either
before or since, for she was a gentle, meek, enduring
old lady in most things. Not all the elder-wine that
ever was mulled could this night wash out the remembrance of this difference between Miss Pole and her
hostess. Indeed, when the elder-wine was brought in,
it gave rise to a new burst of discussion; for Jenny,
the little maiden who staggered under the tray, had to
give evidence of having seen a ghost with her own

eyes, not so many nights ago, in Darkness-lane, the very lane we were to go through on our way home.

In spite of the uncomfortable feeling which this last consideration gave me, I could not help being amused at Jenny's position, which was exceedingly like that of

'Leading questions.'

a witness being examined and cross-examined by two counsel who are not at all scrupulous about asking lead-ing questions. The conclusion I arrived at was, that Jenny had certainly seen something beyond what a fit of indigestion would have caused. A lady all in white, and without her head, was what she deposed and

adhered to, supported by a consciousness of the secret
sympathy of her mistress under the withering scorn
with which Miss Pole regarded her. And not only
she, but many others, had seen this headless lady,
who sat by the roadside wringing her hands as in deep
grief. Mrs. Forrester looked at us from time to time
with an air of conscious triumph; but then she had
not to pass through Darkness-lane before she could
bury herself beneath her own familiar bed-clothes.

We preserved a discreet silence as to the headless
lady while we were putting on our things to go home,
for there was no knowing how near the ghostly head
and ears might be, or what spiritual connection they
might be keeping up with the unhappy body in
Darkness-lane; and, therefore, even Miss Pole felt that
it was as well not to speak lightly on such subjects,
for fear of vexing or insulting that woe-begone trunk.
At least, so I conjecture; for, instead of the busy clatter
usual in the operation, we tied on our cloaks as sadly
as mutes at a funeral. Miss Matty drew the curtains
round the windows of the chair to shut out disagreeable
sights, and the men (either because they were in spirits
that their labours were so nearly ended, or because they
were going down hill) set off at such a round and
merry pace that it was all Miss Pole and I could
do to keep up with them. She had breath for nothing
beyond an imploring 'Don't leave me!' uttered as she
clutched my arm so tightly that I could not have quitted
her, ghost or no ghost. What a relief it was when the
men, weary of their burden and their quick trot, stopped
just where Headingley-causeway branches off from
Darkness-lane! Miss Pole unloosed me and caught
at one of the men.

'Could not you—could not you take Miss Matty round by Headingley-causeway?—the pavement in Darkness-lane jolts so, and she is not very strong.'

A smothered voice was heard from the inside of the chair:

'Oh! pray go on! What is the matter? What is the matter? I will give you sixpence more to go on very fast; pray don't stop here.'

'And I'll give you a shilling,' said Miss Pole, with tremulous dignity, 'if you'll go by Headingley-causeway.'

The two men grunted acquiescence and took up the chair, and went along the causeway, which certainly answered Miss Pole's kind purpose of saving Miss Matty's bones; for it was covered with soft thick mud, and even a fall there would have been easy till the getting up came, when there might have been some difficulty in extrication.

SAMUEL BROWN

The next morning I met Lady Glenmire and Miss Pole setting out on a long walk to find some old woman who was famous in the neighbourhood for her skill in knitting woollen stockings. Miss Pole said to me, with a smile half-kindly and half-contemptuous upon her countenance, 'I have been just telling Lady Glenmire of our poor friend Mrs. Forrester, and her terror of ghosts. It comes from living so much alone, and listening to the bug-a-boo stories of that Jenny of hers.' She was so calm and so much above superstitious fears herself that I was almost ashamed to say how glad I had been of her Headingley-causeway proposition the night before, and turned off the conversation to something else.

In the afternoon Miss Pole called on Miss Matty to tell her of the adventure—the real adventure they had met with on their morning's walk. They had been perplexed about the exact path which they were to take across the fields in order to find the knitting old woman, and had stopped to inquire at a little wayside public-house, standing on the high road to London, about three miles from Cranford. The good woman had asked them to sit down and rest themselves while

'Perplexed about the exact path.'

she fetched her husband, who could direct them better than she could; and, while they were sitting in the sanded parlour, a little girl came in. They thought that she belonged to the landlady, and began some trifling conversation with her; but, on Mrs. Roberts's return, she told them that the little thing was the only child of a couple who were staying in the house. And then she began a long story, out of which Lady Glenmire and Miss Pole could only gather one or two decided facts, which were that, about six weeks ago, a light spring cart had broken down just before their door, in which there were two men, one woman, and this child. One of the men was seriously hurt—no bones broken, only 'shaken,' the landlady called it; but he had probably sustained some severe internal injury, for he had languished in their house ever since, attended by his wife, the mother of this little girl. Miss Pole had asked what he was, what he looked like. And Mrs. Roberts had made answer that he was not like a gentleman, nor yet like a common person; if it had not been that he and his wife were such decent, quiet people, she could almost have thought he was a mountebank, or something of that kind, for they had a great box in the cart, full of she did not know what. She had helped to unpack it, and take out their linen and clothes, when the other man—his twin brother, she believed he was—had gone off with the horse and cart.

Miss Pole had begun to have her suspicions at this point, and expressed her idea that it was rather strange that the box and cart and horse and all should have disappeared; but good Mrs. Roberts seemed to have become quite indignant at Miss Pole's implied suggestion; in fact, Miss Pole said, she was as angry as if Miss Pole had told her that she herself was a swindler. As the best way of convincing the ladies, she bethought her of begging them to see the wife; and, as Miss Pole said, there was no doubting the honest, worn, bronze face of the woman, who, at the first tender word from Lady Glenmire, burst into tears, which she was too weak to check until some word from the landlady made her swallow down her sobs, in order that she might testify to the Christian kindness shown by Mr. and Mrs. Roberts. Miss Pole came round with a swing to as vehement a belief in the sorrowful tale as she had been sceptical before; and, as a proof of this, her energy in the poor sufferer's behalf was nothing daunted when she found out that he, and no other, was our Signor Brunoni, to whom all Cranford had been attributing all manner of evil this six weeks past! Yes! his wife said his proper name was Samuel

'Riding over.'

Brown—'Sam,' she called him—but to the last we preferred calling him 'the Signor'; it sounded so much better.

The end of their conversation with the Signora Brunoni was that it was agreed that he should be placed under medical advice, and for any expense incurred in procuring this Lady Glenmire promised to hold herself responsible, and had accordingly gone to

Mr. Hoggins to beg him to ride over to the 'Rising Sun' that very afternoon, and examine into the signor's real state; and, as Miss Pole said, if it was desirable to remove him to Cranford to be more immediately under Mr. Hoggins's eye, she would undertake to seek for lodgings and arrange about the rent. Mrs. Roberts had been as kind as could be all throughout, but it was evident that their long residence there had been a slight inconvenience.

Before Miss Pole left us, Miss Matty and I were as full of the morning's adventure as she was. We talked about it all the evening, turning it in every possible light, and we went to bed anxious for the morning, when we should surely hear from some one what Mr. Hoggins thought and recommended; for, as Miss Matty observed, though Mr. Hoggins did say 'Jack's up,' 'a fig for his heels,' and called Preference 'Pref,' she believed he was a very worthy man and a very clever surgeon. Indeed, we were rather proud of our doctor at Cranford, as a doctor. We often wished, when we heard of Queen Adelaide or the Duke of Wellington being ill, that they would send for Mr. Hoggins; but, on consideration, we were rather glad they did not, for, if we were ailing, what should we do if Mr. Hoggins had been appointed Physician-in-Ordinary to the Royal Family? As a surgeon we were proud of him; but as a man—or rather, I should say, as a gentleman—we could only shake our heads over his name and himself, and wished that he had read Lord Chesterfield's Letters in the days when his manners were susceptible of improvement. Nevertheless, we all regarded his dictum in the signor's case as infallible, and when he said that with care and attention he might rally, we had no more fear for him.

But, although we had no more fear, everybody did as much as if there was great cause for anxiety—as indeed there was until Mr. Hoggins took charge of him. Miss Pole looked out clean and comfortable, if homely, lodgings ; Miss Matty sent the sedan-chair for him, and Martha and I aired it well before it left

Airing the Sedan Chair.

Cranford by holding a warming-pan full of red-hot coals in it, and then shutting it up close, smoke and all, until the time when he should get into it at the 'Rising Sun.' Lady Glenmire undertook the medical department under Mr. Hoggins's directions, and rummaged up all Mrs. Jamieson's medicine glasses, and spoons, and bed-tables, in a free-and-easy way, that made Miss Matty feel a little anxious as to what that lady and Mr. Mulliner might say, if they knew. Mrs. Forrester made some of the bread-jelly, for which she was so famous, to have ready as a refreshment in the lodgings when he should arrive. A present of this bread-jelly was the highest mark of favour dear Mrs. Forrester could confer. Miss Pole had once asked her for the receipt, but she had met with a very decided rebuff; that lady told her that she could not part with it to any one during her life, and that after her death it was bequeathed, as her executors would find, to Miss Matty. What Miss Matty, or, as Mrs. Forrester called her (remembering the clause in her will and the dignity of the occasion), Miss Matilda Jenkyns—might choose to do with the receipt when it came into her possession —whether to make it public, or to hand it down as an heirloom—she did not know, nor would she dictate. And a mould of this admirable, digestible, unique bread-jelly was sent by Mrs. Forrester to our poor sick conjuror. Who says that the aristocracy are proud? Here was a lady, by birth a Tyrrell, and descended from the great Sir Walter that shot King Rufus, and in whose veins ran the blood of him who murdered the little princes in the Tower, going every day to see what dainty dishes she could prepare for Samuel Brown, a mountebank! But, indeed, it was wonderful to see what kind feelings were called out by this poor man's coming amongst us. And also wonderful to see how the great Cranford panic, which had been occasioned by his first coming in his Turkish dress, melted away into thin air on his second coming—pale and feeble, and with his heavy, filmy eyes, that only brightened a

very little when they fell upon the countenance of his
faithful wife, or their pale and sorrowful little girl.

Somehow we all forgot to be afraid. I daresay it
was that finding out that he, who had first excited our

love of the marvellous
by his unprecedented
arts, had not sufficient
every-day gifts to man-
age a shying horse,
made us feel as if we
were ourselves again.
Miss Pole came with
her little basket at all
hours of the evening, as
if her lonely house and
the unfrequented road
to it had never been
infested by that 'mur-
derous gang'; Mrs. For-
rester said she thought
that neither Jenny nor
she need mind the head-
less lady who wept and
wailed in Darkness
Lane, for surely the
power was never given
to such beings to harm
those who went about

'In Darkness Lane.'

to try to do what little good was in their power, to
which Jenny tremblingly assented; but the mistress's
theory had little effect on the maid's practice until she
had sewn two pieces of red flannel in the shape of a
cross on her inner garment.

O

I found Miss Matty covering her penny ball—the ball that she used to roll under her bed—with gay-coloured worsted in rainbow stripes.

'My dear,' said she, 'my heart is sad for that little careworn child. Although her father is a conjuror, she looks as if she had never had a good game of play in her life. I used to make very pretty balls in this way when I was a girl, and I thought I would try if I could not make this one smart and take it to Phœbe this afternoon. I think "the gang" must have left the neighbourhood, for one does not hear any more of their violence and robbery now.'

We were all of us far too full of the signor's precarious state to talk either about robbers or ghosts. Indeed, Lady Glenmire said she never had heard of any actual robberies, except that two little boys had stolen some apples from Farmer Benson's orchard, and that some eggs had been missed on a market-day off widow Hayward's stall. But that was expecting too much of us; we could not acknowledge that we had only had this small foundation for all our panic. Miss Pole drew herself up at this remark of Lady Glenmire's, and said 'that she wished she could agree with her as to the very small reason we had had for alarm, but with the recollection of a man disguised as a woman who had endeavoured to force himself into her house while his confederates waited outside; with the knowledge gained from Lady Glenmire herself, of the footprints seen on Mrs. Jamieson's flower borders; with the fact before her of the audacious robbery committed on Mr. Hoggins at his own door——' But here Lady Glenmire broke in with a very strong expression of doubt as to whether this last story was not

an entire fabrication founded upon the theft of a cat ;
she grew so red while she was saying all this that I
was not surprised at Miss Pole's manner of bridling up,
and I am certain, if Lady Glenmire had not been 'her
ladyship,' we should have had a more emphatic con-
tradiction than the 'Well, to be sure!' and similar
fragmentary ejaculations, which were all that she
ventured upon in my lady's presence.   But when she

'The boys who stole the apples.'

was gone Miss Pole began a long congratulation to
Miss Matty that so far they had escaped marriage,
which she noticed always made people credulous to the
last degree ; indeed, she thought it argued great natural
credulity in a woman if she could not keep herself from
being married ; and in what Lady Glenmire had said
about Mr. Hoggins's robbery we had a specimen of what
people came to if they gave way to such a weakness ;
evidently Lady Glenmire would swallow anything if

she could believe the poor vamped-up story about a neck of mutton and a pussy with which he had tried to impose on Miss Pole, only she had always been on her guard against believing too much of what men said.

We were thankful, as Miss Pole desired us to be, that we had never been married ; but I think, of the two, we were even more thankful that the robbers had left Cranford ; at least I judge so from a speech of Miss Matty's that evening, as we sat over the fire, in which she evidently looked upon a husband as a great protector against thieves, burglars, and ghosts ; and said that she did not think that she should dare to be always warning young people against matrimony, as Miss Pole did continually ; to be sure, marriage was a risk, as she saw, now she had had some experience ; but she remembered the time when she had looked forward to being married as much as any one.

' Not to any particular person, my dear,' said she, hastily checking herself up as if she were afraid of having admitted too much ; ' only the old story, you know, of ladies always saying, " *When* I marry," and gentlemen, "*If* I marry." ' It was a joke spoken in rather a sad tone, and I doubt if either of us smiled ; but I could not see Miss Matty's face by the flickering fire-light. In a little while she continued—

' But, after all, I have not told you the truth. It is so long ago, and no one ever knew how much I thought of it at the time, unless, indeed, my dear mother guessed ; but I may say that there was a time when I did not think I should have been only Miss Matty Jenkyns all my life ; for even if I did meet with any one who wished to marry me now (and, as Miss Pole says, one is never too safe), I could not take him—I hope he would not

take it too much to heart, but I could *not* take him——or
any one but the person I once thought I should be
married to ; and he is dead and gone, and he never
knew how it all came about that I said "No," when I
had thought many and many a time—— Well, it's no
matter what I thought.   God ordains it all, and I am
very happy, my dear.   No one has such kind friends
as I,' continued she, taking my hand and holding it in
hers.

If I had never known of Mr. Holbrook, I could have
said something in this pause, but as I had, I could not
think of anything that would come in naturally, and so
we both kept silence for a little time.

'My father once made us,' she began, 'keep a diary,
in two columns ; on one side we were to put down in
the morning what we thought would be the course and
events of the coming day, and at night we were to put
down on the other side what really had happened.   It
would be to some people rather a sad way of telling
their lives' (a tear dropped upon my hand at these
words)—'I don't mean that mine has been sad, only so
very different to what I expected.   I remember, one
winter's evening, sitting over our bedroom fire with
Deborah—I remember it as if it were yesterday—and
we were planning our future lives, both of us were
planning, though only she talked about it.   She said
she should like to marry an archdeacon, and write his
charges ; and you know, my dear, she never was
married, and, for aught I know, she never spoke to an
unmarried archdeacon in her life.   I never was ambitious,
nor could I have written charges, but I thought I could
manage a house (my mother used to call me her right
hand), and I was always so fond of little children—the

shyest babies would stretch out their little arms to come
to me ; when I was a girl, I was half my leisure time
nursing in the neighbouring cottages ; but I don't know
how it was, when I grew sad and grave—which I did
a year or two after this time—the little things drew
back from me, and I am afraid I lost the knack, though

'A diary in two columns.'

I am just as fond of children as ever, and have a strange
yearning at my heart whenever I see a mother with her
baby in her arms. Nay, my dear ' (and by a sudden
blaze which sprang up from a fall of the unstirred coals,
I saw that her eyes were full of tears—gazing intently
on some vision of what might have been), ' do you know,
I dream sometimes that I have a little child—always

the same—a little girl of about two years old; she never grows older, though I have dreamt about her for many years. I don't think I ever dream of any words or sound she makes; she is very noiseless and still, but she comes to me when she is very sorry or very glad, and I have wakened with the clasp of her dear little arms round my neck. Only last night—perhaps because I had gone to sleep thinking of this ball for Phœbe—my little darling came in my dream, and put up her mouth to be kissed, just as I have seen real babies do to real mothers before going to bed. But all this is nonsense, dear! only don't be frightened by Miss Pole from being married. I can fancy it may be a very happy state, and a little credulity helps one on through life very smoothly—better than always doubting and doubting and seeing difficulties and disagreeables in everything.'

If I had been inclined to be daunted from matrimony, it would not have been Miss Pole to do it; it would have been the lot of poor Signor Brunoni and his wife. And yet again, it was an encouragement to see how, through all their cares and sorrows, they thought of each other and not of themselves; and how keen were their joys, if they only passed through each other, or through the little Phœbe.

The signora told me, one day, a good deal about their lives up to this period. It began by my asking her whether Miss Pole's story of the twin brothers was true; it sounded so wonderful a likeness, that I should have had my doubts, if Miss Pole had not been unmarried. But the signora, or (as we found out she preferred to be called) Mrs. Brown, said it was quite true; that her brother-in-law was by many taken for her husband, which was of great assistance to them in their profession ; 'though,' she continued, 'how people can mistake Thomas for the real Signor Brunoni, I can't conceive ; but he says they do ; so I suppose I must believe him. Not but what he is a very good man ; I am sure I don't know how we should have paid our bill at the 'Rising Sun' but for the money he sends ; but people must know very little about art if they can take him for my husband. Why, miss, in the ball trick, where my husband spreads his fingers wide, and throws out his little finger with quite an air and a grace, Thomas just clumps up his hand like a fist, and might have ever so many balls hidden in it. Besides, he has never been in India, and knows nothing of the proper sit of a turban.'

'Have you been in India ?' said I, rather astonished.

'Oh yes! many a year, ma'am. Sam was a sergeant in the 31st ; and when the regiment was ordered to India, I drew a lot to go, and I was more thankful than I can tell ; for it seemed as if it would only be a slow death to me to part from my husband. But, indeed, ma'am, if I had known all, I don't know whether I would not rather have died there and then than gone through what I have done since. To be sure, I've been able to comfort Sam, and to be with him ; but, ma'am, I've lost six children,' said she, looking up at me with those strange eyes that I've never noticed but in mothers of dead children—with a kind of wild look in them, as if seeking for what they never more might find. 'Yes! Six children died off, like little buds nipped untimely, in that cruel India. I thought, as each died, I never could—I never would—love a child again ; and when the next came, it had not only its own love, but the deeper love that came from the thoughts of its little dead brothers and sisters. And when Phœbe was coming, I said to my husband, " Sam, when the child is born, and I am strong I shall leave you ; it will cut my heart cruel ; but if this baby dies too, I shall go mad ; the madness is in me now ; but if you let me go down to Calcutta, carrying my baby step by step, it will, maybe, work itself off ; and I will save, and I will hoard, and I will beg—and I will die, to get a passage home to England, where our baby may live ? ' God bless him ! he said I might go ; and he saved up his pay, and I saved every pice I could get for washing or any way ; and when Phœbe came, and I grew strong again, I set off. It was very lonely ; through the thick forests, dark again with their heavy trees—along by the river's side (but I had been brought up near the Avon in Warwickshire, so that flowing noise sounded like home)—from station to station, from Indian village to village, I went along, carrying my child. I had seen one of the officers' ladies with a little picture, ma'am— done by a Catholic foreigner, ma'am—of the Virgin and the little Saviour, ma'am. She had him on her arm, and her form was softly curled round him, and their cheeks touched. Well, when I went to bid good-bye to this lady, for whom I had washed, she cried sadly ; for she, too, had lost her children, but she had not another to save, like me ; and I was bold enough to ask her, would she give me that print. And she cried the more, and said *her* children were with that little blessed Jesus ; and gave it me, and told me she had heard it had been painted on the bottom of a cask, which made it have that round shape. And when my body was very weary, and my heart was sick (for there

were times when I misdoubted if I could ever reach
my home, and there were times when I thought of my
husband, and one time when I thought my baby was
dying), I took out that picture and looked at it, till I
could have thought the mother spoke to me, and comforted me.   And the natives were very kind.   We
could not understand one another; but they saw my
baby on my breast, and they came out to me, and
brought me rice and milk, and sometimes flowers—I
have got some of the flowers dried.   Then, the next
morning, I was so tired ; and they wanted me to stay
with them—I could tell that—and tried to frighten me
from going into the deep woods, which, indeed, looked
very strange and dark ; but it seemed to me as if Death
was following me to take my baby away from me ;
and as if I must go on, and on—and I thought how
God had cared for mothers ever since the world was
made, and would care for me ; so I bade them good-
bye, and set off afresh.   And once when my baby was
ill, and both she and I needed rest, He led me to a
place where I found a kind Englishman lived, right in
the midst of the natives.'

    ' And you reached Calcutta safely at last ? '

    ' Yes, safely.   Oh ! when I knew I had only two
days' journey more before me, I could not help it,
ma'am—it might be idolatry, I cannot tell—but I was
near one of the native temples, and I went into it with
my baby to thank God for his great mercy ; for it
seemed to me that where others had prayed before to
their God, in their joy or in their agony, was of itself
a sacred place.   And I got as servant to an invalid
lady, who grew quite fond of my baby aboardship ;
and, in two years' time, Sam earned his discharge, and

came home to me, and to our child. Then he had to
fix on a trade ; but he knew of none ; and once, once
upon a time, he had learnt some tricks from an Indian
juggler ; so he set up conjuring, and it answered so
well that he took Thomas to help him—as his man,
you know, not as another conjuror, though Thomas has
set it up now on his own hook. But it has been a
great help to us that likeness between the twins, and
made a good many tricks go off well that they made
up together. And Thomas is a good brother, only he
has not the fine carriage of my husband, so that I can't
think how he can be taken for Signor Brunoni himself,
as he says he is.'

'Poor little Phœbe!' said I, my thoughts going
back to the baby she carried all those hundred miles.

'Ah! you may say so! I never thought I should
have reared her, though, when she fell ill at Chunderabaddad ; but that good kind Aga Jenkyns took us in,
which I believe was the very saving of her.'

'Jenkyns!' said I.

'Yes, Jenkyns. I shall think all people of that
name are kind ; for here is that nice old lady who
comes every day to take Phœbe a walk!'

But an idea had flashed through my head : could the
Aga Jenkyns be the lost Peter? True, he was reported
by many to be dead. But, equally true, some had said
that he had arrived at the dignity of Great Lama of
Thibet. Miss Matty thought he was alive. I would
make further inquiry.

Engaged to be married.

 as the 'poor Peter' of Cranford the Aga Jenkyns of Chunderabaddad, or was he not? As somebody says, that was the question.

In my own home, whenever people had nothing else to do, they blamed me for want of discretion. Indiscretion was my bugbear fault. Everybody has a bugbear fault; a sort of standing characteristic—a *pièce de résistance* for their friends to cut at; and in general they cut and come again. I was tired of being called indiscreet and incautious ; and I determined for once to prove myself a model of prudence and wisdom. I would not even hint my suspicions respecting the Aga. I would collect evidence and carry it home to lay before my father, as the family friend of the two Miss Jenkynses.

In my search after facts I was often reminded of a description my father had once given of a Ladies' Committee that he had had to preside over. He said he could not help thinking of a passage in Dickens, which spoke of a chorus in which every man took the tune he knew best, and sang it to his own satisfaction. So, at this charitable committee, every lady took the subject uppermost in her mind, and talked about it to her own great contentment, but not much to the advancement of the subject they had met to discuss. But even that committee could have been nothing to the Cranford ladies when I attempted to gain some clear and definite information as to, poor Peter's height, appearance, and when and where he was seen and heard of last. For instance, I remember asking Miss Pole (and I thought the question was very opportune, for I put it when I met her at a call at Mrs. Forrester's, and both the ladies had known Peter, and I imagined that they might refresh each other's memories)—I asked Miss Pole what was the very last thing they had ever heard about him ; and then she named the absurd report to which I have alluded, about his having been elected Great Lama of Thibet ; and this was a signal for each lady to go off on her separate idea. Mrs. Forrester's start was made on the veiled prophet in Lalla Rookh—whether I thought he was meant for the Great Lama, though Peter was not so ugly, indeed rather handsome, if he had not

been freckled. I was thankful to see her double upon
Peter ; but, in a moment, the delusive lady was off upon
Rowlands' Kalydor, and the merits of cosmetics and
hair oils in general, and holding forth so fluently that I
turned to listen to Miss Pole, who (through the llamas,
the beasts of burden) had got to Peruvian bonds, and
the share market, and her poor opinion of joint-stock
banks in general, and of that one in particular in which
Miss Matty's money was invested. In vain I put in
' When was it—in what year was it that you heard that
Mr. Peter was the Great Lama ? ' They only joined
issue to dispute whether llamas were carnivorous animals
or not ; in which dispute they were not quite on fair
grounds, as Mrs. Forrester (after they had grown warm
and cool again) acknowledged that she always confused
carnivorous and graminivorous together, just as she did
horizontal and perpendicular ; but then she apologised
for it very prettily, by saying that in her day the only
use people made of four-syllabled words was to teach
how they should be spelt.

The only fact I gained from this conversation was
that certainly Peter had last been heard of in India, ' or
that neighbourhood ' ; and that this scanty intelligence
of his whereabouts had reached Cranford in the year
when Miss Pole had bought her Indian muslin gown,
long since worn out (we washed it and mended it, and
traced its decline and fall into a window-blind, before
we could go on) ; and in a year when Wombwell came
to Cranford, because Miss Matty had wanted to see an
elephant in order that she might the better imagine
Peter riding on one ; and had seen a boa-constrictor
too, which was more than she wished to imagine in her
fancy-pictures of Peter's locality ; and in a year when

Miss Jenkyns had learnt some piece of poetry off by heart, and used to say, at all the Cranford parties, how Peter was 'surveying mankind from China to Peru,' which everybody had thought very grand, and rather

'Miss Jenkyns used to say.'

appropriate, because India was between China and Peru, if you took care to turn the globe to the left instead of the right.

I suppose all these inquiries of mine, and the consequent curiosity excited in the minds of my friends, made us blind and deaf to what was going on around us. It seemed to me as if the sun rose and shone, and as if

the rain rained on Cranford, just as usual, and I did
not notice any sign of the times that could be considered
as a prognostic of any uncommon event ; and, to the
best of my belief, not only Miss Matty and Mrs.
Forrester, but even Miss Pole herself, whom we looked
upon as a kind of prophetess, from the knack she had
of foreseeing things before they came to pass—although
she did not like to disturb her friends by telling them
her foreknowledge—even Miss Pole herself was breathless with astonishment when she came to tell us of the
astounding piece of news.   But I must recover myself ;
the contemplation of it, even at this distance of time,
has taken away my breath and my grammar, and unless
I subdue my emotion, my spelling will go too.

We were sitting—Miss Matty and I—much as usual,
she in the blue chintz easy-chair, with her back to the
light, and her knitting in her hand, I reading aloud the
St. James's Chronicle.   A few minutes more, and we
should have gone to make the little alterations in dress
usual before calling-time (twelve o'clock) in Cranford.
I remember the scene and the date well.   We had been
talking of the signor's rapid recovery since the warmer
weather had set in, and praising Mr. Hoggins's skill, and
lamenting his want of refinement and manner (it seems
a curious coincidence that this should have been our
subject, but so it was), when a knock was heard—a
caller's knock—three distinct taps—and we were flying
(that is to say, Miss Matty could not walk very fast,
having had a touch of rheumatism) to our rooms, to
change cap and collars, when Miss Pole arrested us by
calling out, as she came up the stairs, 'Don't go—I
can't wait—it is not twelve, I know—but never mind
your dress—I must speak to you.'   We did our best

to look as if it was not we who had made the hurried
movement, the sound of which she had heard; for, of
course, we did not like to have it supposed that we had
any old clothes that it was convenient to wear out in

'*It was too big for words.*'

the 'sanctuary of home,' as Miss Jenkyns once prettily
called the back parlour, where she was tying up
preserves. So we threw our gentility with double force
into our manners, and very genteel we were for two
minutes while Miss Pole recovered breath, and excited
our curiosity strongly by lifting up her hands in

P

amazement, and bringing them down in silence, as if what she had to say was too big for words, and could only be expressed by pantomime.

'What do you think, Miss Matty? What *do* you think? Lady Glenmire is to marry—is to be married, I mean—Lady Glenmire—Mr. Hoggins—Mr. Hoggins is going to marry Lady Glenmire!'

'Marry!' said we. 'Marry! Madness!'

'Marry!' said Miss Pole, with the decision that belonged to her character. '*I* said marry! as you do; and I also said, "What a fool my lady is going to make of herself!" I could have said "Madness!" but I controlled myself, for it was in a public shop that I heard of it. Where feminine delicacy is gone to, I don't know! You and I, Miss Matty, would have been ashamed to have known that our marriage was spoken of in a grocer's shop, in the hearing of shopmen!'

'But,' said Miss Matty, sighing as one recovering from a blow, 'perhaps it is not true. Perhaps we are doing her injustice.'

'No,' said Miss Pole. 'I have taken care to ascertain that. I went straight to Mrs. Fitz-Adam, to borrow a cookery book which I knew she had; and I introduced my congratulations *à propos* of the difficulty gentlemen must have in housekeeping; and Mrs. Fitz-Adam bridled up, and said that she believed it was true, though how and where I could have heard it she did not know. She said her brother and Lady Glenmire had come to an understanding at last. "Understanding!" such a coarse word! But my lady will have to come down to many a want of refinement. I have reason to believe Mr. Hoggins sups on bread-and-cheese and beer every night.'

'Marry!' said Miss Matty once again. 'Well! I never thought of it. Two people that we know going to be married. It's coming very near!'

'Bread and cheese.'

'So near that my heart stopped beating, when I heard of it, while you might have counted twelve,' said Miss Pole.

'One does not know whose turn may come next. Here, in Cranford, poor Lady Glenmire might have thought herself safe,' said Miss Matty, with a gentle pity in her tones.

'Bah!' said Miss Pole, with a toss of her head. 'Don't you remember poor dear Captain Brown's song "Tibbie Fowler," and the line——

> "Set her on the Tintock Tap,
> The wind will blaw a man till her."'

'That was because "Tibbie Fowler" was rich, I think.'

'Well! there is a kind of attraction about Lady Glenmire that I, for one, should be ashamed to have.'

I put in my wonder. 'But how can she have fancied Mr. Hoggins? I am not surprised that Mr. Hoggins has liked her.'

'Oh!' I don't know. Mr. Hoggins is rich, and very pleasant-looking,' said Miss Matty, 'and very good-tempered and kind-hearted.'

'She has married for an establishment, that's it. I suppose she takes the surgery with it,' said Miss Pole, with a little dry laugh at her own joke. But, like many people who think they have made a severe and sarcastic speech, which yet is clever of its kind, she began to relax in her grimness from the moment when she made this allusion to the surgery; and we turned to speculate on the way in which Mrs. Jamieson would receive the news. The person whom she had left in charge of her house to keep off followers from her maids to set up a follower of her own! And that follower a man whom Mrs. Jamieson had tabooed as vulgar, and inadmissible to Cranford society, not merely on account of his name, but because of his voice, his complexion, his boots,

smelling of the stable, and himself, smelling of drugs.
Had he ever been to see Lady Glenmire at Mrs.
Jamieson's? Chloride of lime would not purify the

'Lady Glenmire.'

house in its owner's estimation if he had. Or had
their interviews been confined to the occasional meetings
in the chamber of the poor sick conjuror, to whom, with
all our sense of the *mésalliance*, we could not help
allowing that they had both been exceedingly kind?

And now it turned out that a servant of Mrs. Jamieson's had been ill, and Mr. Hoggins had been attending her for some weeks. So the wolf had got into the fold, and now he was carrying off the shepherdess. What would Mrs. Jamieson say? We looked into the darkness of futurity as a child gazes after a rocket up in the cloudy sky, full of wondering expectation of the rattle, the discharge, and the brilliant shower of sparks and light. Then we brought ourselves down to earth and the present time by questioning each other (being all equally ignorant, and all equally without the slightest data to build any conclusions upon) as to when IT would take place? Where? How much a year Mr. Hoggins had? Whether she would drop her title? And how Martha and the other correct servants in Cranford would ever be brought to announce a married couple as Lady Glenmire and Mr. Hoggins? But would they be visited? Would Mrs. Jamieson let us? Or must we choose between the Honourable Mrs. Jamieson and the degraded Lady Glenmire? We all liked Lady Glenmire the best. She was bright, and kind, and sociable, and agreeable; and Mrs. Jamieson was dull, and inert, and pompous, and tiresome. But we had acknowledged the sway of the latter so long, that it seemed like a kind of disloyalty now even to meditate disobedience to the prohibition we anticipated.

Mrs. Forrester surprised us in our darned caps and patched collars; and we forgot all about them in our eagerness to see how she would bear the information, which we honourably left to Miss Pole to impart, although, if we had been inclined to take unfair advantage, we might have rushed in ourselves, for she had a most out-of-place fit of coughing for five minutes after Mrs. Forrester entered the room. I shall never forget the imploring expression of her eyes as she looked at us over her pocket-handkerchief. They said as plain as words could speak, 'Don't let nature deprive me of the treasure which is mine, although for a time I can make no use of it.' And we did not.

Mrs. Forrester's surprise was equal to ours; and her sense of injury rather greater, because she had to feel for her Order, and saw more fully than we could do how such conduct brought stains on the aristocracy.

When she and Miss Pole left us we endeavoured to subside into calmness; but Miss Matty was really upset by the intelligence she had heard. She reckoned it up, and it was more than fifteen years since she had heard of any of her acquaintance going to be married, with the one exception of Miss Jessie Brown; and, as she said, it gave her quite a shock, and made her feel as if she could not think what would happen next.

I don't know whether it is a fancy of mine, or a real fact, but I have noticed that, just after the announcement of an engagement in any set, the unmarried ladies in that set flutter out in an unusual gaiety and newness of dress, as much as to say, in a tacit and unconscious manner, 'We also are spinsters.' Miss Matty and Miss Pole talked and thought more about bonnets, gowns, caps, and shawls, during the fortnight that succeeded this call, than I had known them do for years before. But it might be the spring weather, for it was a warm and pleasant March; and merinoes and beavers, and woollen materials of all sorts were but ungracious receptacles of the bright sun's glancing rays. It had not been Lady Glenmire's dress that had won Mr. Hoggins's heart, for she went about on her errands of kindness more shabby than ever. Although in the hurried glimpses I caught of her at church or elsewhere she appeared rather to shun meeting any of her friends, her face seemed to have almost something of the flush

'Mr. Hoggins looked radiant.'

of youth in it; her lips looked redder and more trembling full than in their old compressed state, and her eyes dwelt on all things with a lingering light, as if she was learning to love Cranford and its belongings.

Mr. Hoggins looked broad and radiant, and creaked up the middle aisle at church in a bran-new pair of top-boots—an audible, as well as visible, sign of his purposed change of state; for the tradition went, that the boots he had worn till now were the identical pair in which he first set out on his rounds in Cranford twenty-five years ago; only they had been new-pieced, high and low, top and bottom, heel and sole, black leather and brown leather, more times than any one could tell.

None of the ladies in Cranford chose to sanction the marriage by congratulating either of the parties. We wished to ignore the whole affair until our liege lady, Mrs. Jamieson, returned. Till she came back to give us our cue, we felt that it would be better to consider the engagement in the same light as the Queen of Spain's legs—facts which certainly existed, but the less said about the better. This restraint upon our tongues—for you see if we did not speak about it to any of the parties concerned, how could we get answers to the questions that we longed to ask?—was beginning to be irksome, and our idea of the dignity of silence was paling before our curiosity, when another direction was given to our thoughts, by an announcement on the part of the principal shopkeeper of Cranford, who ranged the trades from grocer and cheesemonger to man-milliner, as occasion required, that the Spring Fashions were arrived, and would be exhibited on the following Tuesday at his rooms in High Street. Now Miss Matty had been only waiting for this before buying herself a new silk gown. I had offered, it is true, to send to Drumble for patterns, but she had rejected my proposal, gently implying that she had not forgotten her disappointment about the sea-green turban. I was thankful that I was on the spot now, to counteract the dazzling fascination of any yellow or scarlet silk.

I must say a word or two here about myself. I have spoken of my father's old friendship for the Jenkyns family; indeed, I am not sure if there was not some distant relationship. He had willingly allowed me to remain all the winter at Cranford, in consideration of a letter which Miss Matty had written to him about the time of the panic, in which I suspect she had exaggerated my powers and my bravery as a defender of the house. But now that the days were longer and more cheerful, he was beginning to urge the necessity of my return; and I only delayed in a sort of odd forlorn hope that if I could obtain any clear information, I might make the account given by the signora of the Aga Jenkyns tally with that of 'poor Peter,' his appearance and disappearance, which I had winnowed out of the conversation of Miss Pole and Mrs. Forrester.

Chapter XIII

HE very Tuesday morning on which
Mr. Johnson was going to show the
fashions, the post-woman brought
two letters to the house. I say the
post-woman, but I should say the
postman's wife. He was a lame shoe-
maker, a very clean, honest man, much
respected in the town ; but he never brought the letters
round except on unusual occasions, such as Christmas Day
or Good Friday ; and on those days the letters, which
should have been delivered at eight in the morning, did
not make their appearance until two or three in the afternoon, for every one liked poor Thomas, and gave him
a welcome on these festive occasions. He used to say,
' He was welly stawed wi' eating, for there were three
or four houses where nowt would serve 'em but he must
share in their breakfast' ; and by the time he had done

his last breakfast, he came to some other friend who was beginning dinner; but come what might in the way of temptation, Tom was always sober, civil, and smiling; and, as Miss Jenkyns used to say, it was a lesson in patience, that she doubted not would call out that precious quality in some minds, where, but for Thomas, it might have lain dormant and undiscovered. Patience was certainly very dormant in Miss Jenkyns's mind. She was always expecting letters, and always drumming on the table till the post-woman had called or gone past. On Christmas day and Good Friday she drummed from breakfast till church, from church-time till two-o'clock—unless when the fire wanted stirring, when she invariably knocked down the fire-irons, and scolded Miss Matty for it. But equally certain was the hearty welcome and the good dinner for Thomas; Miss Jenkyns standing over him like a bold dragoon, questioning him as to his children—what they were doing—what school they went to; upbraiding him if another was likely to make its appearance, but sending even the little babies the shilling and the mince-pie which was her gift to all the children, with half-a-crown in addition for both father and mother. The post was not half of so much consequence to dear Miss Matty; but not for the world would she have diminished Thomas's welcome and his dole, though I could see that she felt rather shy over the ceremony, which had been regarded by Miss Jenkyns as a glorious opportunity for giving advice and benefiting her fellow-creatures. Miss Matty would steal the money all in a lump into his hand, as if she were ashamed of herself. Miss Jenkyns gave him each individual coin separate, with a 'There! that's for yourself; that's for Jenny,' etc. Miss Matty would even

beckon Martha out of the kitchen while he ate his food ;
and once, to my knowledge, winked at its rapid disappearance into a blue cotton pocket-handkerchief.

'*Each individual coin.*'

Miss Jenkyns almost scolded him if he did not leave a
clean plate, however heaped it might have been, and
gave an injunction with every mouthful.

I have wandered a long way from the two letters
that awaited us on the breakfast-table that Tuesday

morning. Mine was from my father. Miss Matty's
was printed. My father's was just a man's letter; I
mean it was very dull, and gave no information beyond
that he was well, that they had had a good deal of
rain, that trade was very stagnant, and there were
many disagreeable rumours afloat. He then asked me
if I knew whether Miss Matty still retained her shares
in the Town and County Bank, as there were very
unpleasant reports about it; though nothing more than
he had always foreseen, and had prophesied to Miss
Jenkyns years ago, when she would invest their little
property in it—the only unwise step that clever woman
had ever taken, to his knowledge (the only time she
ever acted against his advice, I knew). However, if
anything had gone wrong, of course I was not to
think of leaving Miss Matty while I could be of any
use, etc.

'Who is your letter from, my dear? Mine is a
very civil invitation, signed "Edwin Wilson," asking
me to attend an important meeting of the shareholders
of the Town and County Bank, to be held in Drumble,
on Thursday the twenty-first. I am sure, it is very
attentive of them to remember me.'

I did not like to hear of this 'important meeting,'
for, though I did not know much about business, I
feared it confirmed what my father said: however, I
thought, ill news always came fast enough, so I resolved
to say nothing about my alarm, and merely told her
that my father was well, and sent his kind regards to
her. She kept turning over and admiring her letter.
At last she spoke—

'I remember their sending one to Deborah just like
this; but that I did not wonder at, for everybody knew

she was so clear-headed.   I am afraid I could not help
them much ; indeed, if they came to accounts, I should
be quite in the way, for I never could do sums in my
head.   Deborah, I know, rather wished to go, and went
so far as to order a new bonnet for the occasion ; but
when the time came she had a bad cold ; so they sent
her a very polite account of what they had done.
Chosen a director, I think it was.   Do you think they
want me to help them to choose a director ?   I am
sure I should choose your father at once.'

'My father has no shares in the bank,' said I.

'Oh no! I remember.   He objected very much to
Deborah's buying any, I believe.   But she was quite
the woman of business, and always judged for herself ;
and here, you see, they have paid eight per cent all
these years.'

'It was a very uncomfortable subject to me, with
my half-knowledge ; so I thought I would change the
conversation, and I asked at what time she thought we
had better go and see the fashions.   'Well, my dear,' she
said, 'the thing is this : it is not etiquette to go·till
after twelve ; but then, you see, all Cranford will be
there, and one does not like to be too curious about
dress and trimmings and caps with all the world
looking on.   It is never genteel to be over-curious on
these occasions.   Deborah had the knack of always
looking as if the latest fashion was nothing new to her ;
a manner she had caught from Lady Arley, who did see
all the new modes in London, you know.   So I thought
we would just slip down this morning, soon after breakfast
—for I do want half a pound of tea—and then we
could go up and examine the things at our leisure,
and see exactly how my new silk gown must be made ;

and then, after twelve, we could go with our minds disengaged, and free from thoughts of dress.'

We began to talk of Miss Matty's new silk gown. I discovered that it would be really the first time in her life that she had had to choose anything of consequence for herself: for Miss Jenkyns had always been the more decided character, whatever her taste might have been; and it is astonishing how such people carry the world before them by the mere force of will. Miss Matty anticipated the sight of the glossy folds with as much delight as if the five sovereigns, set apart for the purchase, could buy all the silks in the shop; and (remembering my own loss of two hours in a toy-shop before I could tell on what wonder to spend a silver threepence) I was very glad that we were going early, that dear Miss Matty might have leisure for the delights of perplexity.

If a happy sea-green could be met with, the gown was to be sea-green: if not, she inclined to maize, and I to silver gray; and we discussed the requisite number of breadths until we arrived at the shop-door. We were to buy the tea, select the silk, and then clamber up the iron corkscrew stairs that led into what was once a loft, though now a fashion show-room.

The young men at Mr. Johnson's had on their best looks, and their best cravats, and pivoted themselves over the counter with surprising activity. They wanted to show us upstairs at once; but on the principle of business first and pleasure afterwards, we stayed to purchase the tea. Here Miss Matty's absence of mind betrayed itself. If she was made aware that she had been drinking green tea at any time, she always thought it her duty to lie awake half through the night afterward

(I have known her take it in ignorance many a time without such effects), and consequently green tea was prohibited the house; yet to-day she herself asked for the obnoxious article, under the impression that she was talking about the silk. However, the mistake was

'*Over the counter.*'

soon rectified; and then the silks were unrolled in good truth. By this time the shop was pretty well filled, for it was Cranford market-day, and many of the farmers and country people from the neighbourhood round came in, sleeking down their hair, and glancing shyly about, from under their eyelids, as anxious to

take back some notion of the unusual gaiety to the
mistress or the lasses at home, and yet feeling that
they were out of place among the smart shopmen and
gay shawls and summer prints.   One honest-looking

'*The country people came in.*'

man, however, made his way up to the counter at which
we stood, and boldly asked to look at a shawl or two.
The other country folk confined themselves to the
grocery side; but our neighbour was evidently too full
of some kind intention towards mistress, wife, or
daughter, to be shy; and it soon became a question

with me, whether he or Miss Matty would keep their
shopman the longest time. He thought each shawl
more beautiful than the last; and, as for Miss Matty,

'*Our neighbour.*'

she smiled and sighed over each fresh bale that was
brought out; one colour set off another, and the heap
together would, as she said, make even the rainbow
look poor.

'I am afraid,' said she, hesitating, 'whichever I

choose I shall wish I had taken another. Look at
this lovely crimson! it would be so warm in winter.
But spring is coming on, you know. I wish I could
have a gown for every season,' said she, dropping her
voice—as we all did in Cranford whenever we talked
of anything we wished for but could not afford.
'However,' she continued, in a louder and more cheerful
tone, 'it would give me a great deal of trouble to take
care of them if I had them; so, I think, I'll only take
one. But which must it be, my dear?'

And now she hovered over a lilac with yellow spots,
while I pulled out a quiet sage-green that had faded
into insignificance under the more brilliant colours, but
which was nevertheless a good silk in its humble way.
Our attention was called off to our neighbour. He
had chosen a shawl of about thirty shillings' value;
and his face looked broadly happy, under the anticipation, no doubt, of the pleasant surprise he should give
to some Molly or Jenny at home; he had tugged a
leathern purse out of his breeches-pocket, and had
offered a five-pound note in payment for the shawl,
and for some parcels which had been brought round to
him from the grocery counter; and it was just at this
point that he attracted our notice. The shopman was
examining the note with a puzzled, doubtful air.

'Town and County Bank! I am not sure, sir, but I
believe we have received a warning against notes issued
by this bank only this morning. I will just step and ask
Mr. Johnson, sir; but I'm afraid I must trouble you for
payment in cash, or in a note of a different bank.'

I never saw a man's countenance fall so suddenly
into dismay and bewilderment. It was almost piteous
to see the rapid change.

'Dang it!' said he, striking his fist down on the table, as if to try which was the harder, 'the chap talks as if notes and gold were to be had for the picking up.'

"Dang it!" said he

Miss Matty had forgotten her silk gown in her interest for the man. I don't think she had caught the name of the bank, and in my nervous cowardice I was anxious that she should not; and so I began admiring the yellow-spotted lilac gown that I had been utterly condemning only a minute before. But it was of no use.

'What bank was it? I mean, what bank did your note belong to?'

'Town and County Bank.'

'Let me see it,' said she quietly to the shopman, gently taking it out of his hand, as he brought it back to return it to the farmer.

Mr. Johnson was very sorry, but, from information he had received, the notes issued by that bank were little better than waste paper.

'I don't understand it,' said Miss Matty to me in a low voice. 'That is our bank, is it not?—the Town and County Bank?'

'Yes,' said I. 'This lilac silk will just match the ribbons in your new cap, I believe,' I continued, holding up the folds so as to catch the light, and wishing that the man would make haste and be gone, and yet having a new wonder, that had only just sprung up, how far it was wise or right in me to allow Miss Matty to make this expensive purchase if the affairs of the bank were really so bad as the refusal of the note implied.

But Miss Matty put on the soft dignified manner peculiar to her, rarely used, and yet which became her so well, and laying her hand gently on mine, she said—

'Never mind the silks for a few minutes, dear. I don't understand you, sir,' turning now to the shopman, who had been attending to the farmer. 'Is this a forged note?'

'Oh no, ma'am. It is a true note of its kind; but you see, ma'am, it is a joint-stock bank, and there are reports out that it is likely to break. Mr. Johnson is only doing his duty, ma'am, as I am sure Mr. Dobson knows.'

But Mr. Dobson could not respond to the appealing bow by any answering smile. He was turning the note absently over in his fingers, looking gloomily enough at the parcel containing the lately-chosen shawl.

'It's hard upon a poor man,' said he, 'as earns every farthing with the sweat of his brow. However, there's no help for it. You must take back your shawl, my man; Lizzie must do on with her cloak for a while. And yon figs for the little ones—I promised them to 'em—I'll take them; but the 'bacco, and the other things——'

'I will give you five sovereigns for your note, my good man,' said Miss Matty. 'I think there is some great mistake about it, for I am one of the shareholders, and I'm sure they would have told me if things had not been going on right.'

The shopman whispered a word or two across the table to Miss Matty. She looked at him with a dubious air.

'Perhaps so,' said she. 'But I don't pretend to understand business; I only know that if it is going to fail, and if honest people are to lose their money because they have taken our notes—I can't explain myself,' said she, suddenly becoming aware that she had got into a long sentence with four people for audience; 'only I would rather exchange my gold for the note, if you please,' turning to the farmer, 'and then you can take your wife the shawl. It is only going without my gown a few days longer,' she continued, speaking to me. 'Then, I have no doubt, everything will be cleared up.'

'But if it is cleared up the wrong way?' said I.

'Why, then it will only have been common honesty in me, as a shareholder, to have given this good man

the money.   I am quite clear about it in my own
mind ; but, you know, I can never speak quite as
comprehensively as others can ; only you must give
me your note, Mr. Dobson, if you please, and go on
with your purchases with these sovereigns.'

'*He hung back.*'

The man looked at her with silent gratitude—too
awkward to put his thanks into words ; but he hung
back for a minute or two, fumbling with his note.
   'I'm loth to make another one lose instead of me,
if it is a loss ; but, you see, five pounds is a deal of
money to a man with a family ; and, as you say, ten to

one in a day or two the note will be as good as gold
again.'

'No hope of that, my friend,' said the shopman.

'The more reason why I should take it,' said Miss
Matty quietly.   She pushed her sovereigns towards
the man, who slowly laid his note down in exchange.
'Thank you.   I will wait a day or two before I purchase any of these silks ; perhaps you will then have a
greater choice.   My dear, will you come upstairs ?'

We inspected the fashions with as minute and
curious an interest as if the gown to be made after
them had been bought.   I could not see that the little
event in the shop below had in the least damped Miss
Matty's curiosity as to the make of sleeves or the sit
of skirts.   She once or twice exchanged congratulations
with me on our private and leisurely view of the bonnets
and shawls ; but I was, all the time, not so sure that
our examination was so utterly private, for I caught
glimpses of a figure dodging behind the cloaks and
mantles ; and, by a dexterous move, I came face to
face with Miss Pole, also in morning costume (the
principal feature of which was her being without teeth,
and wearing a veil to conceal the deficiency), come on
the same errand as ourselves.   But she quickly took
her departure, because, as she said, she had a bad
headache, and did not feel herself up to conversation.

As we came down through the shop, the civil Mr.
Johnson was awaiting us ; he had been informed of the
exchange of the note for gold, and with much good
feeling and real kindness, but with a little want of
tact, he wished to condole with Miss Matty, and
impress upon her the true state of the case.   I could
only hope that he had heard an exaggerated rumour,

for he said that her shares were worse than nothing,
and that the bank could not pay a shilling in the
pound. I was glad that Miss Matty seemed still a
little incredulous ; but I could not tell how much of

'*The civil Mr. Johnson.*

this was real or assumed, with that self-control which
seemed habitual to ladies of Miss Matty's standing in
Cranford, who would have thought their dignity com-
promised by the slightest expression of surprise, dismay,
or any similar feeling to an inferior in station, or in a

public shop. However, we walked home very silently.
I am ashamed to say, I believe I was rather vexed and
annoyed at Miss Matty's conduct in taking the note to
herself so decidedly. I had so set my heart upon her
having a new silk gown, which she wanted sadly; in
general she was so undecided anybody might turn her
round; in this case I had felt that it was no use
attempting it, but I was not the less put out at the
result.

Somehow, after twelve o'clock, we both acknowledged
to a sated curiosity about the fashions, and to a certain
fatigue of body (which was, in fact, depression of mind)
that indisposed us to go out again. But still we never
spoke of the note; till, all at once, something possessed
me to ask Miss Matty if she would think it her duty to
offer sovereigns for all the notes of the Town and
County Bank she met with? I could have bitten my
tongue out the minute I had said it. She looked up
rather sadly, and as if I had thrown a new perplexity
into her already distressed mind; and for a minute or
two she did not speak. Then she said—my own dear
Miss Matty—without a shade of reproach in her voice—

'My dear, I never feel as if my mind was what
people call very strong; and it's often hard enough work
for me to settle what I ought to do with the case right
before me. I was very thankful to—I was very thankful, that I saw my duty this morning, with the poor
man standing by me; but it's rather a strain upon me
to keep thinking and thinking what I should do if such
and such a thing happened; and, I believe, I had rather
wait and see what really does come; and I don't doubt
I shall be helped then, if I don't fidget myself,
and get too anxious beforehand. You know, love, I'm

not like Deborah.   If Deborah had lived, I've no doubt
she would have seen after them, before they had got
themselves into this state.'

We had neither of us much appetite for dinner,
though we tried to talk cheerfully about indifferent
things.   When we returned into the drawing-room,
Miss Matty unlocked her desk and began to look over
her account-books.   I was so penitent for what I had

' The account-books.'

said in the morning, that I did not choose to take upon
myself the presumption to suppose that I could assist
her ; I rather left her alone, as, with puzzled brow, her
eye followed her pen up and down the ruled page.   By
and by she shut the book, locked her desk, and came
and drew a chair to mine, where I sat in moody sorrow
over the fire.   I stole my hand into hers ; she clasped
it, but did not speak a word.   At last she said, with
forced composure in her voice, ' If that bank goes wrong,
I shall lose one hundred and forty-nine pounds thirteen

shillings and fourpence a year; I shall only have thirteen pounds a year left.' I squeezed her hand hard and tight. I did not know what to say. Presently (it was too dark to see her face) I felt her fingers work convulsively in my grasp; and I knew she was going to speak again. I heard the sobs in her voice as she said, 'I hope it's not wrong—not wicked—but, oh! I am so glad poor Deborah is spared this. She could not have borne to come down in the world—she had such a noble, lofty spirit.'

This was all she said about the sister who had insisted upon investing their little property in that unlucky bank. We were later in lighting the candle than usual that night, and until that light shamed us into speaking, we sat together very silently and sadly.

However, we took to our work after tea with a kind of forced cheerfulness (which soon became real as far as it went), talking of that never-ending wonder, Lady Glenmire's engagement. Miss Matty was almost coming round to think it a good thing.

'I don't mean to deny that men are troublesome in a house. I don't judge from my own experience, for my father was neatness itself, and wiped his shoes on coming in as carefully as any woman; but still a man has a sort of knowledge of what should be done in difficulties, that it is very pleasant to have one at hand ready to lean upon. Now, Lady Glenmire, instead of being tossed about, and wondering where she is to settle, will be certain of a home among pleasant and kind people, such as our good Miss Pole and Mrs. Forrester. And Mr. Hoggins is really a very personable man; and as for his manners, why, if they are not very polished, I have known people with very good hearts,

and very clever minds too, who were not what some
people reckoned refined, but who were both true and
tender.'

She fell off into a soft reverie about Mr. Holbrook,
and I did not interrupt her, I was so busy maturing a
plan I had had in my mind for some days, but which
this threatened failure of the bank had brought to a
crisis. That night, after Miss Matty went to bed, I
treacherously lighted the candle again, and sat down
in the drawing-room to compose a letter to the Aga
Jenkyns, a letter which should affect him if he were
Peter, and yet seem a mere statement of dry facts if he
were a stranger. The church clock pealed out two
before I had done.

The next morning news came, both official and
otherwise, that the Town and County Bank had stopped
payment. Miss Matty was ruined.

She tried to speak quietly to me ; but when she
came to the actual fact that she would have but about
five shillings a week to live upon, she could not restrain
a few tears.

'I am not crying for myself, dear,' said she, wiping
them away ; 'I believe I am crying for the very silly
thought of how my mother would grieve if she could
know ; she always cared for us so much more than for
herself. But many a poor person has less, and I am
not very extravagant, and, thank God, when the neck
of mutton, and Martha's wages, and the rent are paid,
I have not a farthing owing. Poor Martha ! I think
she'll be sorry to leave me.'

Miss Matty smiled at me through her tears, and she
would fain have had me see only the smile, not the
tears.

Chapter XIV

Friends in Need

It was an example to me, and I fancy it might be
to many others, to see how immediately Miss
Matty set about the retrenchment which she knew
to be right under her altered circumstances. While
she went down to speak to Martha, and break the intelligence to her, I stole out with my letter to the Aga
Jenkyns, and went to the signor's lodgings to obtain the
exact address. I bound the signora to secrecy; and
indeed her military manners had a degree of shortness
and reserve in them which made her always say as little
as possible, except when under the pressure of strong
excitement. Moreover (which made my secret doubly
sure), the signor was now so far recovered as to be
looking forward to travelling and conjuring again in
the space of a few days, when he, his wife, and little
Phœbe would leave Cranford. Indeed, I found him
looking over a great black and red placard, in which
the Signor Brunoni's accomplishments were set forth,
and to which only the name of the town where he

would next display them was wanting. He and his
wife were so much absorbed in deciding where the red
letters would come in with most effect (it might have

'Posting the letter.'

been the Rubric for that matter), that it was some time
before I could get my question asked privately, and
not before I had given several decisions, the wisdom of
which I questioned afterwards with equal sincerity as
soon as the signor threw in his doubts and reasons on

the important subject.   At last I got the address, spelt
by sound, and very queer it looked.   I dropped it in
the post on my way home, and then for a minute I
stood looking at the wooden pane with a gaping slit
which divided me from the letter but a moment ago in
my hand.   It was gone from me like life, never to be
recalled.   It would get tossed about on the sea, and
stained with sea-waves perhaps, and be carried among
palm-trees, and scented with all tropical fragrance ; the
little piece of paper but an hour ago so familiar and
commonplace, had set out on its race to the strange
wild countries beyond the Ganges !   But I could not
afford to lose much time on this speculation.   I hastened
home, that Miss Matty might not miss me.   Martha
opened the door to me, her face swollen with crying.
As soon as she saw me she burst out afresh, and taking
hold of my arm she pulled me in, and banged the door
to, in order to ask me if indeed it was all true that Miss
Matty had been saying.

'I'll never leave her !   No ; I won't.   I telled her so,
and said I could not think how she could find in her
heart to give me warning.   I could not have had the
face to do it, if I'd been her.   I might ha' been just as
good for nothing as Mrs. Fitz-Adam's Rosy, who struck
for wages after living seven years and a half in one place.
I said I was not one to go and serve Mammon at that
rate ; that I knew when I'd got a good missus, if she
didn't know when she'd got a good servant———'

'But, Martha,' said I, cutting in while she wiped
her eyes.

'Don't "but Martha" me,' she replied to my
deprecatory tone.

'Listen to reason'———

'I'll not listen to reason,' she said, now in full
possession of her voice, which had been rather choked
with sobbing. 'Reason always means what some one
else has got to say. Now I think what I've got to say

'*Don't "but Martha" me.*'

is good enough reason; but reason or not, I'll say it,
and I'll stick to it. I've money in the Savings Bank,
and I've a good stock of clothes, and I'm not going
to leave Miss Matty. No, not if she gives me warning
every hour in the day!'

She put her arms akimbo, as much as to say she defied me; and, indeed, I could hardly tell how to begin to remonstrate with her, so much did I feel that Miss Matty, in her increasing infirmity, needed the attendance of this kind and faithful woman.

'Well——' said I at last.

'I'm thankful you begin with "well!" If you'd ha' begun with "but," as you did afore, I'd not ha' listened to you. Now you may go on.'

'I know you would be a great loss to Miss Matty, Martha——'

'I telled her so. A loss she'd never cease to be sorry for,' broke in Martha triumphantly.

'Still, she will have so little—so very little—to live upon, that I don't see just now how she could find you food—she will even be pressed for her own. I tell you this, Martha, because I feel you are like a friend to dear Miss Matty, but you know she might not like to have it spoken about.'

Apparently this was even a blacker view of the subject than Miss Matty had presented to her, for Martha just sat down on the first chair that came to hand, and cried out loud (we had been standing in the kitchen).

At last she put her apron down, and looking me earnestly in the face, asked, 'Was that the reason Miss Matty wouldn't order a pudding to-day? She said she had no great fancy for sweet things, and you and she would just have a mutton-chop. But I'll be up to her. Never you tell, but I'll make her a pudding, and a pudding she'll like, too, and I'll pay for it myself; so mind you see she eats it. Many a one has been comforted in their sorrow by seeing a good dish come upon the table.'

I was rather glad that Martha's energy had taken the immediate and practical direction of pudding-making, for it staved off the quarrelsome discussion as to whether she should or should not leave Miss Matty's service. She began to tie on a clean apron, and otherwise prepare herself for going to the shop for the butter, eggs, and what else she might require. She would not use a scrap of the articles already in the house for her cookery, but went to an old tea-pot in which her private store of money was deposited, and took out what she wanted.

I found Miss Matty very quiet, and not a little sad; but by and by she tried to smile for my sake. It was settled that I was to write to my father, and ask him to come over and hold a consultation, and as soon as this letter was despatched we began to talk over future plans. Miss Matty's idea was to take a single room, and retain as much of her furniture as would be necessary to fit up this, and sell the rest, and there to quietly exist upon what would remain after paying the rent. For my part, I was more ambitious and less contented. I thought of all the things by which a woman past middle age, and with the education common to ladies fifty years ago, could earn or add to a living without materially losing caste; but at length I put even this last clause on one side, and wondered what in the world Miss Matty could do.

Teaching was, of course, the first thing that suggested itself. If Miss Matty could teach children anything, it would throw her among the little elves in whom her soul delighted. I ran over her accomplishments. Once upon a time I had heard her say she could play 'Ah! vous dirai-je, maman?' on the piano, but that was long,

long ago ; that faint shadow of musical acquirement
had died out years before. She had also once been
able to trace out patterns very nicely for muslin
embroidery, by dint of placing a piece of silver-paper
over the design to be copied, and holding both against
the window-pane while she marked the scollop and
eyelet-holes. But that was her nearest approach to
the accomplishment of drawing, and I did not think it
would go very far. Then again, as to the branches
of a solid English education—fancy work and the use
of the globes—such as the mistress of the Ladies'
Seminary, to which all the tradespeople in Cranford
sent their daughters, professed to teach. Miss Matty's
eyes were failing her, and I doubted if she could
discover the number of threads in a worsted-work
pattern, or rightly appreciate the different shades required for Queen Adelaide's face in the loyal wool-
work now fashionable in Cranford. As for the use of
the globes, I had never been able to find it out myself,
so perhaps I was not a good judge of Miss Matty's
capability of instructing in this branch of education ;
but it struck me that equators and tropics, and such
mystical circles, were very imaginary lines indeed to
her, and that she looked upon the signs of the Zodiac
as so many remnants of the Black Art.

What she piqued herself upon, as arts in which she
excelled, was making candle-lighters, or 'spills' (as she
preferred calling them), of coloured paper, cut so as
to resemble feathers, and knitting garters in a variety
of dainty stitches. I had once said, on receiving a
present of an elaborate pair, that I should feel quite
tempted to drop one of them in the street, in order to
have it admired ; but I found this little joke (and it

was a very little one) was such a distress to her sense of propriety, and was taken with such anxious, earnest alarm, lest the temptation might some day prove too strong for me, that I quite regretted having ventured upon it. A present of these delicately-wrought garters, a bunch of gay 'spills,' or a set of cards on which sewing-silk was wound in a mystical manner, were the well-known tokens of Miss Matty's favour. But would any one pay to have their children taught these arts? or, indeed, would Miss Matty sell, for filthy lucre, the knack and the skill with which she made trifles of value to those who loved her?

I had to come down to reading, writing, and arithmetic; and, in reading the chapter every morning, she always coughed before coming to long words. I doubted her power of getting through a genealogical chapter, with any number of coughs. Writing she did well and delicately—but spelling! She seemed to think that the more out-of-the-way this was, and the more trouble it cost her, the greater the compliment she paid to her correspondent; and words that she would spell quite correctly in her letters to me became perfect enigmas when she wrote to my father.

No! there was nothing she could teach to the rising generation of Cranford, unless they had been quick learners and ready imitators of her patience, her humility, her sweetness, her quiet contentment with all that she could not do. I pondered and pondered until dinner was announced by Martha, with a face all blubbered and swollen with crying.

Miss Matty had a few little peculiarities which Martha was apt to regard as whims below her attention, and appeared to consider as childish fancies of which

an old lady of fifty-eight should try and cure herself.
But to-day everything was attended to with the most
careful regard. The bread was cut to the imaginary
pattern of excellence that existed in Miss Matty's mind,
as being the way which her mother had preferred, the
curtain was drawn so as to exclude the dead brick-wall

'There!'

of a neighbour's stables, and yet left so as to show
every tender leaf of the poplar which was bursting into
spring beauty. Martha's tone to Miss Matty was just
such as that good, rough-spoken servant usually kept
sacred for little children, and which I had never heard
her use to any grown-up person.

I had forgotten to tell Miss Matty about the
pudding, and I was afraid she might not do justice to
it, for she had evidently very little appetite this day;

so I seized the opportunity of letting her into the secret while Martha took away the meat. Miss Matty's eyes filled with tears, and she could not speak, either to express surprise or delight, when Martha returned bearing it aloft, made in the most wonderful representation of a lion *couchant* that ever was moulded. Martha's face gleamed with triumph as she set it down before Miss Matty with an exultant 'There!' Miss Matty wanted to speak her thanks, but could not; so she took Martha's hand and shook it warmly, which set Martha off crying, and I myself could hardly keep up the necessary composure. Martha burst out of the room, and Miss Matty had to clear her voice once or twice before she could speak. At last she said, 'I should like to keep this pudding under a glass shade, my dear!' and the notion of the lion *couchant*, with his currant eyes, being hoisted up to the place of honour on a mantelpiece, tickled my hysterical fancy, and I began to laugh, which rather surprised Miss Matty.

'I am sure, dear, I have seen uglier things under a glass shade before now,' said she.

So had I, many a time and oft, and I accordingly composed my countenance (and now I could hardly keep from crying), and we both fell to upon the pudding, which was indeed excellent—only every morsel seemed to choke us, our hearts were so full.

We had too much to think about to talk much that afternoon. It passed over very tranquilly. But when the tea-urn was brought in a new thought came into my head. Why should not Miss Matty sell tea—be an agent to the East India Tea Company which then existed? I could see no objections to this plan, while the advantages were many—always supposing that

Miss Matty could get over the degradation of condescending to anything like trade.   Tea was neither
greasy nor sticky—grease and stickiness being two of
the qualities which Miss Matty could not endure.   No
shop-window would be required.   A small, genteel
notification of her being licensed to sell tea would, it is
true, be necessary, but I hoped that it could be placed
where no one would see it.   Neither was tea a heavy
article, so as to tax Miss Matty's fragile strength.   The
only thing against my plan was the buying and selling
involved.

While I was giving but absent answers to the
questions Miss Matty was putting—almost as absently
—we heard a clumping sound on the stairs, and a
whispering outside the door, which indeed once opened
and shut as if by some invisible agency.   After a little
while Martha came in, dragging after her a great tall
young man, all crimson with shyness, and finding his
only relief in perpetually sleeking down his hair.

'Please, ma'am, he's only Jem Hearn,' said Martha,
by way of an introduction ; and so out of breath was
she that I imagine she had had some bodily struggle
before she could overcome his reluctance to be presented
on the courtly scene of Miss Matilda Jenkyns's drawing-
room.

'And please, ma'am, he wants to marry me off-hand.
And please, ma'am, we want to take a lodger—just one
quiet lodger, to make our two ends meet ; and we'd
take any house conformable ; and, oh dear Miss Matty,
if I may be so bold, would you have any objections to
lodging with us?   Jem wants it as much as I do.'
[To Jem :]—'You great oaf ! why can't you back me ?
—But he does want it all the same, very bad—don't

you, Jem ?—only, you see, he's dazed at being called on
to speak before quality.'

 'It's not that,' broke in Jem.   'It's that you've taken

'He's only Jem Hearn.'

me all on a sudden, and I didn't think for to get married
so soon—and such quick work does flabbergast a man.
It's not that I'm against it, ma'am' (addressing Miss
Matty), 'only Martha has such quick ways with her
when once she takes a thing into her head ; and

marriage, ma'am—marriage nails a man, as one may say. I daresay I shan't mind it after it's once over.'

'Please, ma'am,' said Martha—who had plucked at his sleeve, and nudged him with her elbow, and otherwise tried to interrupt him all the time he had been speaking—'don't mind him, he'll come to ; 'twas only last night he was an-axing me, and an-axing me, and all the more because I said I could not think of it for years to come, and now he's only taken aback with the suddenness of the joy ; but you know, Jem, you are just as full as me about wanting a lodger.' (Another great nudge.)

'Ay ! if Miss Matty would lodge with us—otherwise I've no mind to be cumbered with strange folk in the house,' said Jem, with a want of tact which I could see enraged Martha, who was trying to represent a lodger as the great object they wished to obtain, and that, in fact, Miss Matty would be smoothing their path and conferring a favour, if she would only come and live with them.

Miss Matty herself was bewildered by the pair ; their, or rather Martha's sudden resolution in favour of matrimony staggered her, and stood between her and the contemplation of the plan which Martha had at heart. Miss Matty began—

'Marriage is a very solemn thing, Martha.'

'It is indeed, ma'am,' quoth Jem. 'Not that I've no objections to Martha.'

'You've never let me a-be for asking me for to fix when I would be married,' said Martha—her face all a-fire, and ready to cry with vexation—'and now you're shaming me before my missus and all.'

'Nay, now ! Martha, don't ee ! don't ee ! only a man

likes to have breathing-time,' said Jem, trying to possess himself of her hand, but in vain. Then seeing that she was more seriously hurt than he had imagined, he seemed to try to rally his scattered faculties, and with more straightforward dignity than, ten minutes before, I should have thought it possible for him to assume, he turned to Miss Matty, and said, 'I hope, ma'am, you know that I am bound to respect every one who has been kind to Martha. I always looked on her as to be my wife——some time; and she has often and often spoken of you as the kindest lady that ever was; and though the plain truth is, I would not like to be troubled with lodgers of the common run, yet if, ma'am, you'd honour us by living with us, I'm sure Martha would do her best to make you comfortable; and I'd keep out of your way as much as I could, which I reckon would be the best kindness such an awkward chap as me could do.'

Miss Matty had been very busy with taking off her spectacles, wiping them, and replacing them; but all she could say was, 'Don't let any thought of me hurry you into marriage: pray don't! Marriage is such a very solemn thing!'

'But Miss Matilda will think of your plan, Martha,' said I, struck with the advantages that it offered, and unwilling to lose the opportunity of considering about it. 'And I'm sure neither she nor I can ever forget your kindness; nor yours either, Jem.'

'Why, yes, ma'am! I'm sure I mean kindly, though I'm a bit fluttered by being pushed straight a-head into matrimony, as it were, and mayn't express myself conformable. But I'm sure I'm willing enough, and give me time to get accustomed; so, Martha, wench, what's the use of crying so, and slapping me if I come near?'

This last was *sotto voce*, and had the effect of making

'*Soothed by her lover.*'

Martha bounce out of the room, to be followed and soothed by her lover. Whereupon Miss Matty sat down and cried very heartily, and accounted for it by saying that the thought of Martha being married so soon gave her

quite a shock, and that she should never forgive herself
if she thought she was hurrying the poor creature.   I
think my pity was more for Jem, of the two ; but both
Miss Matty and I appreciated to the full the kindness
of the honest couple, although we said little about this,
and a good deal about the chances and dangers of
matrimony.

The next morning, very early, I received a note from
Miss Pole, so mysteriously wrapped up, and with so
many seals on it to secure secrecy, that I had to tear
the paper before I could unfold it.   And when I came
to the writing I could hardly understand the meaning,
it was so involved and oracular.   I made out, however,
that I was to go to Miss Pole's at eleven o'clock ; the
number *eleven* being written in full length as well as in
numerals, and *A.M.* twice dashed under, as if I were
very likely to come at eleven at night, when all Cranford was usually a-bed and asleep by ten.   There was
no signature except Miss Pole's initials reversed, P. E. ;
but as Martha had given me the note, 'with Miss Pole's
kind regards,' it needed no wizard to find out who sent
it ; and if the writer's name was to be kept secret, it
was very well that I was alone when Martha delivered it.

I went as requested to Miss Pole's.   The door was
opened to me by her little maid Lizzie in Sunday trim,
as if some grand event was impending over this work-
day.   And the drawing-room upstairs was arranged in
accordance with this idea.   The table was set out with
the best green card-cloth, and writing materials upon it.
On the little chiffonier was a tray with a newly-decanted
bottle of cowslip-wine, and some ladies'-finger biscuits.
Miss Pole herself was in solemn array, as if to receive
visitors, although it was only eleven o'clock.   Mrs.

Forrester was there, crying quietly and sadly, and my arrival seemed only to call forth fresh tears. Before we had finished our greetings, performed with lugubrious mystery of demeanour, there was another rat-tat-tat, and

'Mrs. Fitz-Adam.'

Mrs. Fitz-Adam appeared, crimson with walking and excitement. It seemed as if this was all the company expected; for now Miss Pole made several demonstrations of being about to open the business of the meeting, by stirring the fire, opening and shutting the door, and coughing and blowing her nose. Then she arranged us all round the table, taking care to place me opposite to her; and last of all, she inquired of me if the sad report was true, as she feared it was, that Miss Matty had lost all her fortune?

Of course, I had but one answer to make; and I never saw more unaffected sorrow depicted on any countenances than I did there on the three before me.

'I wish Mrs. Jamieson was here!' said Mrs. Forrester at last; but to judge from Mrs. Fitz-Adam's face, she could not second the wish.

'But without Mrs. Jamieson,' said Miss Pole, with just a sound of offended merit in her voice, 'we, the ladies of Cranford, in my drawing-room assembled, can resolve upon something. I imagine we are none of us what may be called rich, though we all possess a genteel competency, sufficient for tastes that are elegant and refined, and would not, if they could, be vulgarly ostentatious.' (Here I observed Miss Pole refer to a small card concealed in her hand, on which I imagine she had put down a few notes.)

'Miss Smith,' she continued, addressing me (familiarly known as 'Mary' to all the company assembled, but this was a state occasion), 'I have conversed in private —I made it my business to do so yesterday afternoon —with these ladies on the misfortune which has happened to our friend, and one and all of us have agreed that while we have a superfluity, it is not only a duty, but a pleasure—a true pleasure, Mary!'—her voice was rather choked just here, and she had to wipe her spectacles before she could go on—'to give what we can to assist her—Miss Matilda Jenkyns. Only in consideration of the feelings of delicate independence

existing in the mind of every refined female'—I was
sure she had got back to the card now—'we wish to
contribute our mites in a secret and concealed manner,
so as not to hurt the feelings I have referred to.   And
our object in requesting you to meet us this morning is
that, believing you are the daughter—that your father
is, in fact, her confidential adviser in all pecuniary
matters, we imagined that, by consulting with him, you
might devise some mode in which our contribution could
be made to appear the legal due which Miss Matilda
Jenkyns ought to receive from ——.   Probably, your
father, knowing her investments, can fill up the blank.'

Miss Pole concluded her address, and looked round
for approval and agreement.

'I have expressed your meaning, ladies, have I not?
And while Miss Smith considers what reply to make,
allow me to offer you some little refreshment.'

I had no great reply to make ; I had more thankful-
ness at my heart for their kind thoughts than I cared
to put into words ; and so I only mumbled out something to the effect 'that I would name what Miss Pole
had said to my father, and that if anything could be
arranged for dear Miss Matty,'—and here I broke down
utterly, and had to be refreshed with a glass of cowslip
wine before I could check the crying which had been
repressed for the last two or three days.   The worst
was, all the ladies cried in concert.   Even Miss Pole
cried, who had said a hundred times that to betray
emotion before any one was a sign of weakness and
want of self-control.   She recovered herself into a slight
degree of impatient anger, directed against me, as having
set them all off ; and, moreover, I think she was vexed
that I could not make a speech back in return for hers ;

and if I had known beforehand what was to be said, and had a card on which to express the probable feelings that would rise in my heart, I would have tried to gratify her. As it was, Mrs. Forrester was the person to speak when we had recovered our composure.

'I don't mind, among friends, stating that I—no! I'm not poor exactly, but I don't think I'm what you may call rich ; I wish I were, for dear Miss Matty's sake— but, if you please, I'll write down in a sealed paper what I can give. I only wish it was more : my dear Mary, I do indeed.'

Now I saw why paper, pens, and ink were provided. Every lady wrote down the sum she could give annually, signed the paper, and sealed it mysteriously. If their proposal was acceded to, my father was to be allowed to open the papers, under pledge of secrecy. If not, they were to be returned to their writers.

When this ceremony had been gone through, I rose to depart ; but each lady seemed to wish to have a private conference with me. Miss Pole kept me in the drawing-room to explain why, in Mrs. Jamieson's absence, she had taken the lead in this 'movement,' as she was pleased to call it, and also to inform me that she had heard from good sources that Mrs. Jamieson was coming home directly in a state of high displeasure against her sister-in-law, who was forthwith to leave her house, and was, she believed, to return to Edinburgh that very afternoon. Of course this piece of intelligence could not be communicated before Mrs. Fitz-Adam, more especially as Miss Pole was inclined to think that Lady Glenmire's engagement to Mr. Hoggins could not possibly hold against the blaze of Mrs. Jamieson's displeasure. A few hearty inquiries after Miss

Matty's health concluded my interview with Miss
Pole.

On coming downstairs I found Mrs. Forrester waiting for me at the entrance to the dining-parlour ; she
drew me in, and when the door was shut, she tried two
or three times to begin on some subject, which was so
unapproachable apparently, that I began to despair of
our ever getting to a clear understanding.   At last out
it came ; the poor old lady trembling all the time, as if
it were a great crime which she was exposing to daylight, in telling me how very, very little she had to live
upon ; a confession which she was brought to make
from a dread lest we should think that the small contribution named in her paper bore any proportion to
her love and regard for Miss Matty.   And yet that sum
which she so eagerly relinquished was, in truth, more
than a twentieth part of what she had to live upon, and
keep house, and a little serving-maid, all as became one
born a Tyrrell.   And when the whole income does not
nearly amount to a hundred pounds, to give up a
twentieth of it will necessitate many careful economies,
and many pieces of self-denial, small and insignificant
in the world's account, but bearing a different value in
another account-book that I have heard of.   She did
so wish she was rich, she said, and this wish she kept
repeating, with no thought of herself in it, only with a
longing, yearning desire to be able to heap up Miss
Matty's measure of comforts.

It was some time before I could console her enough
to leave her ; and then, on quitting the house, I was
waylaid by Mrs. Fitz-Adam, who had also her confidence
to make of pretty nearly the opposite description.   She
had not liked to put down all that she could afford and

was ready to give. She told me she thought she never
could look Miss Matty in the face again if she presumed
to be giving her so much as she should like to do.
'Miss Matty!' continued she, 'that I thought was such
a fine young lady when I was nothing but a country
girl, coming to market with eggs and butter and such
like things. For my father, though well-to-do, would
always make me go on as my mother had done before
me, and I had to come into Cranford every Saturday,
and see after sales, and prices, and what not. And one
day, I remember, I met Miss Matty in the lane that
leads to Combehurst ; she was walking on the footpath,
which, you know, is raised a good way above the road,
and a gentleman rode beside her, and was talking to
her, and she was looking down at some primroses she
had gathered, and pulling them all to pieces, and I do
believe she was crying. But after she had passed, she
turned round and ran after me to ask—oh, so kindly—
about my poor mother, who lay on her death-bed ; and
when I cried she took hold of my hand to comfort me
—and the gentleman waiting for her all the time—and
her poor heart very full of something, I am sure ; and
I thought it such an honour to be spoken to in that
pretty way by the rector's daughter, who visited at
Arley Hall. I have loved her ever since, though perhaps I'd no right to do it ; but if you can think of any
way in which I might be allowed to give a little more
without any one knowing it I should be so much
obliged to you, my dear. And my brother would
be delighted to doctor her for nothing—medicines,
leeches, and all. I know that he and her ladyship
(my dear, I little thought in the days I was telling
you of that I should ever come to be sister-in-law

to a ladyship!) would do anything for her. We all would.'

I told her I was quite sure of it, and promised all sorts of things in my anxiety to get home to Miss Matty, who might well be wondering what had become of me—absent from her two hours without being able to account for it. She had taken very little note of time, however, as she had been occupied in numberless little arrangements preparatory to the great step of giving up her house. It was evidently a relief to her to be doing something in the way of retrenchment, for, as she said, whenever she paused to think, the recollection of the poor fellow with his bad five-pound note came over her, and she felt quite dishonest; only if it made her so uncomfortable, what must it not be doing to the directors of the bank, who must know so much more of the misery consequent upon this failure? She almost made me angry by dividing her sympathy between these directors (whom she imagined overwhelmed by self-reproach for the mismanagement of other people's affairs) and those who were suffering like her. Indeed, of the two, she seemed to think poverty a lighter burden than self-reproach; but I privately doubted if the directors would agree with her.

Old hoards were taken out and examined as to their money value, which luckily was small, or else I don't know how Miss Matty would have prevailed upon herself to part with such things as her mother's wedding-ring, the strange, uncouth brooch with which her father had disfigured his shirt-frill, etc. However, we arranged things a little in order as to their pecuniary estimation, and were all ready for my father when he came the next morning.

I am not going to weary you with the details of all
the business we went through ; and one reason for not
telling about them is, that I did not understand what
we were doing at the time, and cannot recollect it now.
Miss Matty and I sat assenting to accounts, and schemes,
and reports, and documents, of which I do not believe
we either of us understood a word ; for my father was
clear-headed and decisive, and a capital man of business,
and if we made the slightest inquiry, or expressed the
slightest want of comprehension, he had a sharp way of
saying, ' Eh ? eh ? it's as clear as daylight.   What's
your objection ? '   And as we had not comprehended
anything of what he had proposed, we found it rather
difficult to shape our objections ; in fact, we never were
sure if we had any.   So presently Miss Matty got into
a nervously acquiescent state, and said ' Yes,' and ' Certainly,' at every pause, whether required or not ; but
when I once joined in as chorus to a ' Decidedly,' pronounced by Miss Matty in a tremblingly dubious tone,
my father fired round at me and asked me ' What there
was to decide ? '   And I am sure to this day I have
never known.   But, in justice to him, I must say he
had come over from Drumble to help Miss Matty when
he could ill spare the time, and when his own affairs
were in a very anxious state.

While Miss Matty was out of the room giving orders
for luncheon—and sadly perplexed between her desire
of honouring my father by a delicate, dainty meal, and
her conviction that she had no right, now that all her
money was gone, to indulge this desire—I told him of
the meeting of the Cranford ladies at Miss Pole's the
day before.   He kept brushing his hand before his eyes
as I spoke—and when I went back to Martha's offer the

evening before, of receiving Miss Matty as a lodger, he
fairly walked away from me to the window, and began
drumming with his fingers upon it. Then he turned

'Drumming with his fingers upon it.'

abruptly round, and said, 'See, Mary, how a good
innocent life makes friends all around. Confound it! I
could make a good lesson out of it if I were a parson;
but, as it is, I can't get a tail to my sentences—only
I'm sure you feel what I want to say. You and I will

have a walk after lunch and talk a bit more about these
plans.'

The lunch—a hot savoury mutton-chop, and a little
of the cold lion sliced and fried—was now brought in.
Every morsel of this last dish was finished, to Martha's
great gratification. Then my father bluntly told Miss
Matty he wanted to talk to me alone, and that he would
stroll out and see some of the old places, and then I
could tell her what plan we thought desirable. Just
before we went out, she called me back and said, 'Remember, dear, I'm the only one left—I mean, there's
no one to be hurt by what I do. I'm willing to do
anything that's right and honest; and I don't think, if
Deborah knows where she is, she'll care so very much
if I'm not genteel; because, you see, she'll know all,
dear. Only let me see what I can do, and pay the
poor people as far as I'm able.'

I gave her a hearty kiss, and ran after my father.
The result of our conversation was this. If all parties
were agreeable, Martha and Jem were to be married
with as little delay as possible, and they were to live on
in Miss Matty's present abode; the sum which the
Cranford ladies had agreed to contribute annually being
sufficient to meet the greater part of the rent, and leaving Martha free to appropriate what Miss Matty should
pay for her lodgings to any little extra comforts required. About the sale, my father was dubious at first
He said the old rectory furniture, however carefully used
and reverently treated, would fetch very little; and that
little would be but as a drop in the sea of the debts of
the Town and County Bank. But when I represented
how Miss Matty's tender conscience would be soothed
by feeling that she had done what she could, he gave

way ; especially after I had told him the five-pound
note adventure, and he had scolded me well for allowing
it.   I then alluded to my idea that she might add to
her small income by selling tea ; and, to my surprise
(for I had nearly given up the plan), my father grasped
at it with all the energy of a tradesman.   I think he
reckoned his chickens before they were hatched, for he
immediately ran up the profits of the sales that she
could effect in Cranford to more than twenty pounds
a year.   The small dining-parlour was to be converted
into a shop, without any of its degrading characteristics ;
a table was to be the counter ; one window was to be
retained unaltered, and the other changed into a glass
door.   I evidently rose in his estimation for having
made this bright suggestion.   I only hoped we should
not both fall in Miss Matty's.

But she was patient and content with all our
arrangements.   She knew, she said, that we should do
the best we could for her ; and she only hoped, only
stipulated, that she should pay every farthing that she
could be said to owe, for her father's sake, who had been
so respected in Cranford.   My father and I had agreed
to say as little as possible about the bank, indeed never
to mention it again, if it could be helped.   Some of the
plans were evidently a little perplexing to her ; but she
had seen me sufficiently snubbed in the morning for
want of comprehension to venture on too many inquiries
now ; and all passed over well, with a hope on her part
that no one would be hurried into marriage on her
account.   When we came to the proposal that she
should sell tea, I could see it was rather a shock to
her ; not on account of any personal loss of gentility
involved, but only because she distrusted her own

powers of action in a new line of life, and would timidly
have preferred a little more privation to any exertion
for which she feared she was unfitted.   However, when
she saw my father was bent upon it, she sighed, and said
she would try ; and if she did not do well, of course she
might give it up.   One good thing about it was, she
did not think men ever bought tea ; and it was of men
particularly she was afraid.   They had such sharp loud
ways with them ; and did up accounts, and counted
their change so quickly !   Now, if she might only sell
comfits to children, she was sure she could please them !

Chapter XV.
A Happy Return.

Before I left Miss Matty at Cranford everything had been comfortably arranged for her. Even Mrs. Jamieson's approval of her selling tea had been gained. That oracle had taken a few days to consider whether by so doing Miss Matty would forfeit her right to the privileges of society in Cranford. I think she had some little idea of mortifying Lady Glenmire by the decision she gave at last ; which was to this effect : that whereas a married woman takes her husband's rank by the strict laws of precedence, an unmarried woman retains the station her father occupied. So Cranford was allowed to visit Miss Matty ; and, whether allowed or not, it intended to visit Lady Glenmire.

But what was our surprise—our dismay—when we learnt that Mr. and *Mrs. Hoggins* were returning on the following Tuesday. Mrs. Hoggins ! Had she absolutely dropped her title, and so, in a spirit of bravado, cut the aristocracy to become a Hoggins! She, who might have been called Lady Glenmire to her dying day! Mrs. Jamieson was pleased. She said it only convinced her of what she had known from the first, that the creature had a low taste. But 'the creature' looked very happy on Sunday at church; nor did we see it necessary to keep our veils down on that side of our bonnets on which Mr. and Mrs. Hoggins sat, as Mrs. Jamieson did; thereby missing all the smiling glory of his face, and all the becoming blushes of hers. I am not sure if Martha and Jem looked more radiant in the afternoon, when they, too, made their first appearance. Mrs. Jamieson soothed the turbulence of her soul by having the blinds of her windows drawn down, as if for a funeral, on the day when Mr. and Mrs. Hoggins received callers; and it was with some difficulty that she was prevailed upon to continue the *St. James's Chronicle*, so indignant was she with its having inserted the announcement of the marriage.

Miss Matty's sale went off famously. She retained the furniture of her sitting-room and bedroom; the former of which she was to occupy till Martha could meet with a lodger who might wish to take it; and into this sitting-room and bedroom she had to cram all sorts of things, which were (the auctioneer assured her) bought in for her at the sale by an unknown friend. I always suspected Mrs. Fitz-Adam of this; but she must have had an accessory, who knew what articles were particularly regarded by Miss Matty on account of their associations with her early days. The rest of the house looked rather bare, to be sure; all except

one tiny bedroom, of which my father allowed me to
purchase the furniture for my occasional use in case of
Miss Matty's illness.

I had expended my own small store in buying all
manner of comfits and lozenges, in order to tempt the
little people whom Miss Matty loved so much to come

' All the smiling glory of his face.'

about her.   Tea in bright green canisters, and comfits
in tumblers—Miss Matty and I felt quite proud as we
looked round us on the evening before the shop was
to be opened.   Martha had scoured the boarded floor
to a white cleanness, and it was adorned with a brilliant
piece of oil-cloth, on which customers were to stand
before the table-counter.   The wholesome smell of

plaster and whitewash pervaded the apartment. A very
small 'Matilda Jenkyns, licensed to sell tea,' was hidden
under the lintel of the new door, and two boxes of tea,
with cabalistic inscriptions all over them, stood ready
to disgorge their contents into the canisters.

Miss Matty, as I ought to have mentioned before,
had had some scruples of conscience at selling tea when
there was already Mr. Johnson in the town, who included
it among his numerous commodities ; and, before she
could quite reconcile herself to the adoption of her new
business, she had trotted down to his shop, unknown
to me, to tell him of the project that was entertained,
and to inquire if it was likely to injure his business.
My father called this idea of hers 'great nonsense,' and
'wondered how tradespeople were to get on if there
was to be a continual consulting of each other's interests,
which would put a stop to all competition directly.'
And, perhaps, it would not have done in Drumble, but
in Cranford it answered very well ; for not only did
Mr. Johnson kindly put at rest all Miss Matty's scruples
and fear of injuring his business, but I have reason to
know he repeatedly sent customers to her, saying that
the teas he kept were of a common kind, but that Miss
Jenkyns had all the choice sorts. And expensive tea
is a very favourite luxury with well-to-do tradespeople
and rich farmers' wives, who turn up their noses at the
Congou and Souchong prevalent at many tables of
gentility, and will have nothing else than Gunpowder
and Pekoe for themselves.

But to return to Miss Matty. It was really very
pleasant to see how her unselfishness and simple sense
of justice called out the same good qualities in others.
She never seemed to think any one would impose upon

her, because she should be so grieved to do it to them. I have heard her put a stop to the asseverations of the man who brought her coals by quietly saying, 'I am sure you would be sorry to bring me wrong weight ;' and if the coals were short measure that time, I don't believe they ever were again. People would have felt as much ashamed of presuming on her good faith as they would have done on that of a child. But my father says ' such simplicity might be very well in Cranford, but would never do in the world.' And I fancy the world must be very bad, for with all my father's suspicion of every one with whom he has dealings, and in spite of all his many precautions, he lost upwards of a thousand pounds by roguery only last year.

I just stayed long enough to establish Miss Matty in her new mode of life, and to pack up the library, which the rector had purchased. He had written a very kind letter to Miss Matty, saying 'how glad he should be to take a library, so well selected as he knew that the late Mr. Jenkyns's must have been, at any valuation put upon them.' And when she agreed to this, with a touch of sorrowful gladness that they would go back to the rectory and be arranged on the accustomed walls once more, he sent word that he feared that he had not room for them all, and perhaps Miss Matty would kindly allow him to leave some volumes on her shelves. But Miss Matty said that she had her Bible and Johnson's *Dictionary*, and should not have much time for reading, she was afraid ; still, I retained a few books out of consideration for the rector's kindness.

The money which he had paid, and that produced by the sale, was partly expended in the stock of tea,

and part of it was invested against a rainy day—*i.e.*
old age or illness.   It was but a small sum, it is true ;
and it occasioned a few evasions of truth and white lies
(all of which I think very wrong indeed—in theory—
and would rather not put them in practice), for we
knew Miss Matty would be perplexed as to her duty
if she were aware of any little reserve-fund being made
for her while the debts of the bank remained unpaid.
Moreover, she had never been told of the way in which
her friends were contributing to pay the rent.   I should
have liked to tell her this, but the mystery of the affair
gave a piquancy to their deed of kindness which the
ladies were unwilling to give up ; and at first Martha
had to shirk many a perplexed question as to her ways
and means of living in such a house, but by and by
Miss Matty's prudent uneasiness sank down into acquiescence with the existing arrangement.

I left Miss Matty with a good heart.   Her sales of
tea during the first two days had surpassed my most
sanguine expectations.   The whole country round
seemed to be all out of tea at once.   The only alteration I could have desired in Miss Matty's way of doing
business was, that she should not have so plaintively
entreated some of her customers not to buy green tea
—running it down as slow poison, sure to destroy the
nerves, and produce all manner of evil.   Their pertina-
city in taking it, in spite of all her warnings, distressed
her so much that I really thought she would relinquish
the sale of it, and so lose half her custom ; and I was
driven to my wits' end for instances of longevity entirely
attributable to a persevering use of green tea.   But the
final argument, which settled the question, was a happy
reference of mine to the train-oil and tallow candles

which the Esquimaux not only enjoy but digest. After that she acknowledged that 'one man's meat might be another man's poison,' and contented herself thenceforward with an occasional remonstrance when she thought the purchaser was too young and innocent to be acquainted with the evil effects green tea produced on some constitutions, and an habitual sigh when people old enough to choose more wisely would prefer it.

I went over from Drumble once a quarter at least to settle the accounts, and see after the necessary business letters. And, speaking of letters, I began to be very much ashamed of remembering my letter to the Aga Jenkyns, and very glad I had never named my writing to any one. I only hoped the letter was lost. No answer came. No sign was made.

About a year after Miss Matty set up shop, I received one of Martha's hieroglyphics, begging me to come to Cranford very soon. I was afraid that Miss Matty was ill, and went off that very afternoon, and took Martha by surprise when she saw me on opening the door. We went into the kitchen, as usual, to have our confidential conference, and then Martha told me she was expecting her confinement very soon—in a week or two ; and she did not think Miss Matty was aware of it, and she wanted me to break the news to her, 'for indeed, miss,' continued Martha, crying hysterically, 'I'm afraid she won't approve of it, and I'm sure I don't know who is to take care of her as she should be taken care of when I am laid up.'

I comforted Martha by telling her I would remain till she was about again, and only wished she had told me her reason for this sudden summons, as then I would have brought the requisite stock of clothes.

But Martha was so tearful and tender-spirited, and unlike her usual self, that I said as little as possible about myself, and endeavoured rather to comfort Martha under all the probable and possible misfortunes which came crowding upon her imagination.

I then stole out of the house-door, and made my appearance as if I were a customer in the shop, just to take Miss Matty by surprise, and gain an idea of how she looked in her new situation. It was warm May weather, so only the little half-door was closed ; and Miss Matty sat behind her counter, knitting an elaborate pair of garters ; elaborate they seemed to me, but the difficult stitch was no weight upon her mind, for she was singing in a low voice to herself as her needles went rapidly in and out. I call it singing, but I daresay a musician would not use that word to the tuneless yet sweet humming of the low, worn voice. I found out from the words, far more than from the attempt at the tune, that it was the Old Hundredth she was crooning to herself ; but the quiet continuous sound told of content, and gave me a pleasant feeling, as I stood in the street just outside the door, quite in harmony with that soft May morning. I went in. At first she did not catch who it was, and stood up as if to serve me ; but in another minute watchful pussy had clutched her knitting, which was dropped in eager joy at seeing me. I found, after we had had a little conversation, that it was as Martha said, and that Miss Matty had no idea of the approaching household event. So I thought I would let things take their course, secure that when I went to her with the baby in my arms, I should obtain that forgiveness for Martha which she was needlessly frightening herself into believing that Miss Matty would

withhold, under some notion that the new claimant
would require attentions from its mother that it would
be faithless treason to Miss Matty to render.

But I was right. I think that must be an hereditary
quality, for my father says he is scarcely ever wrong.
One morning, within a week after I arrived, I went to

'*A complimentary speech.*'

call Miss Matty, with a little bundle of flannel in my
arms. She was very much awestruck when I showed
her what it was, and asked for her spectacles off the
dressing-table, and looked at it curiously, with a sort of
tender wonder at its small perfection of parts. She
could not banish the thought of the surprise all day,
but went about on tiptoe, and was very silent. But

she stole up to see Martha, and they both cried with joy, and she got into a complimentary speech to Jem, and did not know how to get out of it again, and was only extricated from her dilemma by the sound of the shop-bell, which was an equal relief to the shy, proud, honest Jem, who shook my hand so vigorously when I congratulated him, that I think I feel the pain of it yet.

I had a busy life while Martha was laid up. I attended on Miss Matty, and prepared her meals; I cast up her accounts, and examined into the state of her canisters and tumblers. I helped her, too, occasionally, in the shop; and it gave me no small amusement, and sometimes a little uneasiness, to watch her ways there. If a little child came in to ask for an ounce of almond-comfits (and four of the large kind which Miss Matty sold weighed that much), she always added one more by 'way of make-weight,' as she called it, although the scale was handsomely turned before; and when I remonstrated against this, her reply was, 'The little things like it so much!' There was no use in telling her that the fifth comfit weighed a quarter of an ounce, and made every sale into a loss to her pocket. So I remembered the green tea, and winged my shaft with a feather out of her own plumage. I told her how unwholesome almond-comfits were, and how ill excess in them might make the little children. This argument produced some effect; for, henceforward, instead of the fifth comfit, she always told them to hold out their tiny palms, into which she shook either peppermint or ginger lozenges, as a preventive to the dangers that might arise from the previous sale. Altogether the lozenge trade, conducted on these principles, did not promise to be remunerative; but I was happy

to find she had made more than twenty pounds during
the last year by her sales of tea ; and, moreover, that
now she was accustomed to it, she did not dislike the
employment, which brought her into kindly intercourse
with many of the people round about. If she gave
them good weight, they, in their turn, brought many a
little country present to the 'old rector's daughter'; a
cream cheese, a few new-laid eggs, a little fresh ripe
fruit, a bunch of flowers. The counter was quite loaded
with these offerings sometimes, as she told me.

As for Cranford in general, it was going on much as
usual. The Jamieson and Hoggins feud still raged, if a
feud it could be called, when only one side cared much
about it. Mr. and Mrs. Hoggins were very happy
together, and, like most very happy people, quite ready
to be friendly ; indeed, Mrs. Hoggins was really desirous
to be restored to Mrs. Jamieson's good graces, because
of the former intimacy. But Mrs. Jamieson considered
their very happiness an insult to the Glenmire family,
to which she had still the honour to belong, and she
doggedly refused and rejected every advance. Mr.
Mulliner, like a faithful clansman, espoused his mistress's
side with ardour. If he saw either Mr. or Mrs. Hoggins,
he would cross the street, and appear absorbed in the
contemplation of life in general, and his own path in
particular, until he had passed them by. Miss Pole
used to amuse herself with wondering what in the world
Mrs. Jamieson would do, if either she, or Mr. Mulliner,
or any other member of her household, was taken ill ;
she could hardly have the face to call in Mr. Hoggins
after the way she had behaved to them. Miss Pole
grew quite impatient for some indisposition or accident
to befall Mrs. Jamieson or her dependants, in order that

Cranford might see how she would act under the perplexing circumstances.

Martha was beginning to go about again, and I had
already fixed a limit, not very far distant, to my visit,

'*Absorbed in contemplation.*'

when one afternoon, as I was sitting in the shop-parlour
with Miss Matty—I remember the weather was colder
now than it had been in May, three weeks before, and
we had a fire and kept the door fully closed—we saw
a gentleman go slowly past the window, and then stand

opposite to the door, as if looking out for the name
which we had so carefully hidden. He took out a
double eye-glass and peered about for some time before
he could discover it.   Then he came in.   And, all on
a sudden, it flashed across me that it was the Aga
himself!   For his clothes had an out-of-the-way foreign
cut about them, and his face was deep brown, as if
tanned and re-tanned by the sun.   His complexion
contrasted oddly with his plentiful snow-white hair, his
eyes were dark and piercing, and he had an odd way
of contracting them and puckering up his cheeks into
innumerable wrinkles when he looked earnestly at
objects.   He did so to Miss Matty when he first came
in.   His glance had first caught and lingered a little
upon me, but then turned, with the peculiar searching
look I have described, to Miss Matty.   She was a little
fluttered and nervous, but no more so than she always
was when any man came into her shop.   She thought
that he would probably have a note, or a sovereign at
least, for which she would have to give change, which
was an operation she very much disliked to perform.
But the present customer stood opposite to her, without
asking for anything, only looking fixedly at her as he
drummed upon the table with his fingers, just for all
the world as Miss Jenkyns used to do.   Miss Matty
was on the point of asking him what he wanted (as she
told me afterwards), when he turned sharp to me : ' Is
your name Mary Smith ? '

     ' Yes ! ' said I.

     All my doubts as to his identity were set at rest, and
I only wondered what he would say or do next, and
how Miss Matty would stand the joyful shock of what
he had to reveal.   Apparently he was at a loss how to

announce himself, for he looked round at last in search of something to buy, so as to gain time, and, as it happened, his eye caught on the almond-comfits, and he boldly asked for a pound of 'those things.' I doubt if Miss Matty had a whole pound in the shop, and, besides the unusual magnitude of the order, she was distressed with the idea of the indigestion they would produce, taken in such unlimited quantities. She looked up to remonstrate. Something of tender relaxation in his face struck home to her heart. She said, 'It is—oh sir! can you be Peter?' and trembled from head to foot. In a moment he was round the table and had her in his arms, sobbing the tearless cries of old age. I brought her a glass of wine, for indeed her colour had changed so as to alarm me and Mr. Peter too. He kept saying, 'I have been too sudden for you, Matty— I have my little girl.'

I proposed that she should go at once up into the drawing-room and lie down on the sofa there. She looked wistfully at her brother, whose hand she had held tight, even when nearly fainting; but on his assuring her that he would not leave her, she allowed him to carry her upstairs.

I thought that the best I could do was to run and put the kettle on the fire for early tea, and then to attend to the shop, leaving the brother and sister to exchange some of the many thousand things they must have to say. I had also to break the news to Martha, who received it with a burst of tears which nearly infected me. She kept recovering herself to ask if I was sure it was indeed Miss Matty's brother, for I had mentioned that he had gray hair, and she had always heard that he was a very handsome young man. Something of the same kind perplexed Miss Matty at tea-time, when she was installed in the great easy-chair opposite to Mr. Jenkyns's in order to gaze her fill. She could hardly drink for looking at him, and as for eating, that was out of the question.

'I suppose hot climates age people very quickly,' said she, almost to herself. 'When you left Cranford you had not a gray hair in your head.'

'But how many years ago is that?' said Mr. Peter, smiling.

'Ah, true! yes, I suppose you and I are getting old. But still I did not think we were so very old! But white hair is very becoming to you, Peter,' she continued —a little afraid lest she had hurt him by revealing how his appearance had impressed her.

'I suppose I forgot dates too, Matty, for what do you think I have brought for you from India? I have an Indian muslin gown and a pearl necklace for you somewhere in my chest at Portsmouth.' He smiled as if amused at the idea of the incongruity of his presents with the appearance of his sister; but this did not strike her all at once, while the elegance of the articles did. I could see that for a moment her imagination dwelt complacently on the idea of herself thus attired; and instinctively she put her hand up to her throat—that little delicate throat which (as Miss Pole had told me) had been one of her youthful charms; but the hand met the touch of folds of soft muslin in which she was always swathed up to her chin, and the sensation recalled a sense of the unsuitableness of a pearl necklace to her age. She said, 'I'm afraid I'm too old; but it was very kind of you to think of it. They are just what I should have liked years ago—when I was young.'

'So I thought, my little Matty. I remembered your tastes; they were so like my dear mother's.' At the mention of that name the brother and sister clasped each other's hands yet more fondly, and, although they were perfectly silent, I fancied they might have something to say if they were unchecked by my presence, and I got up to arrange my room for Mr. Peter's occupation that night, intending myself to share Miss Matty's bed. But at my movement he started up. 'I must go and settle about a room at the "George." My carpet-bag is there too.'

'No!' said Miss Matty, in great distress—'you must not go; please, dear Peter—pray, Mary—oh! you must not go!'

She was so much agitated that we both promised everything she wished. Peter sat down again and gave her his hand, which for better security she held in both of hers, and I left the room to accomplish my arrangements.

Long, long into the night, far, far into the morning, did Miss Matty and I talk. She had much to tell me of her brother's life and adventures, which he had communicated to her as they had sat alone. She said all was thoroughly clear to her; but I never quite understood the whole story; and when in after days I lost my awe of Mr. Peter enough to question him myself, he laughed at my curiosity, and told me stories that sounded so very much like Baron Munchausen's, that I was sure he was making fun of me. What I heard from Miss Matty was that he had been a volunteer at the siege of Rangoon; had been taken prisoner by the Burmese; had somehow obtained favour and eventual freedom from knowing how to bleed the chief of the small tribe in some case of dangerous illness; that on his release from years of captivity he had had his letters returned from England with the ominous word 'Dead' marked upon them; and, believing himself to be the last of his race, he had settled down as an indigo planter, and had proposed to spend the remainder of his life in the country to whose inhabitants and modes of life he had become habituated, when my letter had reached him, and with the odd vehemence which characterised him in age as it had done in youth, he had sold his land and all his possessions to the first purchaser, and come home to the poor old sister, who was more glad and rich than any princess when she looked at him. She talked me to sleep at last, and then I was awakened by a slight sound at the door, for which she begged my pardon as she crept penitently into bed; but it seems that when I could no longer confirm her belief that the long-lost was really here—under the same roof —she had begun to fear lest it was only a waking dream of hers; that there never had been a Peter sitting by her all that blessed evening—but that the real Peter lay dead far away beneath some wild sea-wave, or under some strange eastern tree. And so strong had this nervous feeling of hers become, that she was fain to get up and go and convince herself that he was really there by listening through the door to his even, regular breathing—I don't like to call it snoring, but I heard it myself through two closed doors—and by and by it soothed Miss Matty to sleep.

I don't believe Mr. Peter came home from India as rich as a nabob; he even considered himself poor, but neither he nor Miss Matty cared much about that. At any rate, he had enough to live upon 'very genteelly'

at Cranford ; he and Miss Matty together.   And a day
or two after his arrival the shop was closed, while
troops of little urchins gleefully awaited the shower
of comfits and lozenges that came from time to time
down upon their faces as they stood up-gazing at Miss
Matty's drawing-room windows.   Occasionally Miss

'Gleefully awaited the shower of comfits and lozenges.

Matty would say to them (half-hidden behind the
curtains), 'My dear children, don't make yourselves
ill;' but a strong arm pulled her back, and a more
rattling shower than ever succeeded.   A part of the
tea was sent in presents to the Cranford ladies; and
some of it was distributed among the old people who
remembered Mr. Peter in the days of his frolicsome
youth.   The India muslin gown was reserved for
darling Flora Gordon (Miss Jessie Brown's daughter).

The Gordons had been on the Continent for the last few years, but were now expected to return very soon ; and Miss Matty, in her sisterly pride, anticipated great delight in the joy of showing them Mr. Peter. The pearl necklace disappeared ; and about that time many handsome and useful presents made their appearance in the households of Miss Pole and Mrs. Forrester ; and some rare and delicate Indian ornaments graced the drawing-rooms of Mrs. Jamieson and Mrs. Fitz-Adam. I myself was not forgotten. Among other things, I had the handsomest bound and best edition of Dr. Johnson's works that could be procured ; and dear Miss Matty, with tears in her eyes, begged me to consider it as a present from her sister as well as herself. In short, no one was forgotten ; and, what was more, every one, however insignificant, who had shown kindness to Miss Matty at any time, was sure of Mr. Peter's cordial regard.

Chapter XVI.
Peace to Cranford.

was not surprising that Mr. Peter became such a favourite at Cranford. The ladies vied with each other who should admire him most ; and no wonder, for their quiet lives were astonishingly stirred up by the arrival from India— especially as the person arrived told more wonderful stories than Sindbad the Sailor ; and, as Miss Pole said, was quite as good as an Arabian Night any evening. For my own part, I had vibrated all my life between Drumble and Cranford, and I thought it was quite possible that all Mr. Peter's stories might be true, although wonderful ; but when I found that, if we swallowed an anecdote of tolerable magnitude one week, we had the dose considerably increased the next, I began to have my doubts ; especially as I noticed that when his sister was present the accounts of Indian life were comparatively tame ; not that she knew more than we did, perhaps less. I noticed also that when the rector came to call, Mr. Peter talked in a different way about the countries he had been in.   But I don't think the ladies in Cranford would have considered him such a wonderful traveller if they had only heard him talk in the quiet way he did to him.   They liked him the better, indeed, for being what they called ' so very Oriental.'

One day, at a select party in his honour, which Miss Pole gave, and from which, as Mrs. Jamieson honoured it with her presence, and had even offered to send Mr. Mulliner to wait, Mr. and Mrs. Hoggins and Mrs. Fitz-Adam were necessarily excluded—one day at Miss Pole's, Mr. Peter said he was tired of sitting upright against the hard-backed uneasy chairs, and asked if he might not indulge himself in sitting cross-legged.   Miss Pole's consent was eagerly given, and down he went with the utmost gravity.   But when Miss Pole asked me, in an audible whisper, ' if he did not remind me of the Father of the Faithful?'   I could not help thinking of poor Simon Jones, the lame tailor ; and while Mrs. Jamieson slowly commented on the elegance and con-venience of the attitude, I remembered how we had all followed that lady's lead in condemning Mr. Hoggins for vulgarity because he simply crossed his legs as he sat still on his chair.   Many of Mr. Peter's ways of eating were a little strange amongst such ladies as Miss Pole, and Miss Matty, and Mrs. Jamieson, especially when I recollected the untasted green peas and two-pronged forks at poor Mr. Holbrook's dinner.

The mention of that gentleman's name recalls to my mind a conversation between Mr. Peter and Miss Matty one evening in the summer after he returned to Cranford.   The day had been very hot, and Miss

Matty had been much oppressed by the weather, in the
heat of which her brother revelled. I remember that
she had been unable to nurse Martha's baby, which had
become her favourite employment of late, and which
was as much at home in her arms as in its mother's, as
long as it remained a light-weight, portable by one so
fragile as Miss Matty. This day to which I refer,

'The Father of the Faithful.'

Miss Matty had seemed more than usually feeble and
languid, and only revived when the sun went down,
and her sofa was wheeled to the open window, through
which, although it looked into the principal street of
Cranford, the fragrant smell of the neighbouring hay-
fields came in every now and then, borne by the soft
breezes that stirred the dull air of the summer twilight,
and then died away. The silence of the sultry atmo-
sphere was lost in the murmuring noises which came

in from many an open window and door ; even the
children were abroad in the street, late as it was
(between ten and eleven), enjoying the game of play
for which they had not had spirits during the heat of
the day.   It was a source of satisfaction to Miss Matty
to see how few candles were lighted, even in the apartments of those houses from which issued the greatest
signs of life.   Mr. Peter, Miss Matty, and I had all
been quiet, each with a separate reverie, for some little
time, when Mr. Peter broke in—

'Do you know, little Matty, I could have sworn you
were on the high road to matrimony when I left England that last time!   If anybody had told me you
would have lived and died an old maid then, I should
have laughed in their faces.'

Miss Matty made no reply, and I tried in vain to
think of some subject which should effectually turn
the conversation ; but I was very stupid ; and before
I spoke he went on—

'It was Holbrook, that fine manly fellow who lived
at Woodley, that I used to think would carry off my
little Matty.   You would not think it now, I daresay,
Mary ; but this sister of mine was once a very pretty
girl—at least, I thought so, and so I've a notion did
poor Holbrook.   What business had he to die before
I came home to thank him for all his kindness to a
good-for-nothing cub as I was?   It was that that made
me first think he cared for you ; for in all our fishing expeditions it was Matty, Matty, we talked about.
Poor Deborah !   What a lecture she read me on having
asked him home to lunch one day, when she had seen
the Arley carriage in the town, and thought that my
lady might call.   Well, that's long years ago ; more

than half a lifetime, and yet it seems like yesterday!
I don't know a fellow I should have liked better as a
brother-in-law. You must have played your cards
badly, my little Matty, somehow or another——wanted
your brother to be a good go-between, eh, little one?'
said he, putting out his hand to take hold of hers as
she lay on the sofa. 'Why, what's this? you're shivering and shaking, Matty, with that confounded open
window. Shut it, Mary, this minute!'

I did so, and then stooped down to kiss Miss Matty,
and see if she really were chilled. She caught at my
hand, and gave it a hard squeeze——but unconsciously,
I think——for in a minute or two she spoke to us quite
in her usual voice, and smiled our uneasiness away,
although she patiently submitted to the prescriptions
we enforced of a warm bed and a glass of weak negus.
I was to leave Cranford the next day, and before I
went I saw that all the effects of the open window had
quite vanished. I had superintended most of the
alterations necessary in the house and household during
the latter weeks of my stay. The shop was once more
a parlour; the empty resounding rooms again furnished
up to the very garrets.

There has been some talk of establishing Martha
and Jem in another house, but Miss Matty would not
hear of this. Indeed, I never saw her so much roused
as when Miss Pole had assumed it to be the most
desirable arrangement. As long as Martha would
remain with Miss Matty, Miss Matty was only too
thankful to have her about her; yes, and Jem too,
who was a very pleasant man to have in the house,
for she never saw him from week's end to week's end.
And as for the probable children, if they would all

turn out such little darlings as her god-daughter, Matilda,
she should not mind the number, if Martha didn't.
Besides, the next was to be called Deborah—a point
which Miss Matty had reluctantly yielded to Martha's
stubborn determination that her first-born was to be
Matilda. So Miss Pole had to lower her colours, and
even her voice, as she said to me that, as Mr. and Mrs.
Hearn were still to go on living in the same house with
Miss Matty, we had certainly done a wise thing in
hiring Martha's niece as an auxiliary.

I left Miss Matty and Mr. Peter most comfortable
and contented ; the only subject for regret to the
tender heart of the one, and the social friendly nature
of the other, being the unfortunate quarrel between
Mrs. Jamieson and the plebeian Hogginses and their
following. In joke, I prophesied one day that this
would only last until Mrs. Jamieson or Mr. Mulliner
were ill, in which case they would only be too glad to
be friends with Mr. Hoggins ; but Miss Matty did not
like my looking forward to anything like illness in so
light a manner, and before the year was out all had
come round in a far more satisfactory way.

I received two Cranford letters on one auspicious
October morning. Both Miss Pole and Miss Matty
wrote to ask me to come over and meet the Gordons,
who had returned to England alive and well with their
two children, now almost grown up. Dear Jessie Brown
had kept her old kind nature, although she had changed
her name and station ; and she wrote to say that she
and Major Gordon expected to be in Cranford on the
fourteenth, and she hoped and begged to be remembered
to Mrs. Jamieson (named first, as became her honourable
station), Miss Pole, and Miss Matty—could she ever

forget their kindness to her poor father and sister?—
Mrs. Forrester, Mr. Hoggins (and here again came in
an allusion to kindness shown to the dead long ago),
his new wife, who as such must allow Mrs. Gordon to
desire to make her acquaintance, and who was, moreover,
an old Scotch friend of her husband's.   In short, every
one was named, from the rector—who had been
appointed to Cranford in the interim between Captain
Brown's death and Miss Jessie's marriage, and was now
associated with the latter event—down to Miss Betsy
Barker.   All were asked to the luncheon ; all except
Mrs. Fitz-Adam, who had come to live in Cranford since
Miss Jessie Brown's days, and whom I found rather
moping on account of the omission.   People wondered
at Miss Betty Barker's being included in the honourable
list ; but, then, as Miss Pole said, we must remember
the disregard of the genteel proprieties of life in which
the poor captain had educated his girls, and for his
sake we swallowed our pride.   Indeed, Mrs. Jamieson
rather took it as a compliment, as putting Miss Betty
(formerly *her* maid) on a level with 'those Hogginses.'

But when I arrived in Cranford, nothing was as yet
ascertained of Mrs. Jamieson's own intentions ; would
the honourable lady go, or would she not ?   Mr. Peter
declared that she should and she would ; Miss Pole
shook her head and desponded.   But Mr. Peter was
a man of resources.   In the first place, he persuaded
Miss Matty to write to Mrs. Gordon, and to tell her
of Mrs. Fitz-Adam's existence, and to beg that one so
kind, and cordial, and generous, might be included in
the pleasant invitation.   An answer came back by
return of post, with a pretty little note for Mrs. Fitz-
Adam, and a request that Miss Matty would deliver

it herself and explain the previous omission. Mrs. Fitz-Adam was as pleased as could be, and thanked Miss Matty over and over again. Mr. Peter had said, 'Leave Mrs. Jamieson to me;' so we did; especially as we knew nothing that we could do to alter her determination if once formed.

I did not know, nor did Miss Matty, how things were going on, until Miss Pole asked me, just the day before Mrs. Gordon came, if I thought there was anything between Mr. Peter and Mrs. Jamieson in the matrimonial line, for that Mrs. Jamieson was really going to the lunch at the 'George.' She had sent Mr. Mulliner down to desire that there might be a footstool put to the warmest seat in the room, as she meant to come, and knew that their chairs were very high. Miss Pole had picked this piece of news up, and from it she conjectured all sorts of things, and bemoaned yet more. 'If Peter should marry, what would become of poor dear Miss Matty? And Mrs. Jamieson, of all people!' Miss Pole seemed to think there were other ladies in Cranford who would have done more credit to his choice, and I think she must have had some one who was unmarried in her head, for she kept saying, 'It was so wanting in delicacy in a widow to think of such a thing.'

When I got back to Miss Matty's I really did begin to think that Mr. Peter might be thinking of Mrs. Jamieson for a wife, and I was as unhappy as Miss Pole about it. He had the proof sheet of a great placard in his hand. 'Signor Brunoni, Magician to the King of Delhi, the Rajah of Oude, and the great Lama of Thibet,' etc. etc. was going to 'perform in Cranford for one night only,' the very next night; and

Miss Matty, exultant, showed me a letter from the
Gordons, promising to remain over this gaiety, which
Miss Matty said was entirely Peter's doing. He had
written to ask the signor to come, and was to be at all
the expenses of the affair. Tickets were to be sent
gratis to as many as the room would hold. In short,

'*The proof sheet of a great placard.*'

Miss Matty was charmed with the plan, and said that
to-morrow Cranford would remind her of the Preston
Guild, to which she had been in her youth—a luncheon
at the 'George,' with the dear Gordons, and the signor
in the Assembly Room in the evening. But I—I looked
only at the fatal words—

    '*Under the Patronage of the* HONOURABLE MRS.
                   JAMIESON.'

She, then, was chosen to preside over this entertainment of Mr. Peter's ; she was perhaps going to displace my dear Miss Matty in his heart, and make her life lonely once more ! I could not look forward to the morrow with any pleasure ; and every innocent anticipation of Miss Matty's only served to add to my annoyance.

So, angry and irritated, and exaggerating every little incident which could add to my irritation, I went on till we were all assembled in the great parlour at the 'George.' Major and Mrs. Gordon and pretty Flora and Mr. Ludovic were all as bright and handsome and friendly as could be ; but I could hardly attend to them for watching Mr. Peter, and I saw that Miss Pole was equally busy. I had never seen Mrs. Jamieson so roused and animated before ; her face looked full of interest in what Mr. Peter was saying. I drew near to listen. My relief was great when I caught that his words were not words of love, but that, for all his grave face, he was at his old tricks. He was telling her of his travels in India, and describing the wonderful height of the Himalaya mountains : one touch after another added to their size, and each exceeded the former in absurdity ; but Mrs. Jamieson really enjoyed all in perfect good faith. I suppose she required strong stimulants to excite her to come out of her apathy. Mr. Peter wound up his account by saying that, of course, at that altitude there were none of the animals to be found that existed in the lower regions ; the game— everything was different. Firing one day at some flying creature, he was very much dismayed when it fell to find that he had shot a cherubim ! Mr. Peter caught my eye at this moment, and gave me such a

funny twinkle, that I felt sure he had no thoughts of
Mrs. Jamieson as a wife from that time. She looked
uncomfortably amazed—

'But, Mr. Peter, shooting a cherubim—don't you
think—I am afraid that was sacrilege!'

'He had shot a cherubim!'

Mr. Peter composed his countenance in a moment,
and appeared shocked at the idea, which, as he said
truly enough, was now presented to him for the first
time; but then Mrs. Jamieson must remember that he
had been living for a long time among savages—all of
whom were heathens—some of them, he was afraid, were
downright Dissenters. Then, seeing Miss Matty draw
near, he hastily changed the conversation, and after a
little while, turning to me, he said, 'Don't be shocked,

prim little Mary at all my wonderful stories. I consider Mrs. Jamieson fair game, and besides I am bent
on propitiating her, and the first step towards it is
keeping her well awake. I bribed her here by asking
her to let me have her name as patroness for my poor
conjuror this evening ; and I don't want to give her
time enough to get up her rancour against the Hogginses,
who are just coming in. I want everybody to be
friends, for it harasses Matty so much to hear of these
quarrels. I shall go at it again by and by, so you need
not look shocked. I intend to enter the Assembly
Room to-night with Mrs. Jamieson on one side and my
lady, Mrs. Hoggins, on the other. You see if I don't.'

Somehow or another he did ; and fairly got them
into conversation together. Major and Mrs. Gordon
helped at the good work with their perfect ignorance of
any existing coolness between any of the inhabitants of
Cranford.

Ever since that day there has been the old friendly
sociability in Cranford society ; which I am thankful
for, because of my dear Miss Matty's love of peace and
kindliness. We all love Miss Matty, and I somehow
think we are all of us better when she is near us.

'Mrs. Jamieson on one side, and my lady, Mrs. Hoggins, on the other.'

The
New Cranford Series.

Crown 8vo., Cloth Elegant, Gilt Edges,

3s. 6d. per volume.

CRANFORD. By Mrs. GASKELL. With Preface by ANNE THACKERAY RITCHIE, and 100 Illustrations by Hugh Thomson.

THE VICAR OF WAKEFIELD. By OLIVER GOLDSMITH. With 182 Illustrations by Hugh Thomson, and a Preface by Austin Dobson.

OUR VILLAGE. By MARY RUSSELL MITFORD. With a Preface by Anne Thackeray Ritchie, and 100 Illustrations by Hugh Thomson.

CORIDON'S SONG, and other Verses. With Illustrations by Hugh Thomson, and an Introduction by Austin Dobson.

COACHING DAYS AND COACHING WAYS. By W. OUTRAM TRISTRAM. With 214 Illustrations by Hugh Thomson and Herbert Railton.

OLD CHRISTMAS. From the Sketch-Book of WASHINGTON IRVING. Illustrated by R. Caldecott.

BRACEBRIDGE HALL. From the Sketch-Book of WASHINGTON IRVING. Illustrated by R. Caldecott.

New Cranford Series—*continued.*

THE ALHAMBRA. By WASHINGTON IRVING. With an Introduction by Elizabeth Robins Pennell. Illustrated with Drawings of the Places mentioned, by Joseph Pennell.

RIP VAN WINKLE AND THE LEGEND OF SLEEPY HOLLOW. By WASHINGTON IRVING. With 53 Illustrations and a Preface by George H. Boughton, A.R.A.

HUMOROUS POEMS. By THOMAS HOOD. With a Preface by Canon Ainger, and 130 Illustrations by Charles E. Brock.

GULLIVER'S TRAVELS. With Introduction by Sir Henry Craik, K.C.B., and 103 Illustrations by C. E. Brock.

REYNARD THE FOX. Edited, with Introduction, by JOSEPH JACOBS. Illustrated by Frank Calderon.

THE SCHOOL FOR SCANDAL, AND THE RIVALS. By R. B. SHERIDAN. With 50 Illustrations by Edmund J. Sullivan, and an Introduction by Augustine Birrell, K.C., M.P.

HOUSEHOLD STORIES. From the Collections of the Bros. GRIMM. Translated from the German by Lucy Crane, and done into Pictures by Walter Crane.

THE FABLES OF ÆSOP. Selected, told anew, and their History traced. By JOSEPH JACOBS. With about 300 Illustrations by Richard Heighway.

MACMILLAN AND CO., LTD., LONDON

Illustrated
Standard Novels.

Crown 8vo. Cloth, 2s. 6d. Cloth Elegant, Gilt Edges, 3s. 6d.

By JANE AUSTEN.

With Introductions by AUSTIN DOBSON.

PRIDE AND PREJUDICE. With Illustrations by Charles E. Brock.

SENSE AND SENSIBILITY. | MANSFIELD PARK.
EMMA. | NORTHANGER ABBEY, AND
| PERSUASION.

With Illustrations by HUGH THOMSON.

By J. FENIMORE COOPER

Illustrated by H. M. BROCK

THE LAST OF THE MOHICANS. With a General Introduction by Mowbray Morris.

THE DEERSLAYER. | THE PIONEERS.

Illustrated by C. E. BROCK

THE PATHFINDER | THE PRAIRIE.

By MARIA EDGEWORTH.

With Introductions by ANNE THACKERAY RITCHIE.

ORMOND. Illustrated by Carl Schloesser.

CASTLE RACKRENT, AND THE ABSENTEE.

POPULAR TALES. | BELINDA.
HELEN. | PARENT'S ASSISTANT.

Illustrated by CHRIS HAMMOND.

By CAPTAIN MARRYAT.

With Introductions by DAVID HANNAY.

JAPHET IN SEARCH OF A FATHER. Illustrated by Henry M. Brock.

JACOB FAITHFUL. Illustrated by Henry M. Brock.

PETER SIMPLE. Illustrated by J. Ayton Symington.

Midshipman Easy   Illustrated by Fred Pegram.
The King's Own.   Illustrated by F. H. Townsend.
The Phantom Ship.   Illustrated by H. R. Millar.
Snarley-yow.   Illustrated by H. R. Millar.
Poor Jack.   Illustrated by Fred Pegram.
The Pirate, and The Three Cutters.   Illustrated
by E. J. Sullivan.
Masterman Ready.   Illustrated by Fred Pegram.
Frank Mildmay.   Illustrated by H. R. Millar.
Newton Forster.   Illustrated by E. J. Sullivan.

By THOMAS LOVE PEACOCK.

With Introductions by George Saintsbury.

Headlong Hall, and Nightmare Abbey.   Illustrated by H. R. Millar.

Maid Marian, and Crotchet Castle.	Melincourt. Misfortunes of Elphin,
Gryll Grange.	and Rhododaphne.

Illustrated by F. H. Townsend.

Westward Ho! By Charles Kingsley. Illustrated
by C. E. Brock.
Handy Andy.   By Samuel Lover.   Illustrated by
H. M. Brock.   With Introduction by Charles Whibley.
Tom Cringle's Log. By Michael Scott. Illustrated
by J. Ayton Symington.   With Introduction by Mowbray
Morris.
Annals of the Parish.   By John Galt.   Illustrated
by Charles E. Brock. With Introduction by Alfred Ainger.
Sybil, or The Two Nations, etc.   By Benjamin
Disraeli.   Illustrated by F. Pegram.   With Introduction
by H. D. Traill.
Lavengro.   By George Borrow.   Illustrated by
E. J. Sullivan.   With Introduction by Augustine
Birrell, K.C., M.P.
Adventures of Hajji Baba of Ispahan.   By James
Morier.   Illustrated by H. R. Millar. With Introduction
by Lord Curzon.

MACMILLAN AND CO., Ltd., LONDON

5.7.08